Untamed Destinies

Sometimes, love is inescapable

Catherine Evans. Kim Petersen. Beth Prentice

A Romance Anthology

The Ivory Veil by BETH PRENTICE
Wildflower by KIM PETERSEN
Storm Struck by CATHERINE EVANS

Kindle: ISBN-13: 978-0-6481595-8-2
Paperback IBSN: 978-0-6481595-9-9
This is a Whispering Ink Press book brought to you by Whispering Ink Press.
Untamed Destinies cover and formatting by Paradox Book Cover Designs.
Storm Struck cover by Paradox Book Cover Designs.
Wildflower cover by Kalosys Art.
Wildflower Edited by Jennifer Collins.
The Ivory Veil cover by Paradox Book Cover Designs.

Untamed Destinies

Sometimes, love is inescapable.

Snuggle up, relax, and prepare to fall in love as you journey through three of the most romantic tales you might ever experience!

Untamed Destinies is the brand-new romance anthology from bestselling authors, Beth Prentice, Kim Petersen and Catherine Evans.

HEAT LEVELS:

The Ivory Veil by BETH PRENTICE ~ Sweet

Wildflower by KIM PETERSEN ~ Sexy

Storm Struck by CATHERINE EVANS ~ Sweet

CONTENTS

Storm Struck By Catherine Evans

The Ivory Veil by Beth Prentice

The Westport Mysteries

Does Grandma
really know best?

The Ivory Veil

BETH PRENTICE
USA Today Bestselling Author

Chapter One

I turned the sign on the door to *Open* and looked out at the dreary morning. Westport was usually sunny, the weather more humid than not. But as the lightning flashed and the rain pelted against the windows, I figured today the weather gods had gotten up on the wrong side of the bed.

"How many brides are going to brave this weather?" I asked Nancy, my manager.

"One, if she wants her dress before the wedding," she replied, her smile bright and fast. Nancy had worked at The Ivory Veil Bridal Boutique for most of her working life, and she knew the shop better than anyone. Lately, menopause had caught up with her which meant that the thermostat had been turned to freezing, but once I'd learned to always carry a sweater to work, we got along just perfectly.

I returned her smile. "Is that bridezilla herself?"

"Yep. Not looking forward to her visit, but as things have been slow around here for some time, we need to keep her happy."

The season of love had been a bit slow lately. Or at least the good citizens of Westport weren't celebrating with weddings.

"Now Gracie," said Nancy, her tone turning serious. "We need you to make sure the shop is tidy. The owner's paying us a visit this morning and we need him to think that we do something around here other than drink coffee."

I scoffed at her sarcasm, lifting a manila folder that held the stock take we'd just completed.

"Why did he want a stock take to be done mid-month?" I asked, thanking every god in existence that the task was behind us.

Nancy shrugged. "He didn't say. He just demanded that we have it to him last week."

"Oops. Maybe that's what he's coming in for. To give us a bollocking for being late with it." Bugger.

"Too bad. I explained to him that the Bridal Expo took up way too much of our time and he'd get the stock take when he got it."

Nancy was one of my favorite people ever. She always stood ramrod straight, her naturally blonde hair now highlighted with small strands of silver and was always tied in the same neat bun at the nape of her neck, and her pearls were real. When I first started here I thought she was very prim and proper. That was until I got to know her.

"We did get a few orders from the expo so that should keep him happy."

"Fingers crossed. But who knows with that man. He continually lifts our sales targets, but for a town of this size I've explained to him that we do extremely well."

Westport isn't the largest town on the east coast. The last census said it had a population of thirty thousand. It pretty much had everything our residents needed with a gorgeous river and easy access to the ocean, one large hospital, one cemetery and one shopping center. Unfortunately, it had more than one bridal boutique, but none of them were quite like ours. The Ivory Veil had been family owned for nearly one hundred years, and even though the décor had changed considerably over that time, it still held the charm of yesteryear. The original white façade was painted with delicate vines of pink flowers, the deep windows displaying our most beautiful dresses. The glass leaded door with the matching transom welcomed our visitors, and the—albeit slightly worn—plush, charcoal carpet gave the shop a feeling of luxury.

I loved everything about it, including how the interior wall color matched the carpet and how it all highlighted the dresses hanging on velvet hangers in neat rows on either side of the room. The shop name was written in large silver scrolled lettering across the wall behind the glass counter and a round ottoman sat in the center of the room, allowing for the bride's family and friends to sit comfortably while they waited for her to try on her perfect dress. That was my favorite part of the job. Matching the dress to its owner. I always got that burning sense of happiness as I watched their faces transform seeing their reflection in the mirror, and for the first time truly believing they were a bride.

My grandmother had never approved of my choice to work here, but I figured she just never understood that feeling you got when you found the perfect dress.

The bell jingled as the door opened and a radiant face beamed back at me as our first customer of the day stepped inside. Nancy immediately slid into professional salesperson mode and greeted her with a smile.

"Quick," she whispered to me, whilst simultaneously moving towards our customer. "Go and tidy yourself up before Marshall gets here."

Oh geez. For her to be saying that at this time of day, the weather had obviously had its effect. Leaving her to it I made my way through to the small kitchen slash storeroom located at the back of the shop, stopping on the way past the dressing rooms to make sure that my appearance was up to standard.

The décor in the dressing rooms matched the shop, only the walls were all mirror, with a black velvet curtain offering privacy.

I groaned at my reflection, my hazel eyes wide as I hurriedly retied my wind swept flaming curls into a ponytail. My lipstick was smudged; my shirt was untucked, and I'd already laddered my stockings. Urgh! No wonder I was single.

The shop bell jingled once again alerting me to more visitors, so I quickly reapplied pink lipstick to my full lips and straightened my shirt, re-tucking it into the band of my black pencil skirt. There wasn't much I could do with the stockings other than take them off, so I pulled the curtain closed, slipped off my shoes, hoisted my skirt up, and started to roll the flimsy silk fabric down my legs.

"I'll be right with you," Nancy's voice floated towards me. "Please look around. Gracie will be able to get you whatever you need."

I looked up into the mirror as muffled footsteps moved towards me and the sound of two men sucking in air filled the dressing room. It would have helped if I'd closed the curtain all the way and hadn't worn a G-string today.

"Mr. M...Marshall," I stammered as his stunned reflection glared back at me. It seemed the younger man standing behind him didn't know where to look.

Hurriedly pulling my skirt down to cover my backside, I spun to face them, but it was difficult with stockings half way down my legs.

Maxwell Marshall was sixty-two years old. He had more hair in his ears than on his head, and had the personality of a toad. I shouldn't really describe him that way. It wasn't fair to toads. He'd been given the bridal shop by his father fifteen years before and he wasn't suited to the job, but he did always pay us on time, so he wasn't all bad.

The man standing next to him was the complete opposite. He was late twenties, smoke grey eyes that held the most incredible blue flecks, and the body of an athlete. As water droplets sat on the ends of his dark lashes, I nearly had an orgasm. Nearly. I knew this man, and he and I weren't friends. But this doesn't mean I didn't consider him hot.

Hurriedly closing the curtain, I spluttered, "So sorry. I'll be right with you." The image of Aaron Douglas's face burned on my retinas. I'd known him my entire life, and to say that it was not a pleasure to see him today was an understatement. But *what* was he doing here?

Once I'd wangled my way out of my stockings, I pushed them into my pocket, noted the color of my cheeks now matched my hair, and faked my confidence. Thankfully the two men had disappeared and I didn't have to face them.

Nancy bustled towards me as the bell alerted me to the disappearance of her customer.

"Where did they go?" she hissed quietly.

I shrugged. "No idea." I didn't fill her in on the details of why I had no idea.

She sighed. "I was expecting Marshall to be on his own. I've got a bad feeling about why Aaron is with him though."

"I'd heard a rumor that he was back in town."

"Yes, but why is he back in town?"

We didn't have to wait long for the answer as footsteps making their way down from the attic echoed around the small shop.

"Ladies," Marshall's authority boomed. "I'm here to announce my retirement. As of yesterday, The Ivory Veil Bridal Boutique is now owned by Aaron Douglas."

Aaron nodded, Nancy sighed, and I groaned.

Mr. Marshall had taken Aaron to the loading area we had out the back of the shop, showing him where we received our deliveries, apparently showing him the ropes. As if he had any idea.

I sat heavily on the nearest chair, pulled my phone towards me, and opened Google.

"What are you doing?" Nancy asked.

"Looking for a new job." According to Google, Bunnings Hardware had vacancies. Surely I could sell tools, and the plant section would be lots of fun. Except on wet days like today. Then it would be miserable.

"Gracie I know that your family has a history with the Douglas's, but do you really feel that you can't work for him?"

"It's more like he'll sack me at the first chance he gets."

"That's not the spirit," she warned. "You have to think good thoughts. You reap what you sow, remember?"

"Yes, but I didn't sow this family feud. I'm just living with the consequences of it."

"What's the feud even about?"

I screwed up my nose as I thought back over my childhood. "I don't remember what started it, but I do know that his family is as much to blame for it as mine."

"It's not about blame."

I sighed. "Nancy, I can't remember him ever doing a nice thing for me."

"Is there a reason he should have? Have you ever done anything nice for him?"

"Well..." I thought of all the interactions I'd ever had with him. "I did save his cat once. But that was because it was really cute and not because it was Aaron's."

"Of course you did." Nancy grinned. "Look, maybe now is a good time to start being nice to him," she advised as the back door opened and the two men stepped inside.

The rain had slowed to a drizzle, but the sky remained gloomy, matching my mood.

"I'll leave you to it Aaron," Marshall said, his grin larger than I'd ever seen it. "If you need anything just ask the girls. Don't ask me, I'm heading out of the country this afternoon. I have a date with Bora Bora."

Lucky him.

"Good luck ladies," he said, addressing us. "I thank you both for your dedication to this business. It's a shame that it's leaving the family after so long, but I have no one to give it to when I die, so I thought I should just enjoy the money while I can."

I couldn't argue with that.

After he left Aaron cleared his throat, gazing at his shoes, his forehead wrinkled. He had a boyish vulnerability about him that if you weren't prepared could take your breath away, yet his masculinity and sexuality aroused hormones in even the most chaste girls.

Just not this girl. Nope. I was immune. A deep sigh rattled my ribcage.

I used the time to assess him properly. The last time I'd been this close to him I'd been screaming at him for hitting my boyfriend. It had been my twenty first birthday party and he'd been at the same bar celebrating his business degree completion. He'd said something to my boyfriend, something had been said back, and a fight had broken out. That had been four years ago and not long after that Aaron left for Europe.

The time had treated him well, apparently. He'd always been athletic, but his body had changed from the slim lean muscles of a swimmer to more defined brawn. The five o'clock shadow that grazed his chin was a good day late, and a raw masculinity lived within the flecks of his eyes.

"I thought you'd like to know what I plan to do with the shop," he said, his deep baritone grating on my nerves.

"That would be a good place to start," Nancy replied. I kept quiet, thinking that working for Bunnings should at least mean that I would get sausages and bread every lunch time. That was a positive, right?

"In the long term I wish to franchise it. I believe it's got a lot of potential, it just needs some attention to the details and some fancy marketing. Luckily, that's what I'm good at," he finished, flashing a megawatt smile towards us. I'd seen the smile a thousand times before. It was designed to win us over, and judging by the dreamy look in Nancy's eyes, it was working. At least on her.

I nudged her with my elbow, hitting her with a glare.

"If you're both happy to stay with the company, I would love to keep you here," Aaron continued.

"What? Even me?" I asked, before I could think.

The megawatt smile faltered. "Yes Gracie. Even you. You're both very good at your jobs and you know this business better than anyone. My skills are taking a failing business and making it a major success," Aaron boasted.

"Gee, you're confident," I snarled.

"Only because I know with your help, we can do it," he returned.

Well, I couldn't argue with that.

Chapter Two

The following morning dawned bright and sunny, which meant the humidity was going to be high. My hair was tamed with a band, my figure accentuated by my little black dress, and as I applied a second layer of mascara I fluttered my eyelids, checking the effect. I wondered who I was trying to impress, but I quickly shrugged it off. I was doing it for myself and no one else.

My alarm dinged alerting me that I needed to leave home now or I wouldn't make it to work in time, so I gave my dog Frankie a pat and slipped my feet into my three-inch heels, pushing my cashmere sweater into my handbag. I'd regret my choice of shoes by the end of the day, but I didn't care. They made my butt look good.

"You be a good boy," I told Frankie, my short haired Dachshund. A little while ago I'd decided that fostering animals was a great thing to do, but as I was now the owner of Frankie, two guinea pigs, three birds and a rat named Geoffrey, I'd quickly learned that fostering wasn't for me. I had no problem with the fostering part, but it seemed that giving them to a new owner wasn't for me. Nancy had mentioned that I had an animal hoarding problem but what would she know? My two-bedroom unit could handle it just fine.

Leaving for work before seven thirty meant I missed the rush of traffic. It also meant I got to work quite early, but I used the time to buy Nancy and I a large cappuccino and a double chocolate muffin each, so my time was well spent.

As I placed the order I wondered whether Aaron would like something, but judging by the way his biceps stretched the fabric of his shirt, I figured he was now a health food nut. He never used to be. I'd caught him in line behind me at Bartley's Bakery more than once in the past.

Only after I collected my order and was fifty meters up the street, did I rethink and ran back to buy him one. After all, Nancy was right. He was my boss now and I needed to make a good impression, and who knew, maybe he still had the occasional treat.

Aaron was already hard at work as I made my way into the shop. The storage room was a mess of boxes, most of which he had opened. He was standing in the middle of it all, scratching his head and looking confused.

I gulped as a small glimpse of his abdomen flashed when he lifted his arms to run his fingers through his hair. I hurriedly took a sip of my coffee.

"Bugger, he's hot," I hissed, under my breath.

"What was that?" he asked, turning towards me, his eyes wide, hysteria lurking within them.

"Ummm, I said it's hot." I lifted the cup as the heat of my face competed with the drink. "I have coffee for you."

He gave a contented sigh and smiled, lighting the room as he stepped over boxes towards me.

I held the cup at arm's length as he accepted it.

"Thanks Gracie," he said, giving me a smaller almost coy smile.

I shrugged. "Don't think anything of it. I always get something for Nancy and I." My words came out much harsher than intended, and guilt momentarily swamped me.

Aaron's smile disappeared, and a small lump formed in my throat.

"What are you doing?" I asked, wanting to dispel the awkwardness that sat in the air.

"Oh, I was wanting to know what all this stuff is. If I'm going to make the business more efficient, it's important."

"You only had to ask."

"Yeah, but I know you and Nancy are busy enough without me annoying you, so I thought I'd be able to figure it out for myself." He looked at the mess he'd made and released a long drawn out breath. "Apparently not."

The helplessness shining from his eyes caused a pull in my belly until I remembered the look he'd given me at my twenty first birthday party. It had stopped me in my tracks and to this day I knew he hated me.

My stomach clenched and I wondered if the milk in my coffee was off.

But Aaron was my boss now and I had two choices. I could quit, or I could put my personal opinions aside, put our past behind us and move forward, hopefully without us killing each other.

I did love working here. I loved the hope and joy that every bride wore like a badge of honor, knowing that she was about to declare a bond with the one she loved the most. I loved being a part of that and I didn't want to leave.

Argh! My shoulders slumped as I placed the bakery box on the table and shuffled towards him.

"How can I help?" I asked, leaning against the door jam.

"You can start by telling me what the heck all this stuff is."

I smiled and stepped into the mess. "Well...where do I begin?"

By the time I had explained the contents of our storage room, I didn't think he was any the wiser as to how a veil turned a woman wearing a white dress into a bride. I gave up trying and ate my chocolate muffin. Some men would never understand.

"Why did you buy a bridal boutique if you don't really care about weddings?"

"I do care about weddings."

"Really?"

He rubbed the back of his neck considering his response. "I may not know the difference between a Cathedral veil and a double tier Waltz veil, but that doesn't mean that I don't know a good business opportunity when I see it."

"So you really believe that you can turn this into a Fortune 500 company?"

"I've done it before with worse businesses than this." Rumors had it that he was successful, so I had no reason to doubt what he was saying.

Okay, so I followed rumors about him, but that didn't mean anything, right?

Nancy bustled in the door, looking more flustered than I'd ever seen her.

"Sorry I'm late," she said, dropping her handbag onto the bench beside the sink.

We didn't open the shop until nine on a Wednesday, which meant that technically she wasn't late. But it definitely wasn't like her.

"Is everything okay?" I asked, as she moved alongside me.

"Yes, everything's perfect. I just had trouble getting out of bed this morning." Her cheeks heated up and she rubbed her lips together, attempting to hide her smile.

Oh oh. I knew that look.

"He was sooo good," she whispered dreamily. Nancy may be in menopause, but her libido wasn't slowing down. She got more action than I ever did.

Before she could tell me any details the bell above the door jingled, alerting us to our first customer of the day.

One close call nicely avoided.

Bridezilla herself had made her way in by lunch time. She was a day late, but she hadn't wanted to get her hair extensions wet so she'd risked not collecting her dress the day her wedding planner had organized. I'd met her wedding planner, and I wouldn't have risked it, but that was just me.

I saw her coming and quickly ducked to the back room, desperately searching for anything that meant I could avoid her. Nancy saw me leave and I heard her sigh all the way to the kitchen, but I'd make it up to her later by listening to her recount her previous evenings encounter.

Actually, it wasn't a hardship. I loved hearing about her adventures. Just not when Aaron was around where he could overhear, because let's face it—that would be embarrassing.

The downside of skipping out on her was that I found Aaron sitting at our little table, scanning our order book.

"Is any of this on computer?" he asked, his eyes meeting mine.

I gulped as I got momentarily lost in their smoky grey depths.

"Ummm, no. Sorry. Nancy's old school. I have tried to talk her around, but she says the old system is fine and if it ain't broke then why fix it." I shrugged, and distracted myself from his stare by opening the fridge and reaching for the jug of water.

I found two glasses, and balancing it all I placed it on the table. However, unexpected nerves got the better of me, and as my hand shook I accidentally knocked the jug over, the liquid pooling on the order book and running across the table to Aaron.

He jumped up but not before the water had spilled into his lap, soaking the crotch of his pants. As the fabric momentarily stuck to his body, my mind blanked and I stumbled to form words.

Instead I heard a faint sigh escape my lips. "Damn." Why did he have to be so damned hot?

Aaron looked at the book, the ink dissolving and numbers infusing with letters. A similar sigh escaped his lips but I was sure it was for a completely different reason.

When he did look at me, a small smile played on his lips. "Looks like we'll be computerizing after all."

"I'm so sorry," I stammered, reaching for the tea towel to mop the mess up. As I debated whether to tackle his crotch or the flood on the table, Aaron took the towel from me. His fingers touched mine and a sizzle ran all the way south.

Oh boy, that couldn't be good.

After he'd dried himself as much as possible the air felt awkward and uncomfortable. I was about to excuse myself, the thought of facing bridezilla far more appealing, when he threw the cloth into the sink and turned towards me.

"Are you okay working with me?" he asked.

Filling my lungs, I bit my bottom lip, considering his question. "Sure."

"You don't sound sure."

"I don't have a lot of choices, do I?" Apparently a diploma in fashion design wasn't useful selling hardware.

"If it helps, I'll only be in store for about a month. I want to bring this place into the twenty first century, then I can run everything remotely."

My stomach twisted. "What does that even mean?"

"It means that you won't have to see me every day."

My mind was cheering, but my stomach tightened and a knot formed in my throat.

"Okay," I managed.

The clock ticked the seconds away as we stood staring at each other. I wasn't sure what he was thinking, but his eyes were soft and held a hint of vulnerability. Gran always told me that the eyes were the window to the soul. Well then Aaron's soul was deep, inviting, and extremely seductive.

"Now," he said, breaking the spell that had been cast. "If Nancy can handle the store for a while, I was hoping that you could help me in the attic?" he asked, pulling the conversation in a much more professional direction.

"What's up there?"

"A lot of boxes, and I was hoping you could tell me what is in them."

To be honest, it was all news to me.

"Lead the way," I announced, following him towards the stairs.

I admitted that the view from behind him was glorious, but I shook myself remembering the time that our family reunions had coincidentally been held in the same park. The consequences had been disastrous, with more than one insult hurled. Sure, it had been my Gran doing most of the hurling, but I was sure his grandfather deserved everything that went his way.

The stairs were narrow and rickety but as I reached the top I looked around me. Aaron pulled a dangling cord and the single overhead bulb dimly lit the room. The space was small, boxes filling almost every square inch of it. Exposed wooden beams, splintery floorboards and the sounds of Nancy bustling around the shop below made me feel like we were a world away from reality, yet the room felt warm and welcoming, despite the dirt and cobwebs that obscured the dormer window.

I believed that all rooms had feelings. Over the years of people living within them, they seemed to absorb an energy that nature hadn't given them. This room was filled with love, security and hope.

A deep sigh rattled from my belly and Aaron looked down at me through his dark lashes.

"Are you okay?"

I nodded as a lump momentarily clogged my throat, wondering what secrets the room held and why it felt so safe.

"Do you feel that?" I asked him.

"Feel what?"

I shook my head. "Never mind."

What God had given him in looks, he'd taken when it came to emotional intelligence.

"I wanted to see what these boxes held," Aaron continued, stepping away from me and towards a stack of cardboard boxes. "I noted they weren't in the stock take."

"I've never been up here. I had no idea these were even here, let alone count any of it. You probably should have asked Nancy for help."

The corners of his lips quivered slightly but he didn't respond. Instead he grabbed the first box and dragged it into the only open space that he could find, the smell of musty cardboard filling the air as he tore it open.

Curiosity got the better of me and I hurried forward, as he unfolded layer after layer of blue tissue paper.

"Blue keeps the white garments white," I explained, looking over his shoulder and enjoying the scent of his shampoo. "We advise all our dresses be stored in it once the wedding is over."

"Well it looks like this box never held any dresses. It's only full of paper and fat moths."

Two hours later we had one box left to open. Dust particles danced in the musty air as the sun streamed through the filthy window. I coughed against it as I wiped my hands on the skirt of my dress, noting the dirt fragments now entwined with the fabric. As a bead of perspiration trickled down from my temple, I discreetly scrutinized Aaron. He still looked cool with barely a mark on him. I'd like to say that was because he'd been doing nothing, but it was just the opposite. He'd been working hard, documenting everything that we'd found before helping me to repack the boxes. So far all we'd uncovered were old payroll ledgers, journals and sewing patterns.

"I'll get that," he said as I moved to pull the last box towards me. It had been pushed to the far side of the attic, the mountain of boxes previously hiding it, but it wasn't cardboard like the others. Instead it was made of carved timber with aged bronze hinges and latch.

"It's okay. I can manage."

"Sure you can," he said, touching my arm. "But I saw a spider run behind it."

The hairs on the back of my neck raised. "I hate spiders!"

"I know."

His eyes held mine for a moment causing a shiver to run down my spine before he stepped behind the box, cupped the Daddy Long Legs in his palm and moved to the small dormer window. Pushing it open, he let the spider run free.

Okay that was pretty heroic, but I wasn't going to let him know that I was impressed by his actions. Or that his eyes had made my heart stutter. Nope, not mentioning that.

As he dazzled me with a smile, I attempted to ignore it all by lifting the latch on the wooden chest.

I expected it to be full of more documents, so I was surprised when a meticulously wrapped garment shone back at me.

"What is it?"

"I think it's a dress," I gushed, as excitement bubbled. "Can you help me get this under the light, please?"

Once the chest was more visible and I gently pulled back the folds of blue tissue, a delicately woven ivory lace gown revealed itself, the exquisite tiny pearls glistening.

I gasped and lovingly stroked the fabric. "Wow."

"Is it okay to lift it out?"

"Yes, but I think we should leave it in the chest and take it straight downstairs to open," I suggested. "This flooring is far too dirty."

Aaron agreed and between the two of us we managed to get it into the showroom, where Nancy was as excited about it as I was.

"In all the years I've worked here I've never seen it before," she exclaimed. "But then I shortened my visits up there as much as possible. Far too many spiders for my liking."

I shivered, grateful that I'd only seen one.

"Well, come on then." She clapped. "Let's have a look at it!" As she directed Aaron on how to handle the delicate fabric, I moved to find a mannequin.

Once the dress was free from its binds, Nancy and I carefully draped it onto the model, standing back to admire its beauty.

"Wow," Nancy gasped.

"Whoa." I whistled.

Aaron sighed. "Pretty."

We both spun our heads towards him.

"That dress is not pretty!" exclaimed Nancy. "It's exquisite."

And it was. The ivory lace bodice with the sweetheart neckline and long sleeves was accentuated as the lace trim crept its way across the silk skirt only stopping as it spilled along the hemline. Creamy pearls were lovingly sewn into tiny silk rosettes as the back plunged to the waistline, and handmade silk buttons trailed the way to the floor.

We were admiring its beauty when the bell jingled and our seamstress walked in, her face flushed from the outside heat.

Chapter Three

"Oh my," she murmured, her hand jumping to her heart as she looked at the dress. "That is quite the thing, isn't it?"

Aaron scratched his head, his brow scrunched.

"Don't you agree?" I asked him as Nancy stepped towards Mrs. Boyce, taking a heavy garment bag from her.

"Yeah, I guess. Is it really that different to any of the other dresses in the store, though?"

I sighed. "When we have a few hours to spare, I'll show you our stock. You'll see that our gowns are indeed beautiful, but this is different."

"How so?" he asked, genuinely perplexed.

Mrs. Boyce stepped close to the fabric, pulling her glasses from her handbag and putting them on. She then peered closely at the lace as she moved around the mannequin, studying it like an anthropologist studied old bones, her inquiring fingers checking every seam. Nancy and I held our breath, watching her moves and waiting for her verdict.

"Well?" Nancy asked her as she stood back and allowed her glasses to hang from their chain.

"It's old. And it's handmade. And there's some embroidery on the inside seam."

Neither Nancy or I had noticed that.

"What is it?" Nancy asked.

Mrs. Boyce undid a few extra buttons and rolled the collar towards her. Swiveling her head to read upside down, she read, "Every touch leaves its trace."

"Poignant."

"Did that get sewn into all our dresses?" I asked.

"I've never seen it before and I've been sewing for this shop just short of ten years."

"So this dress was made with someone in mind?" Aaron asked.

"That would be my guess. Are we selling it on consignment?" Mrs. Boyce asked.

"No. We found it in the attic," I explained.

Felicity Boyce was twelve months off retiring. Her waistline had burgeoned over the years, her gait was stooped, and her libido had retired years ago. Her words, not mine. But her clothes were awe inspiring, stitched with detail and fit her voluptuousness perfectly.

"Well that's quite the find." She smiled, turning her attention to Aaron. If her grin was anything to go by, I figured her libido had just come out of retirement.

"Felicity, this is Aaron Douglas, the new owner," Nancy explained.

Mrs. Boyce didn't hesitate in taking his outstretched hand and holding onto it far longer than what I thought was necessary. When he did manage to get free, Nancy explained to him that Felicity Boyce worked for us on contract, attending to all the necessary adjustments that every bride needed for her dress to look like it was made just for her.

"I'm very pleased to meet you Mrs. Boyce." Aaron beamed.

She swooned slightly. "Please call me Felicity," she gushed.

"How do you know that this dress is handmade?" he asked her.

Her feathers fluffed as he acknowledged her wisdom. "Just look at this sleeve," she explained, her bony fingers caressing the fabric. "My grandmother taught me to sew and to make lace the old-fashioned way. The pattern of the spaces is just as important as the solid work."

"How long would it have taken to make it?"

"At least a year. Some of these patterns are quite intricate, some much easier and quicker. See this knot?" She asked, her lips twisting into a smile.

Aaron nodded, his head moving close to hers as he listened intently. I'd noticed he did that a lot. When he listened to you, he really listened.

"Whoever made this, that's her trademark," Mrs. Boyce explained.

"Do you know who it belongs to?" I asked.

"How would I know such a thing?" she asked, exasperated.

I shrugged. "Well...you know this stuff."

"I can't possibly know every person that makes lace!"

"Sorry," I muttered, my cheeks flaming as Aaron grinned, large and bright.

"I don't know the history of the shop," Aaron stated. "But maybe it belonged to the owner."

Nancy pressed her lips together. "I've worked here a long time and I doubt that."

"I did an essay on the store for my diploma," I announced.

"Really?" Aaron asked, eyebrows raised.

I nodded. "I've had a love affair with this shop for as long as I can remember. When I was little mum would walk me past here to get to the farmers' markets and I have memories of stopping and staring at all the beautiful gowns in the windows, dreaming about the day I would choose one for myself."

"Which one would you choose?" he asked, his voice suddenly husky.

"Until this dress came along I had my heart set on an off the shoulder white A-line dress with a beaded bodice, and tulle skirt." It presently hung in the third row on the left of the room, and I envied every bride who had tried it on. But from this moment on, I knew that dress would be forgotten.

The crinkles around his eyes deepened as a soft smile played on his lips.

"I remember you doing that assignment," added Nancy. "You came in here and hassled me for information." Hassled was a bit harsh, but I guess I did annoy her quite a bit.

"And you put me in touch with the Marshalls," I continued choosing not to argue about semantics. "It was Mary Marshall who gave me all the information I asked for, including a full family history lesson. Neither she or her mother in-law wore that dress."

"You remember such a detail?" Aaron asked.

I scoffed. "Wedding dresses are my thing. Believe me, I remember."

"Well, that still doesn't tell us who the dress belonged to," added Nancy.

"Maybe someone left it here to be sold," suggested Mrs. Boyce.

"I guess it could have been before my time," she acknowledged.

"What should we do with it now?" Aaron asked.

We all shrugged. I didn't know about the others, but I knew that the dress would be dogging my dreams.

The weather had remained sunny and hot for the remainder of the week and then the weekend, but that all changed as an evening storm rolled in the following Monday night. It was my parents' wedding anniversary and the family had been called together to celebrate. I guess thirty years was a milestone as I couldn't even make it past the second date.

"So why don't your dates go further than that?" my sister Annabelle asked. Annabelle was the perfect child. Her auburn hair hung in long flowing locks, she ran yoga classes from her home studio, and her first born was a cherub sent from the gods. Even her husband Darcy reminded me of McDreamy. Not that I was complaining. I loved them all as much as anybody.

"Apparently my expectations are too high," I responded, scanning the menu for what I wanted to order. Mum and dad had chosen a small Italian restaurant for us to get together and celebrate. It was a regular of ours and the owner Mario knew us well.

"Don't tell me—you want your man to be six foot three, dark blonde hair, amazing eyes, and the body of Thor."

That pretty much summed it up.

"What's wrong with that?"

"No man can meet that."

I could think of one.

"And anyway," she continued. "You should be more interested in their personality than their appearance. Take that guy over there. He's been checking you out since you walked in."

She nodded to a guy in the corner, who reminded me of dad.

"Seriously?"

"What's wrong with him? I'm sure he's got a wonderful personality."

"So if looks aren't important, how come Darcy is so damned cute?"

"I just got lucky." She grinned.

"Then I can hang out until I get lucky too."

My nephew Jacob stirred in his pram, and Annabelle turned to settle him.

"I heard that Aaron Douglas is back in town," she said, rubbing Jacob's back to reassure him. He immediately settled, and I immediately prickled.

"You heard right. He's my new boss."

"What?" Mum demanded, cutting in on our conversation. I gritted my teeth and quickly brought my family up to date with my work situation.

"Oh my!" said mum, fanning herself with the menu, her fiery red hair frizzing from the moisture in the air. Her petite nose scrunched as her full lips pursed. "Don't let your grandmother hear that."

"Hear what, Leonie?" Gran asked, shuffling up behind mum. Gran turned eighty last birthday. She was the matriarch of the family and ruled with an iron fist. She was as sharp as a tack, still wore underwear made for twenty-year-olds, and had a beauty spot just above her right lip. It had faded with time, but with the help of make-up it was still noticeable and she wore it with pride, telling the world that it made her look like a super model.

After grandpa passed away three years ago, she now lived alone in the over sixties' village, competing with her friend Doris for the attention of more than one man.

She took the seat between mum and I, and swiveled between us wanting more information, her cloudy eyes not missing a thing.

"Ummm..." I didn't really want to be the one to tell her.

Thankfully the waiter arrived ready to take our orders, which distracted her long enough for mum to change the subject.

We were half way through dinner when Aaron Douglas stepped up to the table.

"Hello Gracie," he said, smiling down at me. I was so surprised I choked on my linguine.

Grandma's mouth fell open and the table went silent. For a Douglas to be that bold was unheard of.

"Aaron," I croaked, as Anabelle hit me on the back.

The sounds of scraping plates, glasses tinkling and silverware clinking, became background noise as he smiled down at me. His white shirt and grey waistcoat accented his eyes, and his tailored pants emphasized his lean hips, and I was positive the drool I wiped from my lips was caused from choking.

The pretty, petite blonde woman who stood alongside him smiled serenely, and I was sure that I heard Angels singing as she gently shook her head, her perfect hair swishing like silk. I gulped and pushed my pasta aside.

"What are you doing here?" spat Grandma, sucking on her dentures and pulling her shoulders back. In her younger days Gran's hair had been long and red. Her personality was similar to that of the Fire Ant, and she had a quick tongue and a heart of gold. Her hair had faded to grey, but her feistiness and quick tongue were sure to still give you a lashing.

"Gracie mentioned that tonight was a family celebration. I saw your party and wanted to pass along my congratulations."

"Thank you, Aaron," murmured mum. Dad had his head down presumably wondering if he could fit in another piece of pizza. Dad never had gotten involved with the whole family feud thing.

"Why would you be talking to Gracie?" Grandma demanded, her eyes narrowed slits.

Oh oh!

"Well here's the thing..." I started as she turned her glare towards me, demanding that I explain.

A blush started around Aarons' collar and only stopped at his ears.

"Sorry," he mouthed as I rapidly glanced between him, his date and grandma.

"Gracie?" she snapped. Silence fell over us and Mario shifted uncomfortably. He'd been on edge ever since Aaron had approached us, probably wondering how he could quickly evacuate the restaurant.

"Ummm, I work for Aaron now," I finished, staring into the depths of my abandoned pasta. "He bought the bridal shop."

Grandma ground her teeth, her eyes narrow fissures. Her shoulders were rigid as she straightened her back considering my words.

"You cannot work for that family," she hissed, her hand grabbing mine protectively.

"Why not?"

Her hand shook as panic filled her eyes. "I forbid it," she spat, acting as if Aaron was invisible.

There was a subtle change in his eyes, but I couldn't put my finger on whether he was annoyed or hurt.

"Forbid?" I asked, dubiously, pulling my fingers free from her grasp.

"Yes! You cannot work there."

"But that's not fair," I returned as mum wrung her hands in her lap. The air prickled with tension and Aaron's date got restless. "How can you say that?"

"You need to do as I say Gracie," Gran responded, her tone deep, her voice just above a whisper. "Please."

"Gran you've never forbidden me to do anything. You're the easy going one remember? Mum's the uptight one." I attempted upbeat, but mum's face had paled and she looked from Aaron, to me, to Gran.

"Mum," she whispered. "This is a conversation for another time."

Aaron coughed, clearing his throat. "I'm sorry to have disturbed you Mrs. Saunders. My intention wasn't to upset anyone. Please forgive me and enjoy your night." He steered his date back out of the room, but before he left his gaze met mine. He gave me a small intimate smile, his shoulders slumped, and I knew just how sorry he was.

Ignoring mum altogether, Gran continued, "Well there's a first time for everything," she said, completely unaware of the pounding of my heart.

"I need the job Gran," I returned as anxiety spiked. "I have rent to pay, mouths to feed."

"Then you can work anywhere you like. Just not there."

"Why not?"

"That family is trouble. You need to stay away from them."

"Yes, that's true," interrupted mum. "Remember the problems you've had with Aaron in the past?" Now that he'd left the room she didn't have the internal conflict about being polite.

"He just seems different now. More mature."

"Once a Douglas always a Douglas," Gran reminded me.

Whatever that meant.

"My friend Bobby owns the fish and chip shop in town. I'm sure he mentioned they're hiring," she explained. "Don't worry, I'll put in a good word for you."

"I don't want to work at a fish and chip shop!"

"Too bad."

And that was the end of the conversation.

As Aaron's BMW whizzed past the rain soaked window, I threw my napkin over my plate, my appetite squashed by the sick feeling consuming my belly, and the burning rage sitting behind my breastbone.

Gran never asked for a lot, and only pulled the matriarch card on special occasions, but I had a feeling this was a subject she wasn't going to negotiate on.

Chapter Four

Nancy looked as horrified as I felt. "You're not going to do it, are you?"

"I don't want to. I love this shop. I always have."

"Then fight to stay here."

"How? You've met my gran. She's a force to be reckoned with. And if I have to choose then of course it will be my family. I love them," I finished quietly, anxiously picking the skin around my fingernail.

"I still have no idea what this stupid feud is even about." Nancy sat heavily on a stool behind the counter. The shop had just opened and so far, no customers were to be seen.

I shrugged. "Me either."

"Then maybe you need to find out. If you can settle the argument she might feel differently."

I considered her words, the implication of diffusing the situation pressing against my chest. My gaze scanned the room and the familiar feeling of belonging panged inside me.

But as the bell above the door jingled and Aaron ambled in carrying a bakery bag and three delicious smelling cups of coffee, I knew the feeling I had was about more than just the shop.

He looked to us and gave a small smile, our eyes only fleetingly connecting before he looked away. The pang next to my heart squeezed and I gasped against it.

"Morning ladies," he said, his long legs covering the ground between us effortlessly.

If I was being completely honest, he looked a bit worse for wear this morning, his sparkling eyes dulled by the dark rings beneath them.

Not that I could talk. I'd had to literally trowel on the concealer to cover the dark bags under my eyes from all the crying I'd done last night, the argument with Gran raw, and the feeling of hopelessness consuming me until sleep had finally won somewhere around 2a.m.

"Did you have a hard night?" Nancy asked him. It was then I remembered his date and the pang near my heart moved to a cramp in my stomach. Oh boy. I was in so much trouble.

"I'm sorry you had to leave early," I said, rubbing my navel as I spoke.

"Don't worry about it. Sophie and I got some take away and took it to my place."

The cramp turned into a convulsion and I worried I might throw up.

"Well that explains the bags under your eyes," Nancy replied, her eyes sparkling with delight.

"I just had trouble sleeping." He shrugged.

"I bet!"

The blush started at his collar and rapidly moved north and I may have vomited in my mouth.

"I couldn't sleep because I couldn't stop worrying about messing up your family dinner," he explained, his eyes glued to mine. "The coffee and cake is my way of saying sorry."

"You have nothing to be sorry about," I managed, swallowing hard against the bile rising in my throat. "You didn't know we were going to be there. But I won't say no to the cake. Triple choc fudge is my favorite," I said, helping myself to a slice—chocolate made everything better, right?

"I know. That's why I picked it." He grinned, his eyes once again holding mine, and my heart skipped a beat knowing that he'd remembered such a detail.

"Has your family ever told you about the feud they have going with mine?" I needed to move the conversation in a different direction to the one my imagination was taking me on. Aaron hated me. I knew that for a fact. But then why was he looking at me with such tenderness?

"Yes, but I don't know what it's about, if that's what you're asking. If we mention your Gran Leonora's name to my grandpa, he just clamps up."

"What about your granny? Would she know?"

"Granny passed away last year," he replied, the light in his eyes dulling momentarily.

"I'm sorry. I didn't know." My family had certainly never mentioned it.

Aaron shrugged. "There's no reason you should have known."

Yeah, but I knew most other things about him, so why had the gossip vine not transmitted that piece of information? I needed to have words with my sources.

I gave him a few minutes lost in his memories before pushing him about talking to his grandpa.

"Would you be able to ask him again?"

"I've tried. Many times. I always get the same response. Why? Is it important?"

I didn't want to make him uncomfortable telling him anymore about my fight with Gran than he already knew. "No reason."

"Okay, if it comes up in conversation, I'll question him some more."

"Thanks."

"Now, I have some information that you might find interesting." A sparkle reignited in his eyes and the dark rings beneath them dulled.

"Oh, do tell."

"Am I right in thinking that your grandmother's maiden name was Murphy?"

"Ahuh. Her family were Irish, hence the red hair which she passed down the generations."

"Well, I was reading through the old payroll journals I found in the attic. Did you know she worked here as a seamstress in 1956?"

My mouth dropped open as a gasp escaped my lips.

"She never mentioned that! Are you sure it's the same person?"

"Leonora Grace Murphy. Date of birth 19th March 1938."

"That's her, but she never told me she worked here. In fact, she's been the biggest advocate for me getting another job." I didn't mention the fact that I was supposed to be handing my resignation in.

"Well according to the payroll she worked here for nearly two years. She would have been sixteen when she started and then she left at seventeen."

"She married my grandpop when she was seventeen," I commented. "Women weren't allowed to work when they were married back then, were they?"

Aaron shrugged, Nancy nodded. "I've heard that too, but I've never married so what would I know?"

"You've never married?" Aaron asked her.

"Nope. I work in a bridal shop but never been a bride," she said, patting his arm. "I love men far too much to marry one."

Aaron raised his left eyebrow.

"Don't ask for details," I warned. "She'll give them to you."

Nancy released a bark of laughter as the bell above the door alerted us to a customer.

"Gracie would you mind coming with me?" Aaron asked as he grabbed the cake box. I followed him from the room as Nancy slipped into professional mode and greeted our customer.

"What's up?" I asked, placing my coffee cup on the counter top, before leaning my back against it.

"I was wondering whether you can ask your Gran if she knew who would have made the dress?"

"That's a really good idea." The dress was presently still on the mannequin but had been pushed to the back corner of the store. More than one customer had commented on it.

"What are you going to do with it?" I asked, a wistful sigh absconding from my lips.

Aaron's brow creased in that adorable way and another sigh escaped me.

I hurriedly shook myself and concentrated on the task at hand.

"I've had an idea and I was hoping you'd like to help me find out its story?"

A flip of excitement thrilled me as I nodded. "I'd love to. I love a mystery!" I mentally added it to the other mystery I needed to solve involving a family feud.

"Good. Then I thought maybe your Gran would be the best place to start seeing how she worked here as a seamstress. I'd like to pay her a visit and ask myself but I don't think that would go down well."

That was the understatement of the year.

"Sure. I'll call around to see her one day this week and I'll ask." Last night's argument sat uncomfortably in my mind.

"You don't want to go now?"

"Now? What's the hurry?"

"I'm going to do a social media campaign about it, highlighting the shop and its history. And there's no time like the present, right? I'm sure Nancy can handle the rush." His sarcastic grin was large and fast.

"I thought you were doing something about that? Aren't our share prices about to go through the roof?"

"We don't have shares," he responded, his grin firmly in place. "But this campaign is going to do a lot for the shop. Trust me."

"My Gran'll be at croquet this morning," I countered, noting the time.

"All the better. More people to question."

I nodded, thinking this would be a great opportunity for me to tell her just how sorry I was that I'd upset her, but I wasn't going to take up her offer of finding me a job. "I'll have to borrow Nancy's car. Mine's in having a service."

"I can drive you. I have a few things I need to do anyway."

I froze. Two reasons. One—I was going to be alone in a confined space with Aaron. What on earth would we talk about? And two—If Gran saw me rock up in his car she'd have a heart attack.

"It's okay," he said, sensing my apprehension. "I'll park around the back of the building where she can't see me."

Aarons' BMW was exquisite. The leather was soft, the air conditioning was set at the perfect temperature, and I could smell his woody aftershave as he fidgeted next to me.

"I never expected you to be a Beemer kind of guy," I said in an attempt to alleviate the awkwardness I felt.

"Really? What did you think I'd drive?"

"I liked the old truck you had before you went to Europe." I'd secretly loved that vehicle. It had been a two door, Ford F100. It was more rusty than red, had no air conditioning and I'd only been a passenger in it once when he'd given a group of us a lift home in the tray.

"I loved that truck too, but Germany taught me an appreciation for vehicles."

"Do you miss Europe?"

"Nope. I enjoyed it while I was there, but in the words of Dorothy—there's no place like home."

"I bet your family was happy to have you back. They must have missed you."

Aaron laughed and the crinkles around his eyes deepened. "Mum did. My brothers—not so much."

"They don't miss the trouble you used to get in, more like," I teased.

"Ha! It was them getting into trouble. I was always helping them out of it!"

I giggled. "Sure. I believe you."

"It's true!"

He pulled up at a red light and swiveled in his seat to face me. The blue flecks in his eyes darkened and humor sat in their depths.

"What about you?" he asked, the humor disappearing as a serious shadow took its place. "You never married what's-his-face."

"If you're referring to Mitch, no. He and I parted ways not long after you left town." Aaron nodded and I figured he already knew that news.

"What about Frankie? I heard you talking to Nancy about him. Sounds like the two of you are pretty close." Aaron gulped and turned his attention to a speck of dust on the dash, looking anywhere but at me.

"Yeah. We're like that," I replied, crossing my fingers and holding them up for him to see. "He takes up far more than his share of the bed and he snores. I honestly never thought I'd share my bed with a snorer, but you can't stop love."

"You love him?" Aaron asked, his voice husky, his eyes jumping to my fingers that I still had crossed.

"Ahuh," I replied. "He's the love of my life."

The light changed and with the hint of a nod, Aaron's jaw tensed as he hit the accelerator, the car rapidly gathering speed and forcing me back into my seat.

"So...will you two get married?"

"Married?" I laughed. "No. Even if they make it legal to marry your dog, I will never marry Frankie."

Confusion creased his brow as he squinted in thought.

"Frankie's my dog," I explained. "He's a short haired Dachshund."

He snapped his head around to look at me, then let out a bark of laughter, his body relaxing back into the leather. "Well that's a relief."

The Westport Croquet club was situated in an activities complex generally suited to the town's older residents. The group of buildings contained the chess club, the croquet club, the bridge club, and one of our many bowls clubs. The grounds on Ivy Road were large, manicured, and well-maintained. Ivy Road was a pretty name, but the reality was that just slightly further along it you would find the Westport rubbish dump. Sure the council kept it clean and neat, but when the wind blew in the wrong direction, the stench was awful.

The car slowed as Aaron indicated into Ivy Road. "Can you drop me here?" I asked, before he could pull up anywhere near the Croquet club.

"But we're a good hundred meters away."

"That's the point. If anyone sees me getting out of your car, I'll be banished to Siberia."

A heaviness settled in the air as he pulled the car to a stop.

"You're hardly dressed for the walk," he commented as his gaze scanned my body.

I followed his eyes to the scooped neckline of my shirt, and my three-inch stilettos, and admitted a hike wasn't what I was thinking of when I dressed this morning. "I'll survive," I commented, opening the door and stepping into the heat.

"You've got my number. Call when you're ready to be picked up. I'll park around the corner so no one sees me lurking. And I'd do up at least two more buttons before some of the men keel over," he suggested, his megawatt smile dissolving the awkwardness.

"Thank you," I mumbled.

I threw my handbag over my shoulder as I stood on the grass footpath and watched him drive away, the purr of the engine even sexier when I was on the outside of the vehicle. But then that could have been enhanced by the man driving it. As he disappeared from sight, I fumbled with my buttons, turned and trudged towards the clubhouse, regretting my choice of footwear.

As I walked my mind ran over Aaron wondering how I'd hated him only a short while ago and how now my heart did a trippy thing every time I so much as thought about him.

But had I hated him?

The faster I walked, the faster my mind whirred over memories. The very first time that I'd ever met him was at a Mickey Mouse birthday party we were both invited to. He pulled my pig tails and teased me about the bow I wore in my hair. I then remembered the times he always seemed to be around whenever trouble was near me, I remembered all the times that his brothers picked fights with my boyfriends, and I remembered how it all culminated on the night of my twenty first birthday. I'd blamed him for it all. Thinking back though, I was having a hard time putting my finger on exactly what he had done wrong. Even the night of my birthday he hadn't thrown the first punch. So what was the feeling that I had for him? Was it hatred? Was it love?

I shook the last thought from my mind. No.

Sure my heart beat faster when he was around, and I may have noticed how sexy he was, and how defined his abs were. But that was lust. That was a completely different thing to love and my hormosnes were just reacting to not having a man for longer than I cared to think about.

"What's a pretty young thing like you doing in a place like this?" a croaky voice called to me, his eyebrows wiggling. "Looking for someone to play with?"

"I'll tell my Gran on you Mr. Wilson," I said, waggling my finger at the innuendo.

He paled, despite the thick sunscreen he'd plastered across his face.

"I'm sorry Gracie! I was just kidding. But I promise not to tell her I saw you getting out of Aaron Douglas's car if you don't tell her what I just said."

"You saw that?" Bugger! "You're supposed to have bad eyesight."

"Not me. I got my cataracts done three weeks ago. I now have the eyesight of an eagle. Well...at long distances anyway. Close up I can't see a bloody thing."

I considered his offer. "You have to pinky promise you won't tell Gran. She'll have a stroke if she finds that information out. I'm supposed to be banned from being anywhere near him."

"So I heard."

I sighed.

"I'm real sorry about that," he continued. "Aaron was always one of the better Douglas boys in my opinion."

"Can you tell Gran that?"

"Nope! Not me. No sirree."

Great.

After we crossed our pinky fingers and both swore to secrecy, I left Mr. Wilson in search of my Gran. I found her sitting under one of the umbrellas sipping an iced tea.

"What are you doing here?" she asked me with a grin. "I'm not complaining. It's a lovely surprise," she quickly added, any awkwardness between us forgotten. Gran was dressed in white from the top of the little hat she wore, right down to the tip of her sensible shoes. She had her croquet mallet resting against the arm of her chair, and the complete attention of Arnold McDonald smiling across the table at her.

"I was in the neighborhood and thought I'd stop by."

"Gracie, do you know that whenever you tell a lie the tips of your ears go red?"

I exhaled. Loudly. "Sorry."

"So what really brings you here today?"

I quickly brought her up to date with how I found the dress (I left out the part of me and Aaron being alone together in the attic). "So I was wondering, as you were once a seamstress for The Ivory Veil did you ever see the dress while you worked there?"

I noticed the subtle straightening of her shoulders and the deepening of her frown when I mentioned her employment, but other than that she kept her expression neutral.

"I don't know what you are talking about, Gracie," she insisted.

"We found the payroll records."

She at least had the grace to blush. "Well, that was for a very short period of my life, and it was so long ago I'd completely forgotten.'

I bit my tongue as the tips of her ears turned red.

"Maybe I can jog your memory," I suggested, pulling my phone from my handbag and retrieving the photo I took of the dress. She was, after all, our best shot at finding out its truth.

"Gracie, do you mind if we do this another time?" she asked, lifting herself to standing. "It's time for my match."

"But it'll only take a second," I pushed, holding the photo up for her to look at.

She released a long pained breath and took the phone from me. As she did I watched her closely. I knew Gran well and I knew her mannerisms. Only what I saw surprised me.

Before she could blink, I saw her eyes mist over, a memory dancing within their depths. With the flutter of her lids, she ground her teeth and handed the phone back to me. "I'm sorry. I've never seen it before."

Why was she lying? What was she hiding?

"I just wondered if you'd know who made it?"

"I'm sorry I can't help you. Now if you'll excuse me I have a match to play." She smacked a hard and fast kiss on my cheek and then shuffled her way towards the green, Arnold McDonald following in her wake.

Chapter Five

The day passed in a blur after that. I accompanied Aaron while he did the things he needed to do, then we headed back to the shop whereby we had a busy afternoon.

He'd been true to his word and had started a series of posts about the ivory lace wedding dress, which he shared to our Facebook and Instagram pages. It didn't take long for our phones to start ringing.

"Aaron can you please update the post to say that the dress is not for sale!" snapped Nancy after the tenth call in a row she'd received about it.

Thankfully I'd been kept busy with fittings, so I hadn't been on phone duty.

Aaron dusted the knees of his navy-blue pants, removing the remnants of dirt from the attic floor.

"Did you find anything useful?" I asked him.

"I've just been going through the old records again. My next post is going to be about the history of the shop so I've taken some photos of the attic and the mound of records that we found, but other than that nope. Nothing useful."

I nodded. He really was full of great ideas.

"I've brought down the patterns," he continued. "I didn't know if Mrs. Boyce would like them."

Behind him was one of the old cardboard boxes. The top was open and I could see the yellowed edges of the pages within.

"I also thought I'd take home some of the old sales logs. The dress might be listed in there somewhere. It puzzles me as to why this one was kept but no others were."

"That's a lot of bed time reading," I commented, knowing I wouldn't make it past the first page before I fell asleep from boredom.

He shrugged. "I don't mind. It gives me something to do in the evening. Plus my bedroom is so much warmer than it is here." He grinned, rubbing the goosebumps from his arms.

"Some days her hot flushes are better than others. Today is a bad day."

"So I'd noticed."

"Hey Nancy," I called as she prepared the shop for the end of day. "Can you give me a lift to Annabelle's, please? She's having an essential oils party and I promised I'd go."

"What's wrong with your car??" she snapped. It seemed that menopause was also making her irritable.

"The mechanic called to tell me that it isn't going to be ready until tomorrow afternoon. Apparently there's something wrong with the thing and they can't get parts for it until then."

"The thing?" Aaron asked, as he lifted the box full of ledgers.

"Yeah. The thing in the motor. It needs a new one." I shrugged. As if I had any idea what the mechanic was actually talking about.

Aaron grinned. "Well, I hope he can get the part he needs. A motor needs its thing."

Smart ass.

"I'm sorry Gracie," interrupted Nancy, pushing the cash from the register into a bag, ready to hand it to Aaron. "I can't give you a lift today. I have somewhere that I need to get to by five past."

"Oh. Okay. No problem." As an afternoon storm had rolled in, I figured a walk was out of question and I'd need to call an Uber.

"I'll give you a lift," Aaron offered.

"It's probably out of your way."

"Where does Annabelle live?"

"Kent Street."

"Awesome. That's not far from me."

"Where do you live?" Curiosity got the better of me.

"The Esplanade."

My mouth fell open.

"But, but that's nowhere near Kent Street. In fact, it's on the complete opposite side of town."

"So I'll be taking the scenic route home," he replied nonchalantly. "Now if you'd like the lift, you'd better grab your bag. Nancy's about to lock up."

Nancy marched towards the door, turning the sign to 'Closed'. "If you're going to be much longer you can lock up yourselves," she snapped.

"Nancy, are you okay?" I asked, rushing to grab my handbag and following her out the door. Aaron was already at his car, loading the cardboard boxes into his trunk.

"I'm fine. I just have a date and I'm telling him that it's over."

"I'm sorry to hear that."

"Don't be. The fool's been two timing me with Marcia Macmillan. Stupid man," she muttered. "Stupid, stupid man."

The mood Nancy was in I didn't doubt that he was about to regret that.

"Well, call if you need a shoulder to cry on," I offered as she locked the door.

"Thank you, but you'll find me celebrating with Thomas Michaels. He's just got out of a relationship and he too needs someone to mop his tears." The spark reignited in her eye and I knew that she was going to be fine.

As she stomped towards her car, I made my way towards Aaron.

"Thank you," I offered as he held the door open for me. I slid onto the leather, and inhaled his scent that hung in the air.

"What time do you have to be there?" he asked.

"Annabelle's? Ummm the party starts at six thirty, so no hurry."

"Good. Then you don't mind if we have a quick stop on the way?"

"Sure. Do whatever you need to do."

The engine roared to life, the vibration travelling through my seat. "What sort of car is this?" Maybe I should save up and buy one for myself.

"It's a BMW 8 series coupe. Twin turbo 8 cylinder 4.4-liter petrol engine with 390 kilowatts of power."

Why did I ask?

"Okay. If you say so."

He looked across at me and smiled. "Trust me."

Funnily enough, I did trust him. And not just about what type of car he drove.

As he expertly maneuvered the vehicle through the streets of Westport the businesses started to disappear and the river soon came into view.

The afternoon storm that hovered gave the usually aqua blue water an almost unreal quality, the low air pressure causing the humidity to sit in close. The BMW pulled to a stop outside Café by the River and Aaron killed the motor.

"Thought we'd have time for a quick coffee," he explained.

I didn't need to be asked twice. I loved this café.

I also loved the iced coffee Aaron bought me and the view that we had looking out across the water from the shade of the large over hanging trees. But I did wonder why he'd brought me here as we slowly walked side by side along the boardwalk as it meandered its way towards the ocean.

"Are you happy with the way things are going at the shop?" I asked.

"Very. I still have a lot to learn and a new system to put into place, but I'm not in a hurry."

"You're happy with me and the way things are going between us?" I meant the question innocently, but Aaron's look sizzled me all the way to my toes.

"Always Gracie. I'm always happy with you."

My belly fizzed with excitement, but I needed to keep this professional as Aaron had the ability to break my heart.

"So this isn't a performance review or anything then?"

He laughed. "No. I just thought it was a lovely afternoon, and what better way to spend it than with great company?"

If I was worried that our time alone would be awkward or that we wouldn't have anything to chat about, I was wrong.

Being with him was easy.

The thought was a little unsettling but I wasn't going to let it spoil the afternoon, instead I relaxed and listened as he recounted his adventures in Europe. It only got awkward once I accidentally brought up a memory from before he left.

"Oh, I had that one!" I squealed as he told me about a Rhianna CD he owned. "Mitch gave it to me for Christmas that year."

Aaron's jaw tensed, his posture tightened and his cup suddenly became the most interesting thing in the world.

"I'm sorry," I said quietly.

"You've got nothing to be sorry about."

"I made things awkward."

"No. Mitch did that."

We continued to walk in silence for a few moments as I considered his words.

"Why did you hate him so much?" I asked.

Aaron stopped walking and turned to face me. His body was only inches from mine and I could feel the heat of his breath as he looked down at me through his dark lashes.

His lips parted as he considered his response. The flecks in his eyes darkened as his brow creased and the boyish vulnerability that shone down at me took my breath away.

The sounds of the afternoon ceased in my mind. The birds stopped singing, the wind stopped whistling through the leaves, and the sounds of nearby laughter disappeared as I waited for him to reply.

Finally, he took a deep shuddery breath and tucked a stray hair behind my ear, his fingers sending a thrill all the way to my soul. As they gently slid down my cheek, I gave an involuntary sigh and turned towards his touch. As his thumb traced a path across my bottom lip I groaned. Aaron lowered his head, his lips parted, his gaze searching. When his mouth hovered above mine he whispered, "He didn't deserve you."

My stomach clenched and my breath got caught in my lungs as I waited for him to close the gap and for his lips to find mine. Instead the loud obnoxious ringing of his phone broke the moment.

"Are you going to get that?" I asked as the sounds of *old bell* killed the mood.

He sighed before turning away, retrieving the call.

As disappointed as I was, I was also grateful for the chance to catch my breath and to regroup my thoughts. Kissing Aaron was very appealing, but was it sensible? No it was not.

I wasn't a rebel. I never did anything wrong or stepped outside the lines, and I wasn't about to start now. Was I?

Argh! Why did this feel so good? Why did I have to be attracted to the one man that I couldn't have?

As he took a few steps away greeting his caller, I swallowed hard, yet I allowed my mind to wander over possibilities of what could be. But then the vision of Sophie standing alongside him in the restaurant filled my mind. She looked good with him, and her family would probably welcome him at the dinner table. Unlike mine.

Annabelle's essential oil party wasn't going to rock my world, but I had to support family, right?

Darcy worked in IT and he was very good at what he did, which meant that he and Annabelle could afford to live in the more affluent part of town. Kent Street was on the hill overlooking Westport, the river and the ocean. Their view was spectacular. Today that view was blocked by the sea of vehicles parked outside her house. Annabelle wasn't only just the perfect child, she was also the perfect friend, hence the packed room I slid into.

She grabbed my arm and pulled me into Darcy's home office. "Do you have a death wish?" she asked, her eyes wide. Her figure hugging purple dress belied that she'd had a baby only a few short months ago.

"What are you talking about?" I dropped my handbag onto Darcy's desk and straightened my shirt.

"You know exactly what I'm talking about. If I'm not mistaken that white BMW you just got out of belongs to Aaron Douglas."

"So?"

"So grandma will be here any minute. If you're unlucky then she'll be passing him as he drives down the street."

"Grandma's coming?"

"Of course she is. She heard that essential oils can help with libido."

I shuddered.

"Maybe you should be buying some," she suggested.

"Nothing wrong with my libido."

"Yeah. I was thinking more of slowing it down."

Maybe that was a good idea as my body still buzzed from Aaron's hand as his fingers had delicately brushed mine before I had gotten out of his car.

"I don't know what you're talking about," I protested as squeals from two of her party guests echoed along the hall. Maybe they'd found the libido oil.

"I saw the way you looked at him in the restaurant."

"How? As if he's just made my life a whole lot more difficult?"

It wasn't a lie. My life had been so much simpler before he'd walked right back into it.

"No. As if all your Christmases just came in one extremely good looking and well-toned package."

I giggled. "Yeah, I'll admit that I may have noticed the package too."

"Tell me, when did Aaron Douglas get so hot?" Annabelle fanned herself dramatically and leaned her backside against the desk.

"He was always hot," I let slip.

She gasped. "You sneaky little...you never told me you had a crush on him!"

"I never did! Honest to god."

She cocked her head to one side, her lips pursed.

"Okay! Maybe I did just a little. But that was a very long time ago before he hated me."

"So what are you going to do about it?"

"Absolutely nothing. You said yourself that if Gran so much as finds out I was in his car, then she's going to kill someone. Not sure if that'll be me or him."

"Maybe he can win her over. He does have a pretty good smile."

"It's not that good," I sulked, picking up Darcy's stapler and fiddling with it. "Anyway, it doesn't matter. He has a girlfriend so Gran doesn't need to worry. It's not like I'm about to hook up with him," I said, my tone flat and monotonous even to my own ears.

Annabelle raised an eyebrow. "She can disappear. I know someone."

"Gran?"

"No! The girlfriend."

My eyes widened as she broke out into a grin and I accidentally squeezed the stapler, lodging a metal bar into my finger.

I cried and Annabelle scoffed taking the device from me and placing it back on to the desk.

"Don't encourage me!" I complained, sucking my finger to stop the blood. "You're supposed to tell me that Aaron and I would never work."

"I'm your big sister. I'm here to fix things for you."

"He hates me, Gran hates him, his family hates ours. That's a lot to fix."

Annabelle pulled me into her arms and squeezed me tight. "I don't think he hates you," she whispered.

I didn't want to admit it, but I thought that too. The memory of his eyes as his fingers caressed my cheek caused my heart to flutter, and my knees to go weak. "That's not helping," I said more to myself than Anna.

Chapter Six

With Annabelle's advice and some amazing essential oils (lavender to help with my anxiety, camphor oil to keep my libido in check, and peppermint oil to keep me focused), I awoke the following day with a plan in mind.

The first part of the plan was to keep my job and Aaron was going to help me do it.

"So you want me to do what?" he asked.

"Have an invitation only event here at the shop. We'll make the dress the focus, the theme fashion from the 1950's."

"And who's being invited?"

"Your family. And mine. Among others."

Aarons' eyebrows disappeared somewhere under his hair.

"You think it's a good idea to have them in the same room together?"

"Sure. Okay no. But they'll be in public. What can they do?"

"Do you remember Christmas of 2001? When the restaurant muddled up its bookings and both our families were there at the same time?"

I bit my thumbnail as the memory caused a shudder to travel all the way to my toes.

"We'll tell them they have to behave."

"What's the purpose of this event?" Aaron asked, sitting heavily on the kitchen chair.

The shop had just opened and I'd started the day full of enthusiasm and great ideas.

"I thought that maybe we can get them together and end this feud once and for all."

Nancy had been leaning against the door jamb listening.

"Not sure about the feud thing, but I think the event is a great idea. You've been getting a lot of attention on social media with the dress, this would be a great way to make the most of it."

"Ahuh," I pushed on. "We could set the room up like a 1950's wedding. One mannequin in the dress we found and another in top hat and tails. We have the arbor already decorated from the expo so it wouldn't take a lot to recreate a wedding scene."

"It would pull in heaps of interest," continued Nancy, getting into the spirit. "And could do a lot to boost our sales, especially as my new man is in radio advertising. He could give us the extra exposure we'd need."

Excitement buzzed as my idea grew. "Please Aaron," I begged. "Please?"

His eyes held mine for a moment and the buzz zinged all the way to my doodah.

"Sure. If you think this is a great idea, then we'll do it. Just tell me what you need from me."

"Money," stated Nancy. "Fake or not, weddings are expensive."

Aaron's grin was large and fast. "Alright. Get me a list of what you need and we'll go shopping."

Phase one, ready and set to go.

"Do we really need this much alcohol?" Aaron complained.

"Yes. If our families are going to be in the same room together, then that box will just be for me."

"Then I'm going to need something much stronger than that." He pushed the trolley loaded with all types of wine, towards the spirits aisle. I watched mesmerized as his eyes travelled along the bottles of whiskey, searching for the one he wanted. His eyes were bright, full of happiness and hope, and I wished—just for a second—that they would look at me like that.

But then at times when he thought I wasn't looking, they had.

Gulping at the thought, I picked up the closest bottle and pretended to study it, all the while attempting to slow my heart rate by reminding myself of why Aaron and I couldn't be together.

"Coming over to the dark side?" he joked, taking the bottle from me, ready to place it in the trolley.

"I think I'm going to need it."

He laughed, the sound dancing across my navel and causing areas to tingle that shouldn't when I was in a public place.

"So once you get everyone together, what's your plan on how to end the feud?"

I'd considered this a lot, and I still had no idea. "I was kind of hoping that would come to me in the moment."

"Hmmm, I think we're going to need a backup plan."

"You mean an escape route."

He laughed. "Yeah, that's a better name for it."

"I was hoping that if we force them to talk to one another, they can hopefully sort their problems out. Something started it, and even if we can learn what that was, it has to be a start, right?"

"I agree getting them together could be the catalyst to get them talking. They're not exactly upfront right now."

I was about to respond when I heard his name being called.

"Aaron!" Sophie bounded towards us, her heels clicking against the tiled floor. She looked particularly pretty in her cut off denim shorts and fitted T-shirt. Her blonde hair was in a messy bun and her make-up was minimal. Yet somehow, she made the whole package look completely ravishing.

It didn't go unnoticed by Aaron as he turned his bright eyes towards her and his smile upped in wattage.

"Hey," he almost sang. "I wasn't expecting to see you here." He greeted her with a hug which she welcomed. Well, I was judging that by the way she clung to him.

Alright, the green-eyed monster was sitting on my shoulder, yelling in my ear. I tried to ignore it by giving Sophie a tiny wave, and busying myself in the vodka aisle, but my gaze kept moving back to them watching as their heads were close, Sophie's giggling wafting towards me.

Aaron looked down at her, his smile reflected in his eyes, his love for her apparent. She gazed up at him, completely in awe and my stomach clenched as a feeling of helplessness smothered me.

I was in so deep it was drowning me. Gran was right—the Douglas men were trouble. Aaron had the ability to destroy me.

I shook myself, relaxing my hold on the vodka bottle in my hand. I needed to focus, get my feelings under control and concentrate. Saving my job would kill two problems with one stone.

It would take my mind off my heart, by giving me something else to focus on, and it would keep me from disemboweling fish.

Aaron had already mentioned that once he had everything in the store updated he would rarely be around. It would be easier then.

I'd only have to chat to him on very few occasions and surely I could talk Nancy into doing that for me. Surely.

His deep gravelly laugh echoed across the aisle, causing my gaze to move towards him.

He moved closer, kissing her cheek.

"I'll see you tonight," he said as she stepped away, her hand lifted in a wave.

"I can't wait. It's going to be amazing!' she trilled.

I'd bet it was.

Chapter Seven

Our family were all busy people. Annabelle had yoga and Jacob, Darcy had a full-time job and his gym membership, dad was the chairmen of the Men's Shed, Mum was on the tennis committee, and Gran had many men to compete for. That meant it was often difficult for us to schedule time together. But we made the effort once a month. Dad would cook a barbeque lunch on a Sunday afternoon and we would all meet up, rain, hail or shine.

Today was that day. Thankfully it was sunny, which meant that while dad cooked, mum and Gran prepared the salad, Darcy swam in the pool with Jacob, and Annabelle and I did whatever we pleased.

We were in the hallway, the cupboard doors wide open blocking the passage. We sat on the floor and had every single photo album that mum owned spread around us, giggling at the things she made us wear. I hadn't mentioned yet that everyone was invited to The Ivory Veil Bridal extravaganza, and I didn't think I would until I was just about to walk out the door.

"Why did she always dress us the same?" I asked, my mind on the photo in front of me. "We're three years apart."

"Oh my god! Don't let Darcy see this." Annabelle's look was sheer horror. "We look like boys!"

I laughed at the colored skivvies and black jeans that we both wore.

"We look like The Wiggles," I added. "I remember begging mum to make me a costume."

"But why did I have to wear it too?" she asked, perplexed.

I flipped the page in the album. "Oh look, we're in matching dresses."

"She was pretty talented with the sewing machine," Annabelle noted, looking over my shoulder and studying the photo. "I can't even sew a button on."

"I didn't inherit her abilities either, but I can find my way around a machine. I had to or I wouldn't have passed my diploma."

"That's right. I remember the wedding dress you made for your finals."

"Yeah, we had to model it for a final fashion show."

"Wasn't it made from calico?" she asked, wrinkling her nose.

"Yep. There's probably a photo in here somewhere."

"No. Mum's digital now. It'll be on the computer."

"Oh here's mum and dads' wedding album!" I pulled an ornate cream, padded photo album from the pile. The pages were yellowed around the edges, each one separated by thin sheets of paper protecting the precious memories.

"Geez, could her sleeves have gotten any bigger?" Annabelle scoffed, as I opened the first page and studied a photo of mum holding onto the arm of grandpa as if her life depended on it.

I giggled. "They were competing with her hair."

I turned the page to see another photo of mum standing with both her parents. Grandpa looked very distinguished in his deep grey suit, pressed white shirt and matching tie, while Gran was wearing a matching top and skirt made in multi-colored silk.

"Oh geez."

I giggled as we turned page after page, laughing at the fashion of the late 1980's.

"What are you girls giggling about?" Gran asked, walking towards us.

"Your choice of outfit for mum's wedding."

"What was wrong with it?"

"Ummm," Where do I start?

"The color for one. It looks like a rainbow threw up all over it," stated Annabelle.

Gran scoffed. "That was all the rage."

"Did you make it, Gran?" I asked. On closer inspection the outfit was extremely well tailored. The shirt had a band of smocking across both shoulders before falling into a V-neckline with handmade buttons, and the skirt was cut on the bias allowing the hem to float around her legs.

"Yes. I made all the dresses, including your mother's and her bridesmaids'."

"At least they were a little less colorful," noted Annabelle, flipping the page and stopping at a photo of wedding party lined up outside the church.

"The color was melon, but it looks pink in the photos. Inside the bodice of your mother's dress had the same fabric."

"That would have been really pretty," I trilled.

"It was. Anyway, lunch is going to be ready in about twenty minutes." With that Gran shuffled her way back down the hallway towards the kitchen, probably to pour herself a brandy.

"Mum still has the dress," Annabelle added. "She was keeping it for one of us to wear when we got married." She shrugged as a grin broke out. "I saved it for you."

Hunph. "Well it has some good points."

"Like what?"

"The lace around the collar is really pretty. Not that I can see it that well."

"It's in the attic if you want to try it on." She was mocking me, but I could honestly see some beauty in the dress.

"Okay. Let's go find it."

We hurriedly restacked the albums and then made our way to the garage. Mum and dad still lived in the same house they had purchased straight after getting married. The paint color had changed as had the carpets, but otherwise everything pretty much remained the status quo.

Annabelle found a ladder and I followed her into the roof space. Years of storage had accumulated, so it took us a few minutes to push the Christmas tree and decorations aside and make our way towards the back.

"Over there!" I pointed to a box marked 'wedding'. Annabelle retrieved the box and ripped back the tape holding it closed.

Mum had done the right thing and had wrapped the dress in blue tissue paper, so after pulling back the layers we found what we were looking for.

Annabelle giggled as I lifted it from its bed, holding it against myself.

It was very different to the last dress that I'd found in storage. This one was vivid white, with large puffy sleeves, a delicate lace collar and itchy tulle leading to a plunging neckline. The skirt was crushed silk and would have had at least two hoops holding it out.

"What were they thinking in the eighties?" Annabelle asked.

"What were they smoking, more like."

"Do you still think it's nice?"

"The collar is. The lace is really pretty. Maybe one day when I get married Mum'll let me pull this one apart and I can use it."

"Hmmm, thinking of getting married, are you?" she teased.

"I've had my dress picked out since I was sixteen. Well, I thought I had."

"Please don't tell me that this one has changed your mind," Annabelle almost begged.

I lowered the dress and sat on the raw timber boards of the attic floor, and recounted the story of how Aaron and I found the ivory dress.

"I have a photo," I finished, retrieving my phone and showing her the shop's Instagram page. Aaron had done an amazing job with the photos and stories posted and already they had several thousand likes. The last post I'd made had fifty likes and I'd been proud of that.

"Wow. That is lovely."

"Just look at the handmade lace," I enthused. "It's so delicate."

Annabelle used two fingers and zoomed the photo in. She scrunched her nose up as she studied it and then looked at me. "It kind of looks like the collar of mum's dress."

I snatched the phone and peered closely at what she was showing me. I then grabbed mum's dress and pulled back the meters of crushed silk until I held the collar in my hand, comparing it to the photo. The tiny rosettes with the iridescent pearls sitting amongst the delicate posies, and the almost invisible knots had me gasping. They were almost exactly the same.

I sunk back on my heels and looked at Annabelle, my thoughts erratic. "So could Gran have made the ivory dress?"

Annabelle looked as unsure as I felt. "Didn't you just say that because it's all handmade then every maker has a unique style?"

"Ahuh. And these do look very similar. But if Gran made this dress then why didn't she just say so? I'd own up to it if it were me. The dress is stunning."

"Is it Gran's wedding dress?"

"No. Her dress was cream satin and had no embellishments."

"Maybe she made if for someone."

"Maybe. But why lie about it?" I sat, thoughtful for a few minutes. As dad's voice called us for dinner, I repacked mum's dress, but not before taking a photo of it.

"Annabelle, don't ask Gran about it today. I want to talk with Mrs. Boyce first. Just to check that what we're seeing is indeed correct."

"Sure. Whatever you think is best."

"Gracie, I meant to tell you," said Gran, stabbing her steak with her fork. "You need to be at Joe's Fishery at nine tomorrow morning."

I stopped, my breath catching, my fork halfway to my lips. "W...why?" I managed, allowing the fork to drop to my plate.

"To start work. He needs someone to clean the fish. One of his deckies is sick, so he has some fill in work for you."

Revulsion rumbled through my belly and I thought I may have just thrown up in my mouth a little.

"Oh mum. Really?" My mum looked as horrified as I felt.

"Ahuh. I had to pull a few strings as there was more than one person after the position, but Joe's father has a thing for me, so I got special privileges."

I stared at her, open mouthed.

"You're welcome," she finished, directing a glare my way.

Perspiration broke out on my forehead as my palms became clammy. There was no way I could clean fish for a living. "But Gran, I love the job I have now!" I protested.

"That maybe so, but there are bigger problems in life, Grace."

Annabelle nudged Darcy. "Are there any jobs going where you work?"

He shrugged, unaware of the fear I was feeling.

"Thanks Anna, but I don't want to work there either."

"I just thought it would be better than gutting fish," she replied.

"I thought they did that on the boat?" asked dad.

"These are special fish," explained Gran.

Special or not there was no way I was removing their intestines.

"But I can't let Nancy down. We've been really busy lately." I hated the idea of arguing with Gran again, but I had to fight for what I believed in.

"Then she should have been more prepared. You've already given notice so what will a few days matter?"

I gulped.

"Gracie you did resign, didn't you?" asked Gran.

"Ummm, well here's the thing..."

The tension around the table grew as everyone stopped eating to observe what was going to happen next.

"Grace Leanne Saunders!" Gran snapped. I jumped, knocking my plate and sending its contents across the table.

"I'm s...sorry," I stuttered as my plate hit my wine glass, which then fell spilling its contents into Darcy's dinner. He jumped to avoid the spillage, bumping Annabelle, who was about to put her steak into her mouth. Instead it slipped, her Diane sauce smearing across her cheek.

Mum sighed, dad moaned, and I cried as a pain started behind my breastbone. That pain increased as Aaron's face filled my mind. Is this what a heart attack felt like?

"I'm not doing it!" I cried. Mum looked close to crying herself, but why I had no idea.

"Stop overreacting," Gran scolded. "You're acting like a child."

"No. I'm not. I don't see you making Annabelle work for Joe."

"That's because she has a sensible husband and a good job."

"So do I. Well, the job bit. Not the husband bit, obviously."

"Everything has a reason and a season," Gran continued, full of wisdom. "Your time at The Ivory Veil has come to an end. Now it's time for a new adventure."

Anger bubbled and my foot tapped with agitation.

"Why do you hate them so much?" I demanded, pushing my chair back and standing. "What did the Douglas family ever do to you? Tell me—why are you lying? What are you not telling us?"

Gran's face froze. Mum sucked in her breath, and Jacob cried.

"Gracie, calm down," suggested mum. "You're upsetting everybody."

"I'm not! Gran's upsetting me. Don't my feelings count for anything around here?"

"Of course they do. But you can't talk to your grandmother like that."

"Then tell her to stop organizing my life. I'm perfectly capable of doing that myself."

Gran stood, her narrowed eyes throwing daggers my way. "And how's that working out for you?" she yelled across the table at me.

"Just fine thanks!"

She grabbed the table for support as she swayed unsteadily on her feet, and Mum dashed to help her. "Come on. Why don't you have a lie down?" she suggested, taking Gran's arm and leading her from the room.

As they made their way past me, her eyes filled with tears. "Stay away from them Gracie. Please."

As she shuffled from the room I remembered the invitations to our event were in my bag, but now didn't feel like a great time to be disbursing them.

The following week was our busiest yet. I'd limited my time alone with Aaron as my emotions threatened to get the better of me whenever he was around, but on the odd occasion it was just the two of us it was easy. He made me laugh, told me countless stories of his childhood and how he was always coming to the rescue of his brothers, and when he thought no one was around, he moved in close. It felt like he had something to say, but I never gave him the chance, the image of

Sophie and my Gran shadowing anything that could ever happen between us.

At night, alone in my bed, I allowed my imagination to run wild, to fill the void that I felt whenever he wasn't there, but at the end of my fantasies I reminded myself of the reasons why it could never be.

I just needed to keep busy, to keep my mind occupied until my heart got over him. Thankfully his social media campaign was working well in getting more visitors into the shop than we'd seen in a long time, and Nancy's new man had managed to get us a few radio ads.

Tonight was the night of our event and Nancy and I were busy getting the shop set up. So far with Aaron's help we'd set up the arbor, had dressed one mannequin in the top hat and tails, and moved the ivory dress to stand alongside it. Pink peonies were bunched in glass vases, white roses enhancing their color. Crystal clear glasses were lined up and ready for the champagne, and the canapés were chilling. We'd pushed the ottoman to one side and had placed a few high backed black velvet chairs around the room and had the soft fragrance of the scented candles filling the air.

"Who would have thought that dress would have become famous around here?" Nancy questioned.

"Not me," I replied. "But Aaron's blog has had tons of interest. Tonight's going to be amazing." Even if it didn't get our families together. I'd left the invitations with Annabelle who had promised to give them to mum and Gran, but so far none of them had RSVP'd.

"Everyone wants a dress just like that one. Too bad we still don't know who made it."

"Gracie!" Aaron called, an urgency in his step as he crossed the floor, stopping behind the counter and unloading the mounds of old papers he was holding.

"What's up?"

"I've been going through these old patterns, wanting to create a display for tonight and look what I came across." He lifted a brown leather-bound book for me to see.

"What is it?"

"It's a sketch book of dresses that once were made here."

His eyes were sparkling with excitement, making my belly clench, as he crooked his finger and beckoned me close.

I rushed to stand next to him, our shoulders barely touching, his heat jumping the void and warming my insides.

"I've seen this book before, but had pushed it aside as I've been too busy. But check this out," he continued, pushing the book towards me as Nancy moved in on the opposite side.

The leather binding was old and cracking, the pages yellowed, but the drawings themselves were perfect, showing minute details of the designs. But he turned the pages, deliberately stopping on one particular drawing, I stared open mouthed, my heart momentarily stopping. For there was the ivory dress that had now become so popular. My fingers lovingly skimmed the page, stopping on the designer's name.

"But this says..." I trailed off, my mind skipping as my thoughts were confirmed.

"Yep. The dress was designed and made by your grandmother. But that's not the most startling part. This is," he finished turning the book to the back page.

A secret envelope was bound to the inside of the cover and I watched in awe as Aaron's long fingers lifted the seal, retrieving a black and white photograph. As he turned the photo towards me the image of a woman wearing the ivory gown shone back at me. She was holding a large bouquet, her veil pulled back to show her long tumbling curls, her radiant smile accentuated by the prominent beauty mark just to the right of her top lip. My Gran.

"Whoa," I whispered.

Aaron gave me time for the image to sink in. When my mind managed to catch up I asked, "Do you think she was just modelling it?"

His response was to silently turn the photograph over.

Written across the back in her large loopy writing were the words 'Every touch leaves its trace. 1957' The same inscription that was embroidered inside the dress.

"Welcome!" Nancy greeted our first guests with a smile. "May I offer you both a glass of champagne?" She expertly guided them towards the makeshift bar, as a waiter miraculously appeared from the back room. It had been Aaron's idea to hire them after I'd protested that I could do the food service, but he'd wanted Nancy and I to enjoy tonight as much as possible.

"Have you heard if your family are coming?" Aaron asked from behind me, his lips close to my ear, his breath causing thrills to travel to inappropriate places. I had been trying my best to get him out of my head, but removing him from my heart was proving difficult.

"No, sorry," I replied, turning to face him. "Yours?"

He nodded. "Yep. They all said they'd be here."

Butterflies zipped around my belly making me feel sick and giddy. "Great."

"Oh, here they are now," he replied, his smile illuminating as the bell above the door jingled.

I took a deep calming breath as his parents and his oldest brother made their way towards him, an older gentleman on his arm. I watched in awe as they greeted each other, their love and respect for one another apparent. Seconds later the bell jingled again and my heart missed a beat.

Sophie looked incredible in her slinky dress with the plunging neckline. Her glossy lips and fake eyelashes would make any man go weak at the knees and I discreetly watched Aaron as he kissed her cheek, my champagne mixing with my stomach acid and those damned butterflies.

He spotted me watching him from behind the rim of my glass and directed his smile towards me.

I had nowhere to run, so I pulled my shoulders back and smiled demurely.

"Gracie, I'd like you to meet my family." Nerves shook in his voice and there was a slight tremble of his hand as he held it out to me.

"My parents—Sally and Erik, and my grandfather Arthur. You already know my brother Damien and his girlfriend Sophie." Wait! *What?* "Guys this is Gracie. Gracie Saunders." He was watching their response, but my mind had frozen on his words about Sophie.

She was Aaron's girlfriend not Damien's. I remember him telling us that. Or did he? I definitely saw him out to dinner with her, and he said that he took her home, but he never did say that she was his girlfriend. But I'd seen the way they interacted. I'd seen the way he looked at her, his eyes soft, his touch gentle. Love and compassion oozed from him as he leaned closer to her, his posture open and accepting.

But hang on, he was looking at his mother the same way.

I gulped as he slapped his brother on the back, his eyes moving to mine, vulnerability lying within their depths.

"Pleased to meet you again, Gracie," Sally said, smiling. "You've grown a lot since I last met you."

I laughed, plastering a fake smile on my lips as I gave her my attention, yet my mind was stuck on Aaron's words.

"It has been a while," I replied.

Arthur stepped forward, his eyes just like Aaron's. They had clouded with age, but I could still see the flecks of blue embedded in the smoky grey depths.

"Gracie," he said, his hand reaching to cup mine. He squeezed tight, his smile small, and I wondered if he was remembering a time long before our family feud. But then maybe he was just wishing we'd give him a glass of champagne. I knew I needed a refill.

"Hey Aaron," Damien said, slapping him on the shoulder. "Thanks for helping Sophie. She told me what you did. How you helped her surprise me for my birthday."

"Yeah," she said, her eyes glistening as they looked at Aaron. "I couldn't have done it without you, mate."

"You two are great together and anything I can do to help that along is my pleasure." Aaron beamed.

While we'd been talking the shop had started to fill, guests now chatting around us as they admired the dress, but all of that was background noise as my thoughts tumbled over Sophie and how she wasn't Aaron's girlfriend. I'd been wrong about them. Oh so wrong.

My pulse raced as my imagination took hold and what if's danced in hope.

What if Aaron did feel the way I hoped he felt? What if I let him say what he needed to say? What if we could solve this family feud? Could the future look the way that I wished it could?

"Aaron, would you mind helping me for a moment?" I asked him, as a waiter stopped to give everyone a glass of bubbly.

"Sure. Is everything okay?"

"Ahuh, I just wanted to ummm…I need help with the ummm…the thingy." What I really wanted was to be anywhere but here, where I could get my thoughts together and ask Aaron how he really felt.

His brows knotted, but he gently touched my lower back as I stepped away from his family leading him towards the wall of dresses that skirted the room.

"Where is this thingy?" he asked, humor dancing in his eyes.

I ignored the pull it caused in my belly and asked, "So Sophie is your brother's girlfriend?"

"Yep. They've been together for a couple of years. Why do you ask?"

"It's just that I thought…I thought that you two…were a, ummm, a couple."

"Sophie and I?"

I nodded, as heat raced from my neck to my ears and my breathing became ragged.

"Why did you think that?"

"Well, I saw you together…"

Everything stilled before he slowly nodded with understanding. "No. Sophie and I have always been friends, but my heart has always belonged to someone else."

I gasped as his fingers gently skimmed my jawline, his touch causing my breathing to become difficult, and a lump formed in my throat as I closed my eyes savoring his closeness. As I reopened them my mind buzzed with his face, so close that I could see the blue flecks in his eyes darken.

A slow, lazy smile played on his lips as his gaze held mine, never breaking. "I thought you knew," he whispered.

I gulped as the noise surrounding me disappeared and I was transported to a place that was only Aaron. The warmth of his skin, the slight coloring of his cheeks, and the rapidness of his breath were all I could see, all I could hear, and his touch caused a longing pang next to my heart.

The sounds of Aaron's family moving towards the ivory gown, zapped me back to the present. I hurriedly shook myself enjoying one last intimate smile.

"So this is the dress we've been hearing about?" Sally asked, unaware of the electricity between us. "Oh, it really is gorgeous," she trilled as Arthur stepped up to it.

Arthur's face paled as he silently stood in front of the mannequin. His gaze slowly took it all in, his grip on his cane tightening. He gulped, as his eyes filled with tears.

What the...

"You've got no right to be looking at that!" A shrill voice sounded from behind me.

I jumped, spinning on my heel as the faces of my family stared back at me.

Gran's face was as red as her hair once was, her mouth was set in a firm line, her shoulders rigid, her eyes spitting fire at Arthur as his mouth hung open.

Sally and Erik groaned, mum took Gran's arm, and Annabelle and Darcy slunk to the edge of the room.

"Gracie, your grandmother scares the shit out of me," Aaron whispered as he moved alongside me.

"She scares me at times too, but she's all talk." My heart pounded behind my ribcage and I crossed my fingers, silently praying that tonight would work the way we'd planned.

"Really?"

"Well no, but she won't hurt you with me standing in front of you." I hoped.

"You'd throw your body on the line for me?"

I'd throw my body anywhere he wanted it.

"Sure."

His sigh was deep and long, but he stepped towards Arthur, ready to help him escape.

I took a deep calming breath, and stepped in front of them all, facing Gran.

Silence had shrouded the room as everyone waited for what was coming next, all enthralled by the drama.

She held my stare as my insides quivered beyond belief, but her stare moved past me, landing on the dress. I heard her small gasp as time stood still, her eyes lost in a memory. Slowly she moved towards the mannequin, her aged bony fingers reaching to caress the lace.

"It's still beautiful," she muttered, all traces of anger dissolving with her touch.

"Yes, it is," I agreed.

As she slowly shuffled around the mannequin, Arthur stepped aside allowing her path. Both families seemed to be holding their breath, muscles tensed and ready to jump to action.

Aaron moved alongside me, his fingers reached out and entwined with mine. His touch brought a reassurance and I knew that no matter what happened next, I needed to make it right. I opened my mouth to speak, but Arthur stopped me with a glance.

"It's time to end this, Leonora," he said, his lips trembling. "It's been going on too long."

Her cloudy eyes misted as tears filled behind her lashes, and she lovingly stroked the gown.

"I loved this dress," she whispered.

"And you looked beautiful in it," Arthur continued.

"How would you know?" she spat back at him.

"Because I saw you. I was there."

Shock froze her glare.

"I had to see you one last time," he finished.

"No. You weren't there." She shook her head vehemently. "You never turned up! I was left standing at the church looking like an idiot in front of all my family and friends. That wouldn't have happened if you'd been there."

Arthur gulped as his eyes filled with tears.

Aaron's fingers tightened around mine and I figured he was having a hard a time as I was piecing this together.

"What do you mean? What happened?" I asked Gran.

"It means that you should never trust a Douglas man, Gracie. Not a single one of them." Her tone was harsh, hiding a barrel load of hurt, as she turned to face me. "They suck you in by telling you how much they love you. That you're the love of their life. They can't live without you! And then, when it matters they don't show up!"

She turned her stare towards Arthur but her tone softened as she lovingly touched the gown. "This dress was mine. It took me months to design, to hand stitch it, but it was worth it. It was everything I dreamt it to be." Years disappeared from Gran as her thoughts moved back in time "My mother warned me about you," she said, blinking and spinning towards Arthur. "I didn't believe her. She kept telling me that I should marry Thomas Ackerman, that he would never hurt me. He was a good man and a good friend, but the heart wanted what the heart wanted."

"You were meant for me." Arthur's voice was so quiet I nearly hadn't heard him.

"Is that so?" she asked, hatred and hurt once again pouring from her every pore. "Then why did you get Ivy Morris pregnant if you loved me so much."

A collective gasp travelled the room.

My breath caught in my throat as I thought of the pain that Gran must have felt learning that the man she loved, the one who had ditched her at the altar, had been sleeping with another woman. No wonder she didn't trust the Douglas men.

"Who's Ivy Morris?" Aaron whispered in my ear. I shrugged. This wasn't my story.

"I never meant to hurt you Leonora. I was about to leave home for our wedding when Ivy showed up on my doorstep. She was bleeding and telling me that she was losing the baby. My baby. But it was a lie. It wasn't mine."

Gran's hand shot to her heart and her knees started to shake. I hurriedly grabbed the nearest chair and helped her sit down, my own heart pounding. She looked shell shocked, her speech momentarily gone.

"I'm sorry Leonora," Arthur continued, shuffling to stand close to her. "I wanted to tell you, but by the time I learned the truth you'd already married Thomas. You seemed happy with your choice. I didn't want to destroy that," he finished quietly.

The clock ticked the minutes away as we all digested the truth.

"It doesn't matter," Gran replied, her voice void of emotion. "If she convinced you that she was pregnant then you had obviously slept with her."

"No, I didn't! She just told me that I did." We all eyed him suspiciously. "You remember how my family was always close to hers? Our parents had parties all the time?"

Gran nodded.

"Well, one night, Ivy got me really drunk. I don't remember a single thing of the night, but the next day she told me that we'd slept together. I later learned that she'd fabricated the whole story. The baby belonged to another man. One who didn't want to know anything about it, so she lied, too ashamed to admit the truth."

Arthur hung his head low, thoughts jumbled on his face. "I was just the gullible idiot who believed her."

"You never told me," Gran said, her voice now shaking, her eyes wide. "You should have told me."

"Would it have changed anything?" he asked. "Would you have left Thomas?"

She slowly shook her head, her eyes falling to her lap, a long breath fleeing her lips. "No. Thomas gave me a good life, and decisions had been made." She lifted her gaze to Arthur. "But you still could have told me before I was humiliated when you didn't turn up."

"I did! I sent Ivy's brother."

"Then how did you see me in the dress?"

"Because I drove past the church on the way to the hospital. You were standing next to the car about to get back into it."

"No one told me that you weren't coming." Grans' eyes were haunted with remembrance. "I waited not wanting to believe it, but eventually even I had to admit the obvious."

"He came back and told me that you were upset but you understood." Confusion sat in Arthur's wrinkles as he squinted.

"Understood! No woman understands something like that happening to her on her wedding day!" Gran shook her head again, tears silently running down her cheeks.

"I'm sorry Leonora. I'm truly sorry. I never meant for any of that to happen. I wanted to marry you, to spend my life with you, and a day hasn't passed where I didn't regret losing you."

Heartache and anguish shone bright in Grans eyes. "It was a lifetime ago. Nothing can be changed."

"Yes it can," I interrupted, thinking without the family feud the future could look different for everyone involved. "You can forgive Arthur for being fooled, for making the choice to stand by a mistake he thought he'd made, and you can know in your heart that the Douglas men are good people."

The problem with pain is that it just doesn't go away once the truth has been set free. Gran struggled with lifelong emotions as her gaze travelled between Aaron and I. He squeezed my hand, transmitting his courage and hope to me with his touch.

Tears once again filled behind her lashes, but she released a long breath, a lifetime of hurt travelling with it. She ground her teeth, her eyes darting between us. "I see the way he looks at you. It's the same way that Arthur once looked at me and it scares me."

Arthur's chin dropped to his chest as sorrow burnished his eyes. "Please Leonora. Don't judge him based on my choices."

Gran considered what he said. "I don't want you to get hurt, Gracie. I love you way too much."

"I know. I love you too and I'm sorry that you were hurt the way you were. But that doesn't mean that my destiny is the same as yours. Please Gran, let me walk my own path."

Her hand reached out and took mine, squeezing tight as a lone tear dampened her cheek. Her gaze moved to Aaron as he held strong. "If you hurt her, I will curse you every day until the day I die. Do you understand?"

Well that certainly lightened the mood.

Aaron placed his hand on my lower back and led me to the rear of the shop. "Let's get out of here," he suggested. "Only our families are left, and they have a lot to talk about. We can clean up tomorrow."

Once the dust had settled, our families had sat down and had a big heart to heart. It turned out that none of them had wanted to feud with each other and even though they weren't going to be BFF's in the next day or so, they all agreed to work it through.

Gran and Arthur were sitting alone discussing life and what it had thrown at them and neither family wanted to stop a discussion that should have happened decades ago.

"Sounds good," I replied, matching his smile.

Aaron silently drove to where the river met the ocean. The sun was setting low in the sky, the radiant colors of red and pink being thrown around haphazardly, it's glow glittering on the swell of the water.

I took a deep breath, filling my lungs with the salty air and released all the tension that had been building.

We walked silently hand in hand along the boardwalk, stopping under a tall willow, its branches draping a curtain of privacy around us.

"So, do we really have our grandparents' blessings?" he asked, his voice low and husky.

"It looks that way," I replied quietly.

Aaron turned his body to face me, his knees only inches from mine. His hands gently cupped my face as his thumbs traced a path across my skin.

"I've been wanting to tell you how I felt for some time now," he explained, his eyes soft and inviting.

I released a deep shuddery breath and took his hands in mine.

"But I need some answers," I said, pulling back with a slight hesitation. "Why me? Why now?" I was looking for reasons that we couldn't be together, as once I'd allow that wall to completely fall, there was no going back.

His eyes narrowed with confusion.

"It's always been you. You're all I ever wanted," he whispered, his voice dancing across my skin.

"But you hated me."

"No. I could never hate you," he challenged.

"I'll never forget that look you gave me at my twenty first."

He sighed. "I hated your boyfriend. You have no idea the things he said about you behind your back." Aaron's hands dropped from mine, hanging at his side as he spoke, the distance between us suddenly cool.

"Is that why you hit him?" I'd since learned what had been said, so it was no surprise.

"I'm sorry. I didn't mean to wreck your party, I just hated the way he spoke about you. But Gracie, I've never hated you. I wanted to be the one with you at that party. I wanted to hold your hand, whisper in your ear and dance slowly. That's all I've wanted since I first met you."

"We were kids when we first met."

"I was nine, you were seven. When you walked into that birthday party and I saw you with that Minnie Mouse bow in your hair, I knew you were the one for me."

"I loved that bow." I replied, surprised that he remembered.

"So did I."

I blinked remembering that day as if it were yesterday.

"You wouldn't talk to me though," he continued, his memories the same as mine.

"My Gran had warned me not to. She told me that your family was not to be trusted."

"We now know that our grandparents had their own agendas."

I took a deep shuddery breath. "Things could have been so different for us."

"It's not too late," he whispered, taking my hand in his. As his long fingers intertwined with mine, a calm settled in my soul. A piece clicked into place and happiness surged.

"Why did you really buy the boutique?"

"It was the only way I could think to get closer to you without you being able to run away," he whispered, his mouth only inches from mine.

As he hovered close, the air turned electric. My lips tingled as our bodies aligned and his hold on my fingers tightened.

"Please don't run away anymore," he begged.

"I never ran away. You did that."

He gulped. "I couldn't watch you and not have you. Europe was as far away from you as I could get. Only problem was, you were in my heart. And it turns out you can't run from that."

That was a pretty good explanation.

"I'll give you everything I have," he continued. "Just please, *please* choose me." His eyes were wide and bright, his voice choked with emotion. His fingers clung to mine and a pang shot to my heart.

No one had ever looked at me the way he was looking at me, and I knew in that moment, that he was the one. "As if I have a choice."

A slow smile tugged at his lips as they parted. He closed the gap between us, his eyes glued to mine. I drowned in their depths, never wanting to resurface, as his hand moved around my waist and he pulled me in tight.

Electricity competed with nerves as butterflies erupted from their cocoons and he lowered his full lips. As their softness caressed mine, the butterflies settled and a contented sigh filled my soul.

I'd found home and I never wanted to leave.

The End.

If you enjoyed Gracie and would like to meet Tilly, I'm offering a free e-book to everyone who signs up to my mailing list. I promise not to spam you and only send out a handful of newsletters a year!
www.bethprentice.com

What are cupcakes made of? Sugar, spice and All Things Nice.

Meet Tilly. She owns a cupcake shop in Price Lane, Westport. All she wants to do is to make the residents love her cakes as much as she does. But on Valentine's Day her worst nightmare comes true—a deformed toe nail is found in one of her cakes.

Is this a new flavor for her menu? Has she dropped her standards of workplace health and safety? Or is someone out to sabotage her?

Luckily for Tilly, the Westport Police Department has a very helpful constable who will help her get to the bottom of it all.

Books By Beth Prentice

The Westport Mysteries
Dangerous Deeds
Give Murder A Hand
Deathly Desire

The Unleashed Mysteries
Killer Unleashed
Deadly Tails

The Aloha Lagoon Samantha Reynolds Mysteries
Deadly Wipeout
Lethal Tide
Invitation To Murder

About The Author

Beth Prentice is the USA Today Bestselling Author of the Westport Mysteries. Killer Unleashed, her GHP debut novel, received a bronze medal in the 2016 Readers Favorite International Book Awards. Her main wish is to write books you can sit back, relax with, and escape from your everyday life...and ones that you walk away from with a smile! When she's not writing you will usually find her at the beach with a coffee in hand, pursuing her favorite pastime—people watching!

Contact.

Website www.bethprentice.com
Facebook bethprentice69
Twitter @PrenticeBeth

Wildflower By Kim Petersen

"Our universe grants every soul a twin - a reflection of themselves - the kindred spirit — This is destiny; this is love."

- Julie Dillon.

Chapter 1

Present Day.

Let the dream die. It was never real.

"Tell that to my heart," Arie Kinard muttered to herself as she gazed at the bathroom mirror. She didn't notice the faint lines greeting the skin around her sleepy, dark eyes. Nor did she notice the morning sun filtering through the window in lazy streaks across the blue-tiled room. She barely noticed anything these days. Not since Charly had severed her from his life as if she were a parasite.

Arie pulled back her long, chestnut-colored hair and secured it into a messy pile on top of her head before sighing so hard that her lips trembled. She absently reached for her toothbrush then, squeezing out the toothpaste as the familiar, dull ache in her heart threatened her emotions.

No, don't cry now!

Those words had become her daily mantra – and all that kept her from totally losing her shit. She shook her head and closed her eyes, swallowing her tears along with the emptiness that edged around her soul like an old relic she couldn't quite forget. A deep breath, and she forced herself into the present – the reality which faced her every day. Her life with her husband and their three daughters. Her life without *him*.

Some days, it worked. Lying to yourself got easier – sooner or later, Arie knew she would coach her heart beyond this point and learn to believe the greatest love she'd ever experienced had been nothing but an illusion. An intense, sweet fantasy designed to totally enrapture and steal her soul. Only, she couldn't speed up the time. And as much as she longed to, she couldn't erase Charly from her memories, either.

Some days were better than others.

Her next breath came with a hefty side of determination while the soft sounds of her daughters beginning to stir drifted along the hall and through the bathroom door. It was an early weekday morning, and the routine was about to kick in at full-force. *Breakfast. Clothes. Lunches. School. Work* – and not necessarily in that order. Well, at least she got to work from her home office. That was something. Although, sometimes Arie wondered if the solitary hours made for too much thinking. As a free-lance journalist, living in her own head was all part-and-parcel with a job like hers, what with all the research and writing. Yet, these days, her thinking had almost bordered on obsession, and she felt sure she might be going a little crazy.

Between the long hours spent researching and writing articles for the various magazines that hired Arie, she was also working on her own side-project. A novel. She figured she had the right material to draw from – a shattered heart and a black void she didn't know how to fill. And working through her feelings with words might help to soothe her heart and find some closure, too... at least, that's what she told herself. One thing was for sure, though, that she was fast mastering the art of make-believe. She'd learned rather well how to mask the pain, and grown used to bluffing her way into happiness.

Fake it till you make it, right? She mused ruefully, scrubbing her teeth a little too hard. *Better get it together and put on your fake-happy face.*

She rinsed her mouth and hovered over the sink, peering closely at her reflection. A strange, thirty-six-year-old woman stared back her. Oh, the image was still familiar – not much had changed there if she didn't count the beginnings of the wrinkles crowing the corners of her eyes, or the random strands of grey springing up at the edge of her hairline. Her face was its usual pale complexion framed with thick hair and dark eyes set above a nose she'd often had trouble forming any judgement of, positive or negative. It was neither small nor large, but it curved a little flat on the end, and her husband Brett loved it. In any case, it wasn't her outer appearance that had changed. It was something deep within her that had transformed – and she knew life would never look the same again.

Arie's thoughts were startled away at the sound of a light knock on the bathroom door.

"Mommy? I'm busting to do a wee!"

Cara, the youngest of her daughters.

Arie sucked in her cheeks as she scrutinized herself a moment longer. Her skin hollowed over the high set of her cheek bones, and today, she was treated to two shadows brimming dark beneath her eyes. Reality set in with the remnants of a sleepless night, and Cara's undeniable urge to pee no less.

"Coming," Arie replied, turning abruptly from the mirror and making for the bathroom door. She filled her lungs with a gulp of air, a brilliant smile stretching across her lips as she flung open the door and greeted Cara. "Good morning, baby girl."

Cara's ankles twisted together, her small frame slightly bent at the knees as she flashed Arie an accusing look. At seven, she was the image of her mother. Dark brown eyes and milky skin, and lustrous tresses that reached her bottom. Only, Cara's dark hair was tinted with golden streaks, just as Arie's had been as a child. Compliments of youth and glorious days playing beneath the Australian sun.

"I'm going to wet myself," Cara said, cringing.

Arie's brows lifted with her grin.

"Well, then – hurry up, buttercup," she said, stifling a chuckle as Cara pushed past her to use the bathroom. She couldn't help but laugh; it wasn't that she relished seeing her daughter struggle with holding her biological needs. It was that Cara's feisty attitude and scrunched-up features were so damned cute, it amused her every time. Well, almost every time.

She left Cara to tend to her needs and padded on bare feet back to her bedroom, pausing when she reached the threshold to see Brett awake and perched on the edge of the bed. His wild hair fell over his face as he leaned forward to pull on his socks before he sat upright and gazed up at her through sleepy eyes.

Arie returned his look with a quick smile.

"Hey," she said, walking past him, further into the room, and beginning to slide the curtains apart.

He grunted a reply and turned back to his socks.

"Is that your idea of saying good morning?" Brett muttered behind her.

Arie's fingers tightened over the curtain, her body stiffening for one split second before she whirled around to face him with a half-smile. He was a good-looking man, she couldn't deny that. His skin was smooth, his face chiselled and yet distinguished, and he was the most upbeat person she'd ever known. Well, that was until his drinking problem caused his behaviour to become erratic. She could never really be sure of his mood until the moment arrived.

Brett's full lips parted with a smile that had once made her heart flutter like crazy. It was wide and magnetic, and could light up the darkest of rooms. He lifted his arms and motioned her closer, grabbing her hips as she stepped into his waiting embrace before he rested his head against her navel and murmured, "I love you, baby."

Arie allowed her hands to fall to the nape of his neck, tangling her fingers in his curls as she gazed at the cream-colored wall and tamed the urge to pull away. Her eyes dropped to him as he lifted his chin and looked up at her. His eyes had used to shine like onyx gems. Now, after years of daily drinking, they were dull and stained, and split red with thin, spidery lines.

He moved his chin and focused up at her, squinting against the morning sunlight breaking through the open curtains.

"I need you to go to the liquor store today and buy some more beer. I won't get the time."

Arie sighed and shook her head.

"Seriously? Didn't you just buy a couple of dozen two days ago?"

Brett scowled and pressed his thumbs deeper into the flesh of her hips.

"Who's counting?" he asked, his tone harsh.

She winced and swallowed back a sharp retort, before she forced a smile and gently removed herself from his grasp.

"Fine, I'll get it for you," she said flatly.

She turned away from him then, stopping as he grabbed her hand and tugged her closer again. Her jaw tightened as she glanced at him.

"Thanks, baby. I love you," he said, his lips breaking into a grin

"Love you, too," she said lightly, before pulling her hand free and heading toward the walk-in closet to dress for the day.

And she did love him.

But she was a different person now and so was he, and she couldn't quite figure out how to slip back into her old life. Truth was, she didn't know if she could. How do you forget the most extraordinary kind of love you've ever known?

She didn't know. But she did know that nothing would ever compare to the love she'd shared with Charly, for that had been a love that transcended time and space. A love that had blossomed in the secretive depths of their souls. A connection so deep, Arie had almost been able to feel every breath he took, and every one of his emotions as he'd experienced them. After months of longing and torment, she had finally come to understand the nature of their sacred bond. Twin Flames. Souls derived from the same energetic cloth.

Charly.

She perched on the edge of the stool she kept in her closet and shut her eyes. A tender smile drifted over her lips as his image floated in her mind and she recalled their first meeting.

It had been the year before, and early spring in New York city. Arie along with four other journalists had met in anticipation of a week-long writing program she'd signed up for at the insistence of her friend, Liza. Liza also happened to double as an editor for one of the magazines Arie routinely submitted her work to. When an opportunity had arisen for one of the magazine's journalists to participate in an intense writing program hosted by the popular American journalist and author, Charly Alba, and his colleague, Ty Nolan, it had been Liza who'd pressed her to attend.

It had been a whirlwind trip that had passed as fast as it had begun – she could've easily learned to forget about him after that. Well, that's what she'd told herself anyhow. She might've, too, had he not pursued her after her return to Australia with a work proposal she couldn't refuse. Looking back, she'd always known he was coming – she'd felt him long before he'd arrived to unravel her life. She'd felt as if she'd known him for a thousand years. And now, she felt as if she'd lost him for a thousand more...

Chapter 2

10 months prior

Arie grasped the strands of her hair and began a fast twirl as she glanced around the crowded New York restaurant. She bit her bottom lip and forced a smile toward her newest acquaintance – a plump American woman with a shock of scorching red curls and cheeks that shined like pink grapefruits when she smiled. Her name was Jane, and Arie thought she looked to be about fifty. She sat across from Arie sipping on white wine and running her mouth as if she hadn't uttered a word in months and needed to make up for it. Arie was certain that the tone of her loud, grating voice could stop a runaway train dead in its tracks.

"The airline food was disastrous. So, me being me, I had to lodge a complaint – I mean, do those people think they're feeding mindless idiots with no tastebuds? We pay a decent dollar to travel by air, ha – and not to mention the risk we take with our lives by choosing—"

Arie supressed a sigh and zoned out, glancing at the other journalists who were part of their group. Aside from herself and Jane, there were three other writers attending the elite program, and they'd all only just met. There was Annie – a young woman from California with cropped, mousy hair and a broad, flattened nose, not to mention golden skin that gleamed fluidly beneath the dim lights of the restaurant. Then there were Scott and Danny. Scott was the oldest of the group. He was gaunt and lofty with a good layer of stark, white hair and faded blue eyes, soft spoken and polite, and Arie knew he was a gentleman if she ever had seen one. Danny, on the other hand, was boisterous and excitable with his lopsided grin and clean-trimmed, nutty-colored hair, plus those twinkling brown eyes of his. He'd flown into New York that morning from

Las Vegas – with no complaints to report. His friendly nature had instantly set Arie at ease.

Well, somewhat. A foreign country plus strangers made for knots in places she'd never known existed. Like the small of her back, for one. It felt as if someone had taken her spine and clenched it between a vice, and it ached like hell. What was that all about? Of course, if Arie was honest with herself, she knew her current state of nervous energy had less to do with foreign country situations, and more to do with the approaching arrival of Charly. But, hey, who wanted to be honest with themselves all of the time?

Not Arie. She'd spent the prior months leading up to this moment diffusing the uncanny sense of utter attraction she'd felt for the man. No. It was even more than that – from the very first exchange of emails they'd shared to iron out the details of the trip, she'd felt an exquisitely unique connection to him. She was drawn to him without any real cause or reason. And the force of what she felt had already begun to possess her more than she cared to admit. She was a married woman, for crying out loud.

She reminded herself of that fact as she fought to reel in her thoughts and ignore the butterflies swirling in her stomach. Butterflies were the enemy tonight, their taunting wings intent on bothering her as she sat with her group and inwardly cursed every single flutter.

Arie and the group were seated in the lounging area of the restaurant, waiting for their hosts to arrive, after which they were set to begin the week with a reception dinner. It was the usual restaurant setting – diffused lighting, thick carpeting, and attractive prints adorning the walls. The other journalists sat across the way and appeared to be engaged in deep discussions as far as she could see. Even if she had wanted to, she wasn't close enough to join their conversations over the noise of the busy restaurant.

She didn't really want to, though. What she needed was a good shot of something. Her gaze fell to Jane's portly fingers as she toyed with her wine glass. Wine. *Where's the wine?* Jane had said it was complimentary. Swivelling around, Arie stretched her neck and scanned the room for signs of a waiter, waitress, or their hosts – anyone - *anything. I just something to take off the edge, sweet lord!*

The room was jammed with patrons while the waiting staff hurried around tending to them – it was hopeless. She pursed her lips and exhaled, squishing the wings now bunching in her stomach as her gaze fell back to Jane, who hadn't shut up the entire time. She gave her a fast nod and a small smile. "Aha," Arie murmured. It was barely audible, but enough to encourage Jane's rolling tongue.

Seven days.

It was a miniscule fraction of her life, but it might feel a little longer if it meant spending her days with Jane in such close proximity. She'd arrived in the States two days prior in order to recoup from the disgustingly long flight from Sydney – and to take the opportunity to explore some of Manhattan before the program began and her days would fill with craft and business matters. She'd been apprehensive about travelling and sight-seeing in such a big city alone, but, to her surprise, she'd actually enjoyed herself. It had been a slice of freedom she seldom got to enjoy these days, and she'd felt liberated.

Jane lowered her voice and leaned closer to Arie, her bosom pressing up beneath her chin, while her grey eyes appeared owl-like through her spectacles.

"And that's how you get a free first-class ticket home, darlin'," she laughed, pushing a fleshy thumb through her tangled hair. "You might want to remember that, especially with the flight you've got to face to get back home. Do you know, I have managed to collect overnight credits in hotels all across America – when I was in San Francisco last fall, I—"

Obviously didn't find a plug for your mouth.

Arie tuned out again, smiling sweetly and making all the right sounds at all the right moments. Having fine-tuned the art of selective hearing at an early age, she'd learned how to skilfully stay in a conversation without actually being a participant – she considered it to be an advantage pertaining to her personality. Still, Arie was always grateful for the talkers among any group, because they were the ones who filled in the awkward gaps that plagued her life when she found herself among new people.

Jane's voice faltered mid-sentence with the tilt of her head. Thin lips spread wide as she lifted an arm and waved furiously, her loose skin wobbling with the movement. The tone of her voice became an excitable pitch as she gushed loudly.

"Oh! Here are our hosts. Finally – I'm starving!"

The instant she heard those words, Arie's attention snapped back to the present with a sharp breath. If she hadn't been tense before, she was a stiff block of ice now, and her heart banged painfully against the impenetrable glacier that had become her ribcage.

Okay - keep cool.

Arie was good at cool. Advantage number two to her personality – she could play a great poker-face when she wanted. It was her inner-self that she could never quite master, but that was a private sanctuary she rarely revealed to others, so that didn't count. She chewed on her bottom lip, took a breath, and lifted her dark gaze to follow Jane's frantic wave. Her heart almost stopped then and there.

Charly Alba.

Well, he was difficult to miss – he stood a good foot taller than most of the folk skimming around the room, and he moved with a confident stride that commanded attention. He was toned and coltish, with a swathe of rust-colored hair that curled against his shoulders and prickled his squared chin, spreading across his jaw in a rebellious shadow. His eyes were the tint of a raging ocean; large and dynamic, yet focused beneath the thick lashes adorning them. When he smiled, the set of his crooked white teeth made for a catchy grin that was hard to ignore.

That wasn't all, though. Not only was Charly Alba a critically acclaimed journalist, he was also a popular author of nonfiction. That fact alone didn't impress Arie. Having spent many hours interviewing dozens of celebrities, she didn't care much for a person's fame or reputation. She was much more interested in the person behind all that bullshit. Those tags, accolades, and statuses were purely derived from the material world, and didn't represent the real essence of a person. Still, most of the population saw only what their eyes revealed, and right now, the people dining and mingling in the restaurant were tripping over themselves to get a better view of Charly Alba.

He strutted into the lounging area like a proud lion – chest raised and chin jutting, his eyes dancing to a tune of their own as they swept over their group and he grinned. He wore a black leather jacket over a crisp, white shirt, with denim jeans that hugged his long legs, and he was closely tailed by Ty Nolan.

"Hey, guys!" Charly crooned, swinging the leather satchel bag he carried from his shoulder to the floor. "I'm so excited to finally meet you all in person."

Arie's eyes settled over him as she rose to her feet with the rest of their group. She hung back and watched as a flurry of greetings ensued, and Ty came to a standstill beside Charly, greeting them all with a smile.

Jane pushed forward with her arms outstretched, her voice rising above the noise.

"Charly, so pleased to meet you," she laughed.

Charly looked at her for a moment, a strained grin curling his whiskers before his eyes grazed past her to level on Arie, who was lingering behind the group. When his smile widened and captured the corners of his eyes, Arie's stomach flipped.

Damned butterflies.

"Ah, hello, Jane. Hold up," Charly said, laughing and side-stepping Jane before making for Arie. "I think the overseas traveller gets the first hug. She's come the farthest to join us."

Arie's mind fizzled and went blank, and she blinked a few too many times before she smiled and tilted her chin. She gazed up at him through her long lashes as he neared her.

"Hi, Charly," she said, trying hard not to sound as awkward as she felt. She quickly broke eye contact, leaning into him and planting a chaste kiss on his cheek. He pulled her in closer, and suddenly her senses were filled with his scent – citrus and woody, with a scant trace of sweat. Man-smell.

She liked it.

Ty moved closer and she struggled to get her thoughts together as he treated her to a big smile, and outstretched arms.

"Arie, so nice to have you here in the States."

Ty's lack of height was accentuated next to Charly; he was thin and wiry, with a coppery, long beard that brushed against the collar of his shirt. His small, brown eyes appeared rat-like, and his facial features were tight and pinched. And he was as bald as a baby's bottom.

"Thanks for having me here in the States," Arie replied with a nervous laugh, while stepping away from Charly and easing into Ty's incoming hug.

She gave Ty a quick squeeze before retreating to her chair to collect her handbag feeling slightly heady and more than a little disturbed. *Keep cool, Arie. Keep cool.* She could tell herself those words till the cows came home, though. While Charly was close by, she knew her body would ignore every syllable.

He is dangerous territory.

There was only one solution to this dilemma, and that was to keep a wide berth between them during her days here. It was only a week, so surely that would work.

Surely.

Chapter 3

Charly stood with his back to Ty and gazed through the hotel window. It was early morning and they were going over the day's schedule over coffee and bagels, after which they'd head off to the office space they'd rented for the week-long program they were currently hosting. Nothing new there. Ty had been a close part of Charly's professional world for some time, and this wasn't the first round of writing programs they'd hosted together. Yet, as he stood peering down 7th Avenue, he found it difficult to focus on Ty's words as the man continued to speak behind him.

That was definitely something new.

Charly hadn't achieved the critically acclaimed status he'd acquired during his career by accident. It had taken a lot of years and gruelling hours to get where he was today – and a generous amount of blood, sweat, and tears. Literally. Charly had ventured into dangerous parts of the world in the name of a story. He had mixed and probed among the likes of the Cartel, human traffickers, serial killers, and perhaps the most wicked of all – politicians. The point was, there was nothing that Charly wouldn't do to secure the best vantage for a story, because he had what it took – drive and determination, and *focus*.

Charly hated feeling out of alignment. Control was important to him. Not so much in relation to people – at forty-three, he'd lived long enough to know you could never really guess the actions of another. And, for the most part, he didn't waste precious thinking time about others. But self-discipline was a crucial part of his life. It gave him structure and boundaries – and he had it all worked out with a wife of twenty-plus years and two teenage sons. He knew where he'd been and he knew where he was going, and nothing was going to deter him from the path he'd mapped out.

Nothing.

So, why was he feeling so out of whack now?

It was the Australian woman, Arie. She had him rattled. She had him fazed and undone – and that had been before he'd even laid on eyes on her. In fact, the moment she'd swept onto his computer screen a few months back, she'd felt like a breath of fresh air. He didn't understand, as this wasn't him. He loved his wife and family. He was a happy man, and he didn't have affairs – well, if he didn't count the time in Brazil when he'd encountered a sultry woman during a feature-piece he'd been covering for the NBN. But that had been a decade ago, and the guilt had almost suffocated him. *Lesson learned.* After that, he'd promised himself he would never commit adultery again – it was vow he'd never broken.

Or intended to, thank-you-very-much.

Only, now, he was finding it hard to crush his fascination with Arie. She was like fire and ice – a rare, unexpected wildflower. A woman-child he wanted to possess. She was gorgeous and sweet, yet witty and confident in a reserved kind of way – she was like a bottomless mystery he longed to explore. And there was a vulnerability about her that almost had him on his knees. Somehow, she'd stirred something deep within him – it was as if her arrival in his life had awakened a part of himself that had remained untouched. And all he wanted to do was inhale her until she filled all of him with her wild spirit.

Crazy. That's what that was.

His eyes glazed against the morning sun bouncing from the window-walls lining the New York street, and for one sweet moment he allowed himself to entertain the notion of her. Then, the pitch of Ty's voice grew behind him, startling him from ideas he knew wouldn't serve him. *Good.* He knew he needed an extra push into reality with Arie filling his days. He spun around and faced Ty, his mind racing to catch up to the conversation.

"Charly? What do you think? Should we cover the features and editorial this morning, and switch it up to non-fictional and fictional conventions after the lunch break?

Charly nodded and strode through the sitting room toward Ty. As usual, when travelling for business together, he and Ty opted to share a two-bedroom suite to cut down on the costs associated with such ventures. Neither of them was particularly wealthy, and besides, it just made sense. The hotel suite's common area was small but clean, and big enough to fit a two-seater sofa setting, a circular dining table, and a kitchenette.

Charly stopped when he reached the table where Ty sat peering up at him. His eyes appeared to be shooting lasers as he narrowed them over Charly. A pen poised in one hand while, in the other, his thin fingers clung to his coffee mug.

"What's got into you?" he asked.

Charly shook his head vaguely and flopped into a chair. His lips pursed beneath his short whiskers and he threw Ty a curt look. "Nothing."

"Is it Mandy?"

"No, why would you bring her up?" Charly asked, reaching for his mug and taking a sip of lukewarm coffee, wondering why Ty had brought up his wife at this moment. He grimaced before setting the mug down and eyeing the bagels with disinterest.

"No reason, really – you guys seem to live parallel lives, is all," Ty said, shrugging. "Like ships passing in the night."

"Hmm... it works for us," Charly replied, suppressing a trace of rising annoyance at the mention of his marriage.

Guilt.

Had to be – but in his own defense, he hadn't done anything wrong. Thoughts didn't count. Besides, with day two of the sessions dawning, he was certain Arie was avoiding him like the plague. She'd barely uttered two words to him since her arrival in the States, and during the workshop sessions, she favored Ty over him with any questions. It was an odd thing because her actions directly opposed the energy he felt emanating from her – it felt raw and unchecked, and alarmingly familiar, and it puzzled him to no end.

Ty got up and began gathering the notepads splayed out over the table. As he leaned forward, the tips of his wiry beard dipped into his coffee mug as he spoke.

"I don't know how you do it, man – I'd go crazy in a marriage like that. Either that, or my wife would kill me first," he laughed. "But then again, you guys have been together for so much longer than me and Rach. Old man," he added with a wink.

Charly gave a half-laugh, his thoughts dragging back to his wife. He sighed. Mandy was the last thing he wanted to think about. It wasn't that their marriage suffered from the way they arranged their lives – on the contrary, the two of them had an ongoing system that worked for them. Mandy was a middle school teacher. She was clever and organized, and perhaps a tad bossy at times, but that was nothing he couldn't handle. Most importantly, though, his wife appreciated systems. Charly liked systems, too. Systems implied practical methods, and if he was anything, he was pragmatic.

He hadn't spoken to Mandy since he'd left their home in Chicago a few days before, but that wasn't unusual for their relationship. Considering he'd travelled quite a lot over the years while chasing stories, they'd grown accustomed to long stretches of silence between them. He chewed on his bottom lip for a second, and decided he'd call Mandy that afternoon and check in on her and the boys. With that thought firmly staked into his mind, he felt a whole lot better. *Yeah, that's probably what I need, a good dose of Mandy to chase away ardent fancies involving a woman I'd probably never see again after the end of this week.*

Charly stood up abruptly, snapping his laptop closed and almost missing the peculiar expression on Ty's face shown when he'd paused and watched him stuffed his gear into his bag. It was the thick drawl of Ty's voice that pricked his attention.

"So, any thoughts about our attendees?" Ty asked.

"Huh?" Charly lifted his chin, curling a lock of hair behind his ear as he caught the mocking flicker in his friend's eyes. He ignored it and shrugged before looking back at his bag and fiddling to secure the buckles. "They seem like nice people."

"That all?"

Charly frowned.

"What do you mean?" he asked, finishing with the buckles and slugging the bag across his shoulder. He glanced at Ty, then spun his heels in a semi-turn and began to make for the hotel door.

Ty grabbed his own bag and followed close behind, his sly laugh grating against Charly's nerves.

"I mean, you didn't happen to notice the stunning brunette with the hair, the curves and lips, and the... oh... and the breasts to die for?"

Charly paused and reached for the door handle, glaring over his shoulder at Ty, who stood behind him with a smirk. He shook his head and forced a laugh. "Nah," he said, and then he yanked the door open and slid out into the hotel corridor, deliberately taking extra-long strides toward the elevator, so that Ty had walk doubly fast to keep in pace.

Stupid frickin question. I didn't notice her at all.

Chapter 4

Arie cherished the quiet morning hours. To her, the soft light of a new day was another chance at creating her life just as she wanted it. Not to mention that these small hours somehow felt sacred and hallowed. It wasn't that she was unhappy. Over the years, Arie had learned that happiness couldn't be dependent upon the circumstances of life, but had to be found from within if it was going to inform your experiences – a fact she had discovered the hard way, when her first husband had thought her face was a good place to vent his frustrations.

It had taken Arie years to summon the courage to leave that violent world behind, and several more to work through the pain and torment the abusive relationship had left etched into her heart and soul. As dark as those years had been for Arie, she knew she wouldn't have gone back to change her life-course, even if she could have – for out of the darkness is born light and evolution. Without those horrific experiences, she never would've discovered and appreciated the beauty of her true inner self, her passion to write, or learned the simplest pleasures of "just being".

Right now, Arie was enjoying taking a moment of "just being" on a bench in Central Park while she sipped on an extra-large Starbucks as the city came to life around her. She smiled and raised her chin toward the weak, morning rays, marvelling at the contrasting energy between the southern and northern hemispheres. She couldn't articulate it, but the atmosphere in America differed from her homeland – it was neither better nor worse. Just different. Strange thing was, it also felt familiar.

Arie figured the sense of familiarity was due to the underlying pull she'd always felt toward America. She'd often dreamed of obscure aspects of the States – specific visions like subway signs, lake shores, and homes – none of which she could explain. Then, one day, she'd visited a psychic medium. The woman had been graceful, friendly, and mysterious, and she'd read Arie's palm and used a crystal as a tool to receive information from the other side. It had been during that reading that Arie had learned about mirrored souls splitting to incarnate the earth simultaneously.

At first, Arie had dismissed the idea and taken no notice of the woman's unusual words – it sounded completely irrational to think that a part of her soul lived and breathed in another body elsewhere in the world. There was only one of her, of that she was certain. But then the woman had asked her if she'd ever felt an unexplainable magnetism toward America. That had been when Arie could no longer deny the odd tingles prickling the hairs on the back of her neck and skimming down her spine – for the psychic woman had gone on to reveal that that was the country where her twin soul lived, and that that explained the visions and strong bonds Arie felt around the idea of the States.

"Excuse me, miss?"

Arie gasped as thoughts of the woman and her predictions were interrupted, pulled back to the present with the sound of a gruff voice. She blinked a couple of times before her eyes settled on a man hovering at the far end of the park bench where she sat.

A thick layer of grime filled the crinkles of his pasty skin, his hazel eyes appearing hollow and faded beneath a mat of stringy silver hair. He was as thin as a garden rake, his clothes ragged and filthy, and he twisted a black plastic garbage bag between fraying, fingerless gloves.

Arie smiled up at him. The small gesture was enough to encourage him to shuffle closer and sit down beside her. His eyes darted to meet hers before falling to his quivering thumbs, and he mumbled, "Wondering if you could spare a dollar?" His stiff whiskers stretched with a waning smile.

"Sure," Arie replied, shifting her bottom to stuff a hand into her jeans pocket and fish for some notes. She produced a five-dollar bill and handed it to him. "Here, take a fiver."

The man's eyes widened over the bill. Half a beat passed before he gingerly took the money and treated her to a stained, crooked grin.

"Thank you, and god bless," he uttered, shoving the money into his jacket pocket. "Are you English?"

"Australian," Arie said, wondering why Americans always seemed to misjudge her Australian accent as English. As far as she was concerned, the Pommie accent sounded nothing like the Aussie accent – which was strong, distinct, and twangy.

"Ah... here for pleasure?" the old man asked.

When Arie looked at him, she noticed a light spark flash across his dull eyes. She shook her head.

"More of a work-related thing."

"Oh," he murmured. He groaned then as he stretched awkwardly to his feet and picked up his garbage bag, slinging it over one shoulder. He held her gaze as he began to back away slowly, and then he moved his chin slightly and motioned with his free hand to someplace behind her. "The universe sure has funny way of orchestrating the unions," he added.

"What do you mean?" Arie asked as she frowned and turned to peer over her shoulder to where the old man had gestured. She froze instantly then, her insides racing with a dazzling zing that caught her pulse and flooded her being – Charly and Ty were headed straight for her. She whirled back around to the man, her jaw gaping when she realized he was nowhere to be seen.

She hardly had time to process the homeless man's vanishing act because, suddenly, Charly's smooth, fruity voice drowned in her ears as he called her name. She groaned inwardly, and silently cursed the immediate reaction his voice generated in parts of her body she'd rather not think about – especially in his company.

Does his voice have to sound so damned sexy?

She wasn't ready for him yet – by her clock, there was still half an hour before their workshop was due to begin. It was time she needed to erect the invisible walls around her unreasonable emotions and get her cool face together. Now, she'd just have to wing it – she hated winging it. For a brief moment, she actually considered pretending she hadn't heard him call her name. *Yeah, I'll just get up and walk off in the other direction.* She could do that. But the thought fizzled somewhere in the grey matter of her brain as the sound of their footsteps thudded closer behind her.

Too late.

"Hey, there she is," Ty said as he stepped around the park bench and faced her, Charly sidling up beside him. Ty grinned down at her and gestured toward the Starbucks takeaway cup she gripped in her hand. "That cup mightn't survive the next sip if you keep holding it that tight," he added with a laugh.

"Huh?" Her eyes dropped to the cup and then darted back up at him before she relaxed her fingers and gave a sheepish grin. "I didn't expect to see you guys so soon."

"No? You didn't plan on seeing us this morning?" Charly asked.

Mmmm... niiiice.

"What? Umm... yeah, of course."

Oh my god – you're an idiot.

Arie swallowed hard, smiling while she duelled with the rising heat threatening to expose her. It sprung from her heart, flowing into her organs before lingering between her legs like an exquisite burn. Her gaze drifted casually over him, and her jaw clamped shut and she ignored his amused smile as she mentally pulled herself together.

You're a cool cat, remember – get it together.

Her lips spread into a wide grin. She was all lynx now.

"I guess we should get to the office, then," she said lightly, gathering her bag and coffee before standing up. Then she whirled around in the direction of their building and began to move away.

"Right on," Charly murmured.

Exactly.

Arie barely heard the tease in his voice over the incessant thump of her heart and the loud thoughts scrambling through her mind like a mini-cyclone.

Chapter 5

Time is merciless.

Charly had never had problem with time before. Usually, he found that time worked in his favor. That was because he knew how to use the concept to his advantage. Long gone were days of idling about on social platforms like Facebook and Twitter. For the most part, he considered social media to be toxic – just another way to control and manipulate the population. Conformity wore many jackets. But social media *did* have its uses to someone in his profession. So, he used various online mediums wisely, and in such a way that it didn't crunch against his precious time. But it was a *lack* of time on Charly's mind right now – and he had no way to wind back the clock to begin the week over again.

The days had flown by, and Charly knew he should be feeling elated. He was pleased with how the week had unfolded – just not entirely on the usual high he experienced at the completion of events such as these.

He and Ty had nailed it. They'd covered everything from feature writing and editorials to interview skills, data media, and production – they'd even ventured into discussions about writing full-length nonfiction and fiction, the latter being an idea Charly had been toying with for some time. The intimate size of the group had meant they could deliver an optimal course structured by the needs of their attendees. But even though Charly had revelled in the sense of comradery among the group and enjoyed every moment in their company, he couldn't shake the dull ache of melancholy expanding somewhere in his chest.

He dodged a pile of garbage strewn across the curb and frowned beneath his sunglasses as he and Ty walked the couple of blocks toward the office-space for the last time that week. The morning air was crisp and heavily laced with the odor of trash as garbage collectors snaked slowly along the New York streets in filthy trucks. Even over the noise of the truck engines and the occasional hollering echoing along the buildings, his thoughts were stolen by images of Arie.

Her distinct, pale features radiated against the length of her dark hair while her eyes pierced into his soul and imprinted against his mind like an enchanting depiction. For an instant, he'd considered he might be losing his mind – sure, he wasn't immune to attractive women; he *was* a man after all. But there was something different about Arie, and part of him knew he was utterly bewitched by her.

And that part was proving to be a pain in the ass – and central to the inner conflict that'd been driving him nuts all week. He'd thought a few phone calls to Mandy might help ease the temptation straining against his will. Yet, hearing his wife's voice had done nothing to soothe the titillating spell which the curvy Australian woman had cast over him. And he wasn't sure how he felt about her flying out of the States and away from him so damned soon.

Argh! I need to meditate.

It was true. He hadn't done a session all week, what with travelling and everything else happening. And he could sure feel the difference between the extended intervals between meditation sessions. The practice soothed his soul

– entering the higher realms through meditation kept him centered and gave him clarity. It was through the ancient practice that he'd been able to discover his inner being and reach sacred heights. That's what he needed... a good session of meditation and he'd be back to normal. Besides, no good would come from pining over a woman he couldn't have.

Right?

Right. Thinking of meditation and higher realms triggered something in Charly's mind. He'd already acknowledged to himself that Arie was different; he'd never met her before this program, and yet she felt so familiar. Being around her felt natural – a strange kind of natural, like her presence ignited an awareness inside of him that he was yet to fully realize. It felt almost... *divine*.

What if she was my... He halted abruptly as one thought materialized above the jungle tangling though his mind.

"Hey, Ty," he said.

Ty stopped walking in front of him, taking a sip from the takeaway coffee cup he held and half-turning to glance at Charly.

"Yeah?"

"Do you think you and Rachael are soul mates?"

Charly had at least twelve years on Ty, but he knew Ty and his wife had been childhood sweethearts and married for some time. It was a valid question.

The puzzled expression creasing Ty's face suggested otherwise, though, as his bushy brows lifted and his parched lips formed an "O" before transforming into a cheesy grin.

"Hmm... let me think on that one," he said with an exaggerated drawl. He tilted his chin and feigned a thoughtful frown, before his grinned so wide, his face almost spit in two. "Woo-woo – what in the world has got into you, man? Twilight zone catching you early?" he laughed.

Charly scowled and ran his fingers through his hair with a shrug.

"Nothing has gotten *into* me – you're a married couple with kids, so it's a normal frickin question."

"Ah, the rusher kicks in. Throw it to the quarterback dude, what's your deal?"

"Dick," Charly said, scowling and brushing past him. Seriously, there were times when Ty excelled at stroking the nerves that annoyed him the most. Ty was a dear friend and he loved him, but sometimes even love couldn't appease his brash, jarring traits.

Ty caught up to Charly to fall into step beside him as they slowed and reached the office building. They were silent for a moment before Charly glanced at Ty and took an even breath. He knew he had to remind himself that, at thirty-three, Ty was a lot younger than he was – a fact he'd do well to remember in the future.

"Sorry, man," Ty muttered with a sheepish grin. "I didn't mean to offend – you okay?"

Charly nodded before pushing on the heavy glass doors and stepping into the building's lobby. He paused to slide his sunglasses to the top of his head and gaze around the vast space. He was greeted by a standard Manhattan office lobby, complete with an admin counter, oversized armchairs, and polished, marbled floors.

"Yeah, I'm fine," he said.

"Good. Last day and celebratory dinner tonight – you all set to return home in the morning?"

Charly's whiskers curved with his smirk as he looked back at Ty. "Of course – you know I travel light," he said, turning his gaze forward. He began to move, but stopped short and froze when he saw Arie.

She was sitting on one of the armchairs with her opened laptop perched on her lap. Her fingers twirled in the ends of her long strands of hair that fell over her brow and wisped against her chin, her dark lashes lowered as she focused on the screen in front her.

The moment was fleeting, yet it seemed to stand still. Charly vaguely heard the other workshop participants as they spilled into the lobby behind them and greeted Ty, robust laughter catching their words. All he really heard was the shallow sound of his breath hitching in his throat as his world zeroed in around Arie. He took a step away from the chattering group, his jaw slackening slightly while his chin fell to the side and his chest swelled against his ribcage. He couldn't take his eyes off her.

Then, in one fluid movement, she lifted her eyes to meet his, and he was no longer – his heart leapt and slid from his chest along an invisible cord to entwine with hers, and the room seemed to dissolve beneath his boots. He was floating someplace in the in-between and he wanted to stay there forever.

She smiled briefly, and he mirrored her expression with his own before her eyes dashed from his and his heart catapulted back through his ribcage with a silent crash. Reality blasted through his awareness with a sharp breath and Ty's voice drumming in his ear.

"Ready to go up, man?" Ty said.

"I'm ready," Charly replied, keeping his eyes forward and setting off toward the elevators. All the while, his pulse raced and heart thundered.

What the frig was that?

Chapter 6

Eye language.

There was no way Arie could escape the neurochemical rush spiralling through her brain when Charly's gaze locked onto hers from across the room. Suddenly, she felt clammy all over, her body responding in ways that'd caught her completely off guard. And her heart – it seemed to erupt from her chest in a silent explosion. Her breath stagnated and she smiled – and it wasn't the cheerful variety of smile, either. No, it was quick and fleeting, the type of smile that only reached the very edges of your lips and dissolved just as fast. The type created by high levels of bodily stimulation that had her insides reeling.

Shit. Shit. Shit.

If she could actually form words in her head, she was certain that word would've been it. She tore her eyes away from him, swinging her gaze toward Jane, who'd called her name and begun waddling in her direction. All the while, Arie remained totally aware of his every movement as he turned and walked off with the others in the group.

She smiled again. This time, her lips spread wide, reflecting the burst of elation now catching in her mind and shimmering to every region of her body as the kickback set in. *Wow.* The reaction was beyond her control and unmistakeable, but it was exactly what she'd been avoiding all week long. Still, she couldn't deny the blissful feelings curling through her bloodstream and resonating in her heart.

Here she'd been – waiting in the lobby with her email for company and minding her own business – and now she knew she'd be pondering the moment for the better part of the day. At the very least.

Was that so bad?

Arie wasn't sure anymore. All week, she'd found herself counting. Days. Hours. Minutes. Tallying up the time she couldn't recreate.

Moments that would be forever lost to her – vanished along with the opportunities to talk to Charly. It was a strange thing, because at any one of those given moments, she'd been utterly aware of his presence and what he was doing. She'd taken to stealing glances at him when he wasn't looking, and wondered if he'd done the same.

She'd told herself it was okay – avoiding him was the right thing to do. She was a loyal wife, dammit. Yet, her heart and soul told her a different story – and she knew a part of herself would regret the time she'd never taken to just be in his company during her trip abroad. Minus the inner wrestling driving her insane, of course. Regrets or no regrets, this was her last day in New York, and she intended on making the most of it.

With that thought dousing the sizzle charging like a hot current through her pulse, she began to pack away her laptop as she greeted Jane.

"Morning," Arie said, eyeing the banana Jane clenched between her fingers. The yellow skin was bruised and soft, the flesh mushy looking. She grimaced. "Breakfast?"

"Yep, the hotel was handing them out for free this morning," Jane replied. Her chest puffed as she took a bite, talking with her mouth full. "You didn't get one?"

"Nah – I like my bananas firmer."

Among other things...

Jane grunted. "Too bad – I never miss out on a freebie."

Arie laughed and stood up, slinging her backpack over a shoulder.

"I seriously hadn't noticed that about you." She gestured toward the elevators with a flick of her hand. "C'mon, let's catch up with the others."

The loose skin beneath Jane's chin trembled with her laugh as she started forward beside Arie.

"Gotta get what you can while the offerings are ripe, honey," Jane said.

"Hmm... I think you nailed that one with that banana."

"Hey, if it's free, I'm taking. I don't get a whole lot of the good free stuff in my life these days," Jane muttered. They reached the elevators and she stamped a thumb against the button to request a ride, leaving a thick slick of banana flesh in her wake.

"Like what?" Arie asked, scrunching her nose as she studied the gluggy, bruised banana flesh now covering the button.

Jane's eyes narrowed as she gave Arie a hard stare, her teeth scraping bits of banana from her lips. When Arie swung her eyes back to Jane, it was difficult not to grin. Then, Jane's expression dropped, her chest heaving as she sighed.

"Like... love," she said softly.

"Oh."

Arie's mind stretched with the words that failed her as she tried to think of a suitable reply. Truth was, she wasn't always the greatest at discussing delicate topics with people close to her – let alone those she barely knew. She wanted to look away, to change the subject, but the wistful look glazing over Jane's eyes tugged on her conscience. She chewed on the insides of her cheeks for a moment before the right words sprung in her mind.

"Well, you know what I always say about love?" she asked, continuing before waiting for a reply. "I say, love is like a wildflower. It's usually found in the most unlikely of places."

Jane's expression brightened with her smile, her grey eyes glinting through her glasses. "I like it," she said, nodding.

Arie gave her a wink. "Not bad, eh?"

Not bad at all.

Jane commented, "My ex-husband was an asshole – I caught him cheating more than once. What about you? Are you still in love with your husband?"

Arie's brows raised. Her mind went blank before she snapped back her thoughts and replied. "Ah – yeah, of course," she stammered.

"Lucky you. Must be the love of your life, then?"

Charly's eyes burned in Arie's mind instantly.

Geez, how did we get so personal all of a sudden?

She squirmed, dropping her eyes to her boots while her suddenly sweaty palms clutched at the strap of her bag. Thankfully, she found respite in the form of the soft chime signalling the arrival of the elevator as it rang out over them. She didn't hesitate – she nodded her reply before she turned and flounced into the small space, her backpack bumping against her tailbone with the speed of her gait.

"Gee, this week has gone by so fast," Jane said as she meandered over the elevator threshold behind Arie. "I can't wait for the last dinner tonight; should be fun."

Arie nodded. "Yeah, this entire week has been a great experience," she replied, deliberately turning her gaze up toward the numbers indicting the floor levels, each one flashing with the ascending elevator.

She was all out of talk for the moment, and grateful Jane seemed to be, too. They fell silent as the elevator shifted upward at a rapid pace. Then, Jane's voice broke the faint noise of the cable mechanisms whirling in the background.

"Ha – wildflower."

"So, your kids must miss you?" Charly asked.

Arie glanced up at him with a nod. They were walking back towards their respective hotels after dinner, and somehow they'd broken away from the rest of the group that strolled along in high-spirited banter behind them.

"Yeah," she said, matching his strides with her own in perfect unison. The New York streets were thriving with activity – people pushing their way along the pavements while others hustled on grimy street corners. Horns beeped, drivers hollered, and the night sky offered a lucid backdrop against a pale moon.

Arie saw none of it. These were the final moments of her time with Charly – not to mention, the first time all week they were actually alone. She was too busy soaking him up to pay attention to her surroundings. Plus, after two margaritas during dinner, she was feeling rather chilled and chatty.

Liquid courage. Gotta love it.

"And your husband? He must be missing you, too?" Charly asked casually.

"What's not to miss, right?" Arie laughed. "Seriously, I think he's finding it a challenge going it alone with the kids."

He looked at her with a half-laugh, his blue eyes luminous against the city lights.

"What does he do?"

"Works for himself. He's an engineer," she said, frowning. "How about you? Your family must be missing you, too?"

He shrugged and dug his hands into the pockets of his jeans. "Meh – they're used to my absences," he said.

He lowered his chin and looked her way again, the intensity in his eyes instantly smothering her thoughts. Not that she was thinking anything rational. How could she? It was those damned margaritas. The tangy tequila shots had done more than just go to her head – they'd totally liquidated all traces of her cool face.

"You've been pretty quiet all week – I hope you found the trip worth it. Did you enjoy the writing program?" he asked.

Ohhh... that voice is sexy as sin.

Her breath quickened, and she shivered. It was the cool night air whispering against her skin, not the fact that the sound of his voice made her want to melt in a puddle at his feet. She cleared her throat. *Get it together, Arie!*

"Yeah, I loved every minute of my time here," she said, turning her eyes forward and trying to focus on the path ahead of them instead of his closeness. "It's good to talk shop with other writers in person. I meet a lot of people, but mostly online."

"Me, too. Goes with the turf in our business."

She threw him a quick look, her mouth forming words before she had a chance to screen them. "You can always get a feel for people through online correspondence, though – feel their energy through email and such. Opening an email from someone is like opening a fragment of their essence. I feel it strong with some people, at least, others not so much."

Oh god – now he's going to think I'm a lunatic.

Charly's whiskers curled with his grin.

"Yeah, yeah. I know what you mean," he said.

Do you? Do you really know that I'm trying to explain something I don't even understand?

Her chest tightened and she fell silent as they walked, rounding the corner to the street of her hotel. For some reason, she felt compelled to at least let him know something before their time was up – anything to communicate the bizarre sense of connection she felt with him. But she was tongue-tied, and she had nothing that wouldn't sound crazy. Thoughts strung out in her mind like cryptic messages she couldn't decipher, and then suddenly, her breath was snatched away when Charly's hand accidently brushed against hers.

The contact was fast and fleeting, but it gripped every one of Arie's senses. It felt flawlessly divine – like a delicate shot of heat. An acute, energetic current rippled up her arm, radiating toward her heart before gracefully teasing its way between her thighs. Her mind scrambled as Charly widened the distance between them, carefully adjusting his gait to the far side of the pavement as they slowed at the doors to her hotel.

She supressed the insatiable sense of hunger scorching though her body while her heart plummeted at his reaction to their unexpected contact. Obviously, he hadn't experienced the same kickback as her – he couldn't have moved to get further away from her if he'd tried. Her eyes skirted to the ground and she bit her bottom lip before her gaze lifted to meet his.

"Do you think it's a coincidence our names are so alike?" she blurted out.

Umm... hello, lunacy. Why the hell did you say that?

She didn't know the answer to that question, but as soon as the words fell from her mouth, she wished she could collect them back with the tip of her tongue.

Charly laughed, the corners of his eyes crinkling as he tilted his head and watched her with amusement. But, when he spoke, his low and husky voice revealed other things on his mind.

"I don't believe in coincidences, Arie."

"Me, either," she replied, grinning up at him.

She thought about saying something else – but anything that came to mind would probably sound just as foolish as her last attempts at conversation. And besides that, she was beginning to distrust the escalating drum of her heart.

A silent moment passed between them as Ty and the rest of the group sidled up and gathered around them to say their final goodbyes. Their attention shifted to a round of warm hugs and farewells as the group prepared to part ways for the last time. When Arie had made the rounds and it was time to say goodbye to Charly, she moved closer gradually, tilting her chin and meeting his gaze with her dark stare.

"Well, I guess we'll keep in touch online – email, Facebook," she said.

Charly grinned and stretched his arms out for an incoming hug. "For sure, safe travels. Let us know when you arrive home in one piece."

When she stepped into his arms, she pressed her nose against his hair falling over his shoulders and closed her eyes for a beat. She inhaled his scent one last time – woody, masculine undertones filling her senses until she was heady. It felt good. Too good.

"Will do. Bye, Charly," she uttered before pulling herself away from him in a hasty retreat.

She repeated the last words louder and gave a tiny wave before she whirled around and rushed for the hotel doors without looking back at him. *Well, that was that,* she thought as she walked briskly through the lobby toward the elevators. It was probably just as well, too. Now she could get on with her life as normal and forget all about Charly Alba and this craziness.

Yep. Adventure complete.

Goodbye, Charly Alba.

Chow, baby.

Adios.

Au revoir.

Auf Wiedersehen.

It's all over, red rover.

Yes, she was flying back home to her husband the following day, and she was looking forward to seeing him and the kids, for sure. She just had to forget how Charly's arms had felt like paradise.

Chapter 7

"Mom, can I get a tattoo when I'm fifteen?" Mia asked, swivelling the kitchen bench stool from side to side as she sat and watched Arie prepare dinner.

Mia was fourteen going on twenty – and if the conditions were right, she could just about pass for a twenty-year-old, too. She was a product of Arie's first marriage, and a lot fairer than her mother with long, dark blond hair. Her vivid green eyes were garnished with thick black lashes, and perched wide above the most chiselled nose Arie had ever seen. And she was fast developing curves in all the right places – a fact that Arie didn't take care to spend time pondering.

Arie paused, knife mid-air as she sliced an onion. She lifted her chin and gave her eldest daughter a crazy face – her nose wrinkling furiously while her eyeballs almost popped from their sockets and her lips curled into something that'd crack mirrors for sure.

"Wait – before you say a word, hear me out," Mia added before Arie had a chance to respond verbally.

Okay – this might be half amusing, Arie thought. She relaxed her features into a more sombre expression and waited for her daughter to state a case she'd never win. She couldn't blame her, though; Mia mightn't share the same physical attributions as Arie, but Arie had been just like her as a teenager – rebellious, spirited, and always up to something. Arie couldn't decide if that was a good thing or not.

"So, like, all I want is a semi-colon and a full stop – it's tiny, and... like, did you know if you get tatts on your palms, they'll fade away after a few years anyway? So..." Mia's voice trailed off, her eyes widening before she continued. "So, it means 'stop and take a breath' – you know, just chill. And all I need is your written consent."

"Which you won't be getting," Arie said, smiling sweetly.

Dramatic eye roll.

"But, why not? Like, it's a great omen, and it would be hardly visible," Mia argued.

Arie nodded and turned back to the onions, wincing as she fought the zingy vapors stinging her eyes.

"Yeah, it *will* be hardly visible, because it will be, like, *invisible*," she said, emphasizing the last of her words as a lone tear erupted from her eye.

Damned onion.

Exaggerated sigh with dramatic eye roll. "You never let me do anything remotely interesting. Why not, though?" Mia pressed.

Arie put the knife down and backed away from the killer onion, her gaze softening over her daughter.

"Because, Mia – you have the rest of your adult life to permanently ink your body if you so choose. Choices and desires change as you grow and experience new things. What you want now will be very different in five, ten years' time. You never stop learning, wanting, and changing, even when you're my age – it's how we're designed to create and evolve," Arie said, pausing to give her a cheeky grin. "Besides, you're not marking that beautiful skin under my watch. It's a non-negotiable no, kitten."

"Whatever," Mia replied, pulling her lips together and swinging off the stool before she stalked from the kitchen.

Yep, whatever.

Arie smirked. She knew Mia hated her little speeches about life – but it never stopped her from dishing them out.

The instant she was alone, it didn't take long for Arie's thoughts to run away from her again. Six weeks had passed since she'd returned from the States, and she'd been so glad to get back onto Australian soil and see her family again. Yet, no matter how hard she tried, she just couldn't get Charly out of her mind. They'd exchanged a few emails regarding an article assignment Charly and Ty had given the group before the end of the program. When she'd completed the task, the emails had dwindled and she now faced radio silence.

It was probably for the best – the last thing she needed was complications in her life. Not to mention that he lived on the other side of the world. It was an impossible situation, and entertaining the notion of him any further was both fruitless and unproductive. All she had to do was let time fade the memory of him. Easy peasy – she was certain. Although, she *was* grateful for the distractions her work and family provided, for those were the only times her thoughts were completely clear of him.

Dreaming, on the other hand, was beyond her control. He crashed into her dreams with a tenacious energy, leaving his mark against her subconscious mind so she'd be sure to remember him upon waking. And given her track record, Arie knew, she only ever recalled the dreams that were significant to her waking life. The messages were always clear – Charly was thinking of her as much as she thought about him. A lot of good that would do either of them.

Arie's vision glazed over as she began heating a frying pan. She tossed the onions into the pan, along with some garlic and chopped bacon, and stood over the hotplate pushing the ingredients around with a wooden spoon without really seeing them. Images of last night's dream played across her mind like a repetitive movie she couldn't stop. An odd sense of inner knowing flooded through her as the sequence played out for the umpteenth time that day.

Arie gazed up at the ceiling fan as it circulated warm air over her body. She didn't know where she was; she only knew she was in a hotel room someplace in America. The room was small and sparingly furnished, the bed soft and unremarkable, and she was alone.

She wasn't worried at all – there were no resistant or discordant feelings rifling through her. No concern over her whereabouts as she relaxed under the balmy breeze of the fan. She just was. Then, the door swung open and Charly stood at the threshold watching her, as if it were the most natural thing in the world. A smile caught his lips while she sat up on the mattress and motioned for him to come closer.

His distinct, woody scent invaded her senses when he stopped beside the bed and gazed down at her. He smelled like heaven-on-a-stick to Arie.

"Hi," he said, stretching his hands toward her.

"Hey."

She clasped his hands, entwining her fingers through his as he gently tugged her to her feet beside him. Then, he leaned closer, his warm breath tickling her ear and sending a delicious shiver down her spine as he whispered.

"We're going to work together," he said. He pulled back to face her, uncurling his fingers from hers before cupping her chin in his hands and smiling. "You're all I ever wanted, Arie."

Arie's breath surged and mingled with the humid air as she exhaled, her heart leaping with the words she'd never known she'd longed to hear. She didn't say a thing – words failed her, and as he lowered his face closer to hers, the world diffused beneath her feet. Desire. Anticipation. Wanting. Oh, how she wanted to kiss those lips! Her quickened pulse felt like fire in her veins – she wanted to feel him now. Her eyes locked onto his as she closed the space between them, circling her hands around his neck and tangling her fingers in his hair as she crushed her lips against his.

She was a thirsty, wild cat drinking from the earth's sweetest spring, and she couldn't get enough of him. His mouth felt soft and warm, and contrasted with the roughness edging his lips as his whiskers grazed her skin, their lips parting and tongues entwining, and... oh, he tasted so good, and she melted into his chest and gave herself to the moment with total abandonment. Then, the moment was over and he slowly pulled away from her, leaving her wanting more while her mind scattered and her swollen lips pouted.

Wait, what? Why?

She frowned, the words whirling through her mind and catching beneath her tongue as she watched Charly back away from her.

A smile played in Charly's eyes before he turned from her, and without another word he strutted towards the hotel door. Her frown deepened, and she strained to piece together his motions as she watched him open the door and disappear from view. Her heart banged against her ribcage rebelliously while her gaze fell and lingered over the shiny door handle as if her stare might will him back to her – but then something else took hold. A fermenting, vile sensation nudged its way from her heart and settled in her gut, tightening *her lungs along its path. It twisted and wrenched, and it felt horrible. Guilt.*

"Hey, baby!"

Arie jumped and whirled around so fast that she almost shed her skin.

Shite!

It was Brett.

Lashes blinked over her dark eyes momentarily as she was dragged from the remnants of her dream back to the present. She snuffed the dream beneath a smile, watching as Brett dropped his bag on the kitchen benchtop and approached her.

"Hey, babe, how was your day?" she asked, stepping into his open arms and leaning into his chest. The odor of beer and sweat immediately assaulted her nostrils.

He leaned in to brush his lips against her forehead, mouthing his next words against her skin. "Good. Yours?"

"Mine was good, too," she replied.

She stifled a grimace and untangled herself from his arms before searching his eyes to gage his mood along with his level of intoxication – an exercise that'd become her daily habit.

Brett's pupils were dilated and blended with the dark shade of his irises, his vision blurred into focus as he gazed her with a lopsided grin and reached for her hand.

"You okay?"

Arie nodded and slipped her fingers from his as she backed away toward the hotplate. He appeared mellow. *Good.* She relaxed a little before she picked up the spoon and turned to the sizzling pan.

"Yeah, why?"

"You seem different since you arrived back from the States – distant," he said, coming up behind her and wrapping his arms around her waist.

She shrugged. "Just busy, that's all."

His voice lowered and he grazed his lips against her earlobe. "You sure?"

She tried not to tense.

"I'm sure," she said lightly as the sound of footsteps thudded against the set of timber stairs leading to the upper level of the house. Arie began to relax as a high-pitched voice echoed from the staircase.

"Daddy! Daddy, you're home!"

It was their middle daughter, Isobel, and she squealed in delight as she ran into the kitchen toward her father.

From the moment she'd been able to walk and talk, Isobel had become the 'daddy's girl' of the family. Now, nine years later, nothing had changed. Her favorite pastime of all was hanging out with Brett in his garage-cum-workshop. The two spent hours together doing things Arie considered to be boring. But Isobel loved to learn about the mechanics of anything Brett happened to be working on, and Arie appreciated that about their daughter. She was also the easiest of their daughters to please with her kind nature and charitable traits – and physically, she was the perfect blend of both Brett and Arie, with wild chestnut curls, golden skin, and exotic, almond eyes. In short, the girl was a delight.

"Hey, hey, baby girl," Brett said, pulling away from Arie and bending on his haunches as Isobel flung herself into his waiting arms.

Arie glanced at them with a smile, watching as Isobel's eyes squeezed shut and she pressed her cheek against her father's chest.

"I missed you, Daddy," she said, stretching her arms further around him. "I've been waiting to show you the Lego technic forest machine I built today – wanna come see?"

Brett laughed and stood up. "Sure, lead the way," he said.

"C'mon," she exclaimed, taking his hand and tugging hard as he pretended to resist. Her features knitted together as she frowned up at him. "Daddy?"

"Huh? What?"

"C'mon, then – hurry up!"

Brett chuckled and threw Arie a wink. "Back soon," he said before he allowed Isobel to lead him from the kitchen.

Arie responded with a grin while she grabbed some minced meat from the fridge and turned back to the pan, taking her time with adding the meat and separating the chunks with the end of the wooden spoon. Really, she was grateful for her family – she loved them to pieces and they loved her, too. They lived near the coast in a beautiful house with stunning ocean views, and for the most part, their home was warm and homey, its energy tranquil. Things could be a lot worse - she shouldn't have any reservations.

Everything is as it should be.

The words drifted in her mind and she began to feel she could believe them. That was it – there would be no more thinking about Mr. American Pie, and no more dreams to be sure. No, she had to anchor herself into the now and forget all about him. Her life was sweet, and she was going to stop this nonsense. She nodded to herself to emphasize the fresh sense of determination springing up in her gut.

Arie's thoughts were interrupted by the faint ding of her iPhone signalling an incoming email. She added tomato paste and water to the meat mixture before leaving the pan to simmer and going for her phone, which she'd left lying on the kitchen bench. She leaned against the bench and clicked her screen open and navigated to her emails. Her eyes widened, her interest instantly captured by the lettering on her screen – an email from Charly with the subject text:

Are you interested in working with us?

Her heart skipped a beat and she frowned while she pressed a finger to open the email. The text was simple and to the point, yet she read the words at least three times before they seeped into her consciousness and curled the edges of her lips into a wide smile.

Hey Arie,

Ty and I have a project we've been working out behind the scenes. We need two other journalists to get involved, and we think you might be the perfect addition for the project. We'd love to set up a Skype meeting if you're interested, so we can pitch you our idea and discuss.

Look forward to hearing from you.

Sincerely,

Charly.

Arie's hand dropped to the bench and her mind shifted into overdrive.

What could they possibly want me for?

She didn't know, but as she rushed toward her office to reply to Charly, all previous thoughts about casting him from her mind fell to the side like scattering dominoes, and her heart soared.

"Special are the stars in the sky. Special is the order of the universe; the mysteries of space, time and the multiverse in which we live. And special doesn't scratch the surface of what one's twin flame is to them."

~ Xavier Eastenbrick

Chapter 8

Hot damn! That is one foxy lady.

Charly grinned and leaned back in his office chair, looping his fingers together and cradling the back of his neck. He'd just finished up a Skype meeting with Arie and Ty, and to say he was pleased with the outcome of the call was an understatement. He couldn't explain it, but since parting ways with Arie in New York, he'd experienced an overwhelming urge to keep her a part of his life.

No, there was more to it than that – it was like a need he couldn't deny.

Charly didn't believe in coincidences. The fact that he'd long been toying with an idea for a project that would work well with the added mix of a female counterpart hadn't been lost on Charly. And after getting a taste for Arie's work when she'd submitted her article assignment following the New York workshop, he'd had no doubts she'd be the perfect addition for the job. Convincing Ty hadn't been hard, either. All that had been left for him to do was to approach Arie with his idea and hope for the best. Luckily, he hadn't had to wait long for her reply. As it was, the anticipation he'd felt surrounding the entire process had almost suffocated him.

Now that she'd agreed to work with them and they'd ironed out all the details, Charly was flooded with a sense of relief. And after a good dose of that candied, Aussie accent of hers... perhaps a little elation, too. She was like syrup for his ears, and wonder for his eyes. Normally, he wasn't all that big on extended conversation, but he knew he could listen to her voice and watch her all day long. His chest pushed against his shirt while thoughts buzzed around his head like honey bees – and why not? He could be a bee for a moment. A Charly king-bee tasting the sweet nectar of a wildflower – his wildflower.

Hold up – wildflower? Where the hell did that come from? What are you thinking, dick?

He was being ridiculous. The woman belonged to another man and lived in Australia, no less. This was business and nothing more, and they were bringing in one other journalist to join their team for this project. Granted, Arie would be the only woman among them, but she just happened to be the perfect candidate for the project – an in-depth series about cultural diversity and gender-related challenges facing artists across the world. Naturally, a woman's point of view was required to complete the series authentically – and who better than an Australian woman?

A beautiful Australian.

Shut up, Charly.

He sat upright and set about getting back to work again. Irrational moment over. He wasn't an impractical man. Sure, at times, he was prone to chasing shiny objects and wild ideas – a trait that served him well when he was out in the field investigating stories. But, as far as he was concerned, the moment he crossed over the threshold back to his real life, the buck stopped and his feet became rooted firmly in reality. While he did believe there was a higher phenomenon at work in their world, it wasn't his business to try to understand the mysteries of the divine. Besides, if Charly was good at anything, it was the uncanny ability to shut out situations that threw him off balance and interrupted his life.

So, why did you lure Arie back into your life?

Because she feels like the part of yourself you never knew you were missing.

Bullshit. Mandy is your woman and always will be.

Now, who's lying?

Shut up, Charly!

Charly moaned aloud. The truth was, inner dialogue like this had become his constant companion of late. A royal pain-in-the-ass companion. Admittedly, he might've had a chance to forget about Arie if she hadn't kept appearing in his meditations and dreams. She was like a mystical spirit haunting him every chance she got – it was those dark eyes that affected him the most. They seeped into his consciousness like beautiful gems glittering with love.

Maybe she's an angel.

Now, you're being an idiot.

He laughed out loud, a smile still lingering at the corners of his lips as he turned back to the computer screen and pulled up an image of her. He tilted his head and rubbed his fingers over the short whiskers covering his chin, utterly losing himself in her picture.

What is it about this woman?

He didn't know. But if he was truly being honest with himself, he knew she represented something significant in his life – something deep, and at a level his heart and soul were privy to. Unfortunately, his heart and soul had failed to inform his brain of their secrets, and he was scrambling to play catch-up.

As Charly gazed at Arie's picture, he recalled their last conversation in New York, and how good it had felt to be close to her. That moment, when their hands had accidently collided, it had felt like a flashing streak of lightning racing through his system and striking his heart. The sudden surge had caught him off guard and he'd instinctively widened the space them. Oh, he'd liked it, but he was a man who didn't deal well with sudden emotions gusting through him like mini tornadoes – his analytic nature spilled into even the most delicate of situations. And he'd needed to process the incident before he could figure out what it meant.

Maybe. Just maybe, she could be someone important in my life.

Charly leaned closer to the computer screen and sighed. His eyes hazed, lips slackening along with the tantalizing daydreams capturing his mind. He was processing so deeply now, he failed to hear Mandy as she padded through his office door and sidled up behind him.

"She's attractive."

"Huh?" Charly straightened up, turning his chin to gaze up at his wife. He gave a fast nod and deliberately relaxed his shoulders. "Yeah."

He extended an arm and reached for her hand as she swung her gaze from the monitor down to him. Mandy was tall for a woman, a fact that suited Charly just fine due his own height. She was lithe and bony, with shoulder-length hair the color of straw. Her pale complexion was dotted with light ginger freckles which had always appealed to him. But it was really her firm ass and her fickle attitude that'd hooked him back in his early twenties.

Hazel eyes narrowed as Mandy studied him for a moment, before her thin brows raised. "Who is she?" she asked.

He shook his head. "Arie Kinard, the Australian woman who attended the New York writing program last spring," he said casually. He half-turned back toward his desk, grabbing the mouse with his free hand and clicking Arie's image from the screen.

"Hmm... you didn't mention how beautiful she was," Mandy said, slipping her hand from his and watching him closely.

Too closely.

Charly tried not to squirm beneath her piercing stare. His thick brows knitted with his scowl. "Who cares what she looks like? She's business –

end of story," he snapped, rising to his feet next to her.

She nodded slowly while her eyes still bore into his. When she spoke, her voice pinched tight. "Okay. Well, dinner is ready. Are you coming?"

"Yep," he replied, forcing a smile. "Let's eat."

He felt odd as he followed his wife from the room – he'd been with her for most of his adult life, and she knew him better than anyone. He loved her. Yet, it wasn't until recently that he'd begun to feel as if something was missing from his marriage. His life. And it wasn't anything tangible. Sometimes, he felt like an empty carcass starving for something he couldn't quite figure out.

He had to admit that those feelings had been simmering below the surface for some time now. He just hadn't wanted to acknowledge them. But what do you do, right? He was a family man with a mortgage and responsibilities. This was the life he'd chosen, and the life he appreciated, too.

He hadn't asked for anything different.

Or have I?

Charly frowned as he rounded the corner to the kitchen and made for the table. His sons, Jamie and Jack, sat across from one another – their arms flailed around, eyebrows raised, tongues flapping as they enthusiastically discussed the rules of a PS4 game.

At seventeen, Jamie was the eldest of the two and heading into his final year of high school. He mirrored the image of Charly, but for the fact that the color of his hair was a blend of chestnut and honey, and cropped much shorter. But his eyes were the exact shade of blue as Charly's, and they churned like the ocean with the flare of his passions. Jack was fourteen, and a throwback from older Alba generations. He was as fair as a silver moon, and just as interesting with his upbeat and quirky personality. His eyes were like crystals, his features strong and sharp, and Charly called him his walking encyclopedia. The kid never stopped devouring information – a fact that delighted both Mandy and Charly.

They barely glanced at Charly as he sat down at the table, but they both threw a fast greeting his way before continuing their conversation at full speed. He didn't mind. Listening to their debate made for interesting entertainment, and besides that, he had other things on his mind.

Like her.

He knew he had to find a way to bury the discordant feelings, but he was savvy enough about universal laws to know that nothing ever occurred without having attracted it in the first place. Had he attracted Arie into his life? He figured he had. But he was clueless as to why. Whatever the reason, he knew he could never find the answers outside of himself. He had to look within and go from there.

He was also beginning to realize that, sometimes, all it took was a chance encounter to ignite the flames of change. The question was, did he want change?

Chapter 9

Charly: Do you feel that gender identity is used as a method of self-definition for writers?

Arie: Absolutely! Moreover, people in general. Gender identity has definitely acted as an external barrier toward the undervaluing, under-publishing and under-representation of work by female writers.

Charly: How so?

Arie: Historically, female authors have been required to hide their gender in order to be taken seriously as writers. Men on the other hand, gather creative fuel from their identity and the ability to express from it — whatever the experience might be.

Charly: Sounds interesting, can't wait to see you write it all up. I know you're gonna blow my mind.

Arie: Hope so! LOL!

Charly: What's to hope? You already have.

Arie: Really? Wow. Thanks!

Charly: Yeah, really. That's why I was just about to change my profile picture.

Arie: Huh?

Charly: To try and keep up with your glamorous photo.

Arie: Oh! Now I'm blushing…

Charly: I'd like to see that.

Arie: Well, I'm glad you can't.

Charly: Then don't blush, you're a beautiful woman.

The night was still, the ocean waves that usually lulled Arie to sleep were silent, and the humid air clung to her skin like a heavy cloak. Even with the breeze of the overhead fan drifting over her, Arie couldn't get comfortable. It was that along with her incessant thoughts keeping her awake in the dark as she lay in her bed beside Brett.

She closed her eyes and tried to block out the faint drum of Brett's snoring. Images of Charly instantly greeted her. His blue eyes seemed to penetrate into her soul, accompanied by a burst of energy that flashed through the center of her being like a luminous blaze.

What is that?

Arie had no idea, but the zingy feelings had become a familiar friend and, somehow, she knew it had something to do with Charly. She couldn't remember the exact moment when she'd come to grasp the depth of her feelings for Charly. It was more like a slow burn that had gently curled through every channel of her body – charring and awakening invisible barriers along the way. Then, when the flames had finally consumed the very last inch of her resistance, it had been too late. She had become his, and she was his for the taking.

No. It was more than that... it was as if he had triggered the rawest parts of herself, and she'd ventured into an internal volcano waiting to erupt at any moment. Her emotions swung from the highest love she had ever experienced, to delving into the darkest pits of torment. All of which puzzled her.

The best part?

The best part was when they transcended from their physical bodies and consciously coupled together in the higher realms. She groaned inwardly, and shuddered with pleasure while Charly's presence swirled all around her. Shifting away from Brett, she curled her body with her back to him while every one of her cells began to tingle on high alert as she invited Charly closer.

He didn't hesitate. He came to her with a desire so deep that it cracked through any invisible walls she may have tried to erect. Her lips trembled, and she gave a breathless sigh as she surrendered to his energy with a hunger that matched his own.

His soul spoke to her in ways that reached the core of her essence. She was unbarred and exposed, and her heart thumped wildly as she opened up to him like an unfurling petal. A luxurious rush twisted down Arie's spine when she felt him ease inside of her – he felt strong and masculine, and beautiful and ardent, and he spilled into her body with a sense of completeness.

"Arie." His voice was an echo whispering against her soul. "I've been searching for you."

"I'm here, my love. I've been searching for you, too," she replied, circling her hands around his neck and pulling him closer still.

There was nothing she could hide from him, and there was nothing that she wanted to hide from him. Her breath stole away somewhere in the depths of her lungs as his body deliciously entwined with hers and every inch of him filled her. He was hard and pulsing, his wanting traced with a slight sense of aggression that swelled between her thighs and dampened her panties.

She cupped her breasts and squeezed; her swollen nipples were so hard, she ached to feel him take them in his mouth and swallow them whole – to consume all of her tingling flesh and claim her soul as his own.

"Charly."

Ecstasy rippled from her crown to her toes and crashed against her throbbing clitoris. Her body writhed on the mattress in a film of sweat, and she thrust her hips forward and bit down on her quivering lips, trying to tame her rapid panting. She balanced on the very edge of desire – unmade and vulnerable to his deliberate manipulation, and she wanted to scream out loud.

"Please," she silently begged. "Please."

He ebbed and flowed within her, and all the while her body began to wind tight, the tension building to an impossible height, and she thought she'd lose her mind. Then, he entered her and she thanked the heavens, and moaned softly while she clenched against his cock and their hips began to sing to a beautiful rhythm.

His gruff moan rang in her ears, his breath hot against her lips, and it was enough to send her over the edge to spiral into the wonderous depths of passion. Her body fluttered violently, her vagina pulsing hot as she exploded, and her head was lost somewhere in a dizzy bliss as she burst into a euphoric buzz.

And then he was gone as fast as he'd arrived, leaving her breathless and feeling barren, and she gripped her chest in an attempt to ease the great, big hole in her heart that ached like hell.

Arie pulled her body into a tight ball, her mind whirling with the remnants of Charly's visit while her eyes stung hot with tears. She didn't know what was happening to her, and she struggled to comprehend the dynamics playing out between herself and Charly. It was foreign and surreal, and she thought that perhaps it was her imagination tricking her. Yet, somewhere deep inside, she knew it was more real to her than anything she'd encountered in the physical world.

Charly had become her lover.

Chapter 10

Twelve.

That was the number of weeks Arie had been working closely with Charly on their project – and the number of weeks required for her to realize she was in way over her head. She was like a wild moth drawn to the radiance of the light. She cared not if the heat of the light was deadly to her heart, or if it might burn to a blackened husk in a vain attempt to get closer to him – all thoughts of sanity had drowned beneath his blaze, and all she wanted to do was to bask in the wondrous feelings of love.

It sounded crazy, even to herself – to fall so deeply in love with a man she barely knew. After all, she had a very analytical mind, and a logical one, too. She was the one that pulled situations apart, then separated, mulled, and pieced them back together before repeating the process numerous times. She'd do this until she had successfully solved the issue at hand and filed the particulars into suitable sections of her mind. She wasn't crazy, but she was an overthinker. Yet, no amount of analyzing the current situation could place it into any comfortable compartments in her mind.

Stupid love.

Stupid heart.

Those very thoughts drifted through Arie's brain as she pulled her car into the driveway of her home. She'd just finished making the rounds and dropping the girls off at school, and now a quiet day of writing in her office lay spread before her. She loved her days alone in the house. These hours were the only times she had to herself – utter isolation to explore her thoughts and write her heart out. Sometimes, she'd plug in her earbuds and treat herself to a blast of music while cleaning the house between bouts of writing, even breaking out her dance moves. She might be fast heading toward forty, but she still had it. She could think of nothing better than a day alone enjoying her own company. Well, maybe she could. But she knew she shouldn't.

She also knew the wisest thing to do with Charly was to keep their relationship strictly business. Of course, that was the right thing to do. But despite her logic, Arie had never been fond of rules. Besides that, her heart wouldn't let her.

Can you fault the heart?

Arie wasn't so sure, and she could hardly contain the urge to find out more about him. She found herself wanting to chat with him about subjects outside of their project discussions. He was an interesting man and he fascinated her. He was smart, quirky and quick-witted, and his mind was like a cryptic puzzle she longed to figure out. Plus, she adored his sarcastic sense of humor.

Was that so bad?

Well, it couldn't be all that good, considering they were both married. The thing was, something had recently begun to shift between her and Charly. He was treating her differently, and she couldn't quite pin him down. He and Ty had created an online workspace where they and their other co-worker, Stevie, could all communicate and seamlessly share files relating to the project. During the first few weeks, Charly had been super helpful with easing her transition into their production schedule. He'd been friendly and accommodating, offering her loads of support and guidance. There was a gentleness about the way he spoke to her, and with each interaction, she felt his growing fondness toward her.

Now, Arie wasn't a stupid woman, but gaging people's feelings wasn't always her strongest suit. Despite her own irrational feelings and dreams of Charly, she'd been surprised at first when she'd finally figured out that he might possess deeper feelings for her, too.

That was when it had all begun to change. Suddenly, Arie had found herself longing to hear from him. She couldn't help it – she was hooked, but confused and conflicted with the torrent of feelings gripping her every waking hour, and the intensity of him was consuming.

Problem was, between their telepathic communication, their unworldly encounters, and their professional relationship, Arie was caught in a strange zone she couldn't decipher. To make matters worse, the more of herself she revealed to him, she seemed to ignite a hot and cold reaction from him, and she wasn't certain how to handle it.

Today was no different. Arie's mind buzzed as she made a cup of tea before settling into her office and firing up her computer. She switched on her Sony Bluetooth speaker and tuned into some relaxing music while she waited for the computer to load. When it did, she immediately brought up the workspace website she shared with Charly, Ty, and Stevie. A delighted surge sprinkled down her spine when she noticed Charly was already online.

"Helloooo, baby," she murmured, her lips curving into a smile.

The blue light indicting he was active also activated a slight pulse that lingered around Arie's naval and idled between her thighs. Who was she kidding? Those unusual sensations she was experiencing in those areas of her body seemed to be a constant reminder of him – especially during his waking hours. It was like an invisible magnetic chord stretching between them, and it was growing stronger every day. She wondered if he'd felt something similar.

She scanned the message he'd left for her in the general feed.

Charly: Hey Arie, loved your piece about female voices in the arts and the widening gap needing to be filled! I can really feel your empathy in your writing. Nice work! I wonder if we should investigate why and how Australian women feel limited. Are they struggling with self-limiting beliefs at the core level? Fear of breaking so-called societal rues and boundaries surrounding role expectations? And how do personal belief systems inform decision making? What do you think?

I think I've just gone back on all of my personal belief systems.

Arie: Hi Charly! Glad you liked the piece – thank you! I'm already on it and getting my hands dirty digging in the Australian soil. I have to tell you, though, us Aussies excel at small poppy syndrome. This is probably one core level for artists of both genders.

Charly: Tall poppy syndrome?

Arie: Yeah. The term is used in Australia to describe cultural aspects where people of high status are resented, criticized or cut down for their success.

Charly: Oh… you Aussies have some interesting terminology!

Arie: You don't know the half of it, mate :)

Charly: America's where it's at, then. LOL!

Literally.

A shot of energy burst through Arie's system. She shivered, and watched the screen for a moment. He wouldn't say much more unless she applied a little coaxing. She wanted to apply. She drummed a fingernail against her keyboard before she switched her screen to personal messaging and began to type.

Arie: Do you fear breaking the rules and boundaries?

Charly: Rules and boundaries have never suited me. I've always tended to push against authority;

that's why I love doing what I'm doing – I get to push boundaries without the risk, and live vicariously through the shady people I interview. LOL! Meanwhile, I pay my taxes and don't go around murdering people because I don't wish to harm others.

Do you fear breaking the rules?

Vicariously?

That one word stuck out in her mind like a sore thumb. It drifted through Arie's mind and began to unsettle her. Is that what I am to him? A safe way he could sample a love affair without feeling as if he were cheating? Were they cheating? Did emotional, out-of-body affairs really count? And, more to the point, was this even real, or was she just imagining the entire thing?

She frowned and chewed her bottom lip as she peered at the screen.

She found it difficult to distinguish her feelings between his often-aloof attitude toward her during their professional exchanges and the moments when his soul wrapped around hers in a blanket of pure love. In short... it was a total mindfuck. Meh. What the heck – he'd just asked her a direct, personal question. She wasn't about to let one little word get in the way of keeping him engaged. She swallowed her doubt and focused on the monitor.

Arie: Ha! Rules are meant to be broken I say!

Charly: LOL! Rebel. I like it ;)
Arie: Always the rebel. You make me laugh, I'm
really enjoying working with you.
Charly: I'm enjoying working on this project with
you too. It's been amazing and I LOVE working
with you!

Her heart sang as she read his text, and she grinned. She hesitated for a moment before typing the next words.

Arie: Do you believe people can communicate in
spirit? Like, on a soul level or something?
Charly: Sure. I definitely think there's more to the
universe than can be explained, and I'm not sure
we're all just flesh and blood.

Okay – that's encouraging. She decided to venture a little further, to feel him out some more. She had to know if he was really present during their telepathic encounters.

Arie: Don't judge okay. Sometimes, I feel your
energy speaking to me, I feel you so strongly, it's
almost as if you're standing right next to me.

Long pause. Admittedly, she knew those words might come across as a bit 'out there', but at same time, she sensed an uncanny familiarity about him that allowed her to say things she normally wouldn't dream of saying. She squirmed in her chair as she sensed his discomfort emanating through the monitor. Then, finally.

Charly: Okay.

Okay? That's all?

Arie shook her head and frowned. Suddenly, she wanted something from him. *Needed* something from him – an acknowledgement of some sort. She had to know she wasn't going crazy. Always an upfront kind of person, she could think of nothing better than the truth.

> Arie: You're judging? It gets even better; you come to me in my dreams, too. Help me out here, am I totally mad? Does this spook you?
>
> Charly: I'm not easily spooked, Arie, and I'm not judging you. I think dreams can reveal a lot about ourselves. They can show us truths we'd rather not face. You're not mad at all.
>
> Arie: Thank god! I'm finding my emotions are shifting from one extreme to another – I have these super-elated bubbles filled with love. Filled with you. Then, I come crashing down and I feel so depleted and... depressed. I don't understand what's happening.
>
> I know I shouldn't, but I think about you much more than I should.

Major long pause.

Arie cringed and knotted her fingers together so tight that her knuckles grew white as she waited for his response.

Oh my god! Why did I tell him that? Idiot.

She almost didn't want to look when his reply finally appeared on the screen. Her breath hitched as she read the text, while her heart dropped somewhere near her feet and her thoughts gnawed chunks in her brain.

Charly: Our desires can often cause suffering. Although, I've found that altering your diet helps with extreme mood swings like you describe. It's scientifically proven that omitting foods like sugar and caffeine help to manage mental disorders. I've completely cut these from my diet, and feel all the better for it.

You should probably stop thinking about me so much! LOL!

Huh? What exactly did all that mean?

He'd totally deflected her deepest confessions – swept aside her feelings – and now she really did feel like an idiot. The beginnings of a blush stung her cheeks as she turned back to the keyboard. She needed to leave this conversation right now.

Arie: Then it's probably best that you stop thinking about me, too.

Charly: Ha ha! That's a great one!

Yeah, great one.

How did she know he thought about her?

Because his energy had merged with her own and imprinted upon her soul like a sacred stamp. Although, that didn't stop her heart from splitting in her chest as clicked him away from her screen.

Chapter 11

"So, what's up with you and Arie?" Ty asked, stroking his beard while his eyes narrowed over Charly like glass beads.

Charly shrugged and slumped back against his seat. He reached for his glass of water, taking a long sip before he answered, "What do you mean?"

Charly and Ty sat in their regular booth facing each other in a Chicago diner. The booth was tucked away from the noise of the usual, buzzing lunch crowd in the far back of the room. It was Charly's favorite spot. He liked it because the booth was partially sectioned off from the rest of the diner and the position provided a clear view of Michigan Avenue.

Ty gave a half-laugh, his fingers now working to knead the whiskers around his lips.

"C'mon, man. The tension between the two of you online isn't half obvious. Hell, it almost feels like an intrusion when I comment or post about something related to the project. I'm sure Stevie has picked up on it by now, too. So, what gives?"

Charly scowled and peered out the window. The streets were slick and wet, and a light fog hung over the city. He scraped his teeth over his lips while his thoughts ran in circles. This whole thing with Arie was getting him so wound up, he was starting to feel a little out of control. He'd never wanted anyone this much in his entire life, and it was eating him from the inside out – maybe confiding in Ty would help. He turned back to Ty.

"Is it that obvious?" he asked.

"Yeah," Ty said, shaking his head. His gaze sharpened and he leaned forward over the table. "What the hell are you doing, man? You know it's crazy, right? I mean, you're both married to other people, both have kids, and then the big kicker – she lives in Australia, dude."

"I'm well aware of those facts, Ty. Thanks for the recap," Charly muttered.

"Ha. You might be aware of the facts, but it's not stopping you from encouraging her... I can tell she's developed feelings for you. And you know what? I can't speak for Stevie, but it makes me feel awkward. This is supposed to be a professional relationship – not perfect match or dial–a–date."

Charly's eyes razored in on Ty. His muscles tensed defensively before he reconsidered his instinctual reaction to Ty's comment. Maybe this was exactly what he needed to hear to snap him out of the infatuation he had for Arie. He gave a rueful laugh before glancing out the window again.

"Do you really think I wanted this?"

"You tell me," Ty replied, straightening his back and watching Charly carefully.

Charly screwed up his lips and shook his head. "She's under my skin, Ty. She's a beautiful woman..." he said, his voice trailing off as her image flashed through his mind. He noted the upbeat of his heart and the familiar feelings she provoked within him and sighed. Arie made him feel like a man. She gave him a sense of renewed hope and opened his mind in ways he'd never imagined. She made him feel higher.

"And? There are millions of beautiful women in the world, but I don't see you falling to pieces over all of them," Ty snapped.

"She's not like any of them – she's different."

"Regardless..." Ty paused and cocked his head to side as he regarded Charly. His eyes widened over him before he frowned. "Oh, you're in love with her."

It was more of a statement than a question, and the truth of his words struck the deepest chord in Charly's soul. He clenched his jaw shut and dropped his gaze to the table.

Love is nothing but a lucid dream that keeps waking me.

Ty peered around the diner before lowering his voice to a confidential tone and leaning forward again. "Look, I know you, Charly – you're a practical man, so you can't *really* be in love with her. You just love chasing shiny new things, is all; and yeah, she's shiny alright." He laughed. "But her shine won't work for you – for us. Sometimes your head gets lost up in the clouds, and I'm the one that reels you back to earth. This, whatever it is, isn't good for you, or Arie. It can't work, so what's the point of prolonging the inevitable? You've gotta stop this now – before it goes too far."

It already has.

But Charly nodded anyway, his heart squeezing as he uttered his next words. "You're right. It not a viable situation."

Ty's cheeks balled with his grin and he nodded fast before he turned toward the laptop he had set up on the table between them. He flipped the screen closed and grabbed his bag to pack it away, his mouth offering a running dialogue as he did so.

"Damned right it's not a viable situation – you have to be polite and cordial toward her until we finish the project. After that, we can ditch her and move on; no more Arie means no more complications, right?" he asked.

"Right," Charly said, shifting uncomfortably. He swung his gaze away from Ty, every one of his nerve endings beginning to feel fidgety. As far as he was concerned, the conversation was over. He gathered his bag and slid from the booth before pausing for a beat and looking down at Ty. He was busy fiddling around with his gear, a triumphant expression painting his features. Suddenly, Charly felt agitated. "I need some air," he added before turning and strutting from the diner without waiting for a reply.

Once out on the street, he didn't wait around for Ty. He couldn't – he needed time to process alone and get his shit together. He needed to walk and blend into oblivion – to become another faceless guy haunting the Chicago streets for a few sweet minutes and try to train his heart to let go of Arie.

He pulled the hoodie of his sweater over his head and shoved his fists deep into his pockets before he set off down Michigan Avenue toward DuSable Bridge and the river. All the while, Ty's words repeated in his mind and began to stir a tinge of resentment in him. Oh, he knew Ty was right. It was pointless to pursue anything more than a business relationship with Arie. Yet, Ty didn't realize how deep the connection was between them, and Charly couldn't find the right words to articulate it properly.

Somehow, Charly knew it wouldn't matter anyway – neither Ty nor anyone else could really understand what was happening between himself and Arie. Hell, he didn't even get it. All he knew was that the woman seemed to mirror him and arouse his most inner feelings – good and bad. It was as if he could feel her emotions at any given time, and like his thoughts weren't always his own. And, his desire for her was indescribable, and bordered on being beyond healthy – he *needed* to feel her. He *needed* her closer.

Shit, shit, shit!

Charly's gait quickened, and he ignored his phone vibrating in his pocket as he reached the bridge and stopped to gaze at the water. He leaned over the rough bridge wall and tried to gather his thoughts. The cool air sharpened his nose and tore through his lungs as he thought about her.

She danced in the dense mist that clung over the water's surface. Her hips swayed provocatively, and she whispered his name and slinked along with the white, silent fog as it crawled along the glass towers bordering the river.

She was everywhere – she sweetened his dreams, and shined with the stars at night. She was the beat of his heart, and the owner of his soul. And he loved her – he loved her so much, their separation felt like pain.

Was loving her so wrong?

Arie had blasted into his life and crashed against every one of his convictions, catching him unaware and ensnaring him with her charms. He was afraid of the closeness he felt with her, and scared to acknowledge their intense bond. It was unusual and confronting; between the telepathic communications and their transcended meetings that defied space and time, he was utterly baffled. Yet, he could neither affirm or deny the words she'd typed on his screen about their connection.

To say he was conflicted with his feelings was an understatement – it was pure torment to be denied her, and yet, his desire was accompanied by a hefty side of guilt. Every time he looked at his wife, it was guilt that simmered like potent poison in the depths of his gut.

So, he'd been trying to distance himself from Arie, and preserve what was left of his heart – the part he'd kept guarded from feeling unwanted pain. But it was becoming near impossible to reject her, and if he was being honest with himself, he knew he didn't want to.

Argh!

Charly cranked his neck and gazed up at the sky. It was grey and dismal, and he was greeted by a fine drizzle that fell in his eyes and clung to his lashes. He took a slow breath, and silently willed the rain to wash away his worries – to bring him the clarity he so desperately needed. Then he lowered his chin and caught sight of a couple rushing in his direction. He didn't really see their faces. All he saw was the way their fingers entwined and the invisible threads that bonded them. They seemed to glow and thrive in each other's presence as they laughed and scrambled to cross the bridge.

A tingle emerged at the base of Charly's neck. It lingered there before it gathered momentum and spiralled down his spine, spreading through his entire being. It felt beautiful and divine, as if he were sprinkled with golden dust. His lips curved into a smile as he surrendered to the feelings. And then, the haze in his mind lifted, and clarity found him – and he knew that whatever was happening between him and Arie was much bigger than either of them.

She is part of me.

His heart almost burst with the revelation, and he was filled with a sense of happiness so deep that he wanted to run through the streets and dance with the buskers like a crazed lunatic.

Screw Ty and his biased opinion – he didn't know. He was an outsider looking in, and Charly suspected he had his own agenda at heart, and that somehow, he felt threatened by Arie.

When Charly turned away from the bridge and began the trek back to the office, he walked with a new sense of hope – the impossibilities of the situation had dissolved and he knew anything was possible. A love that felt so right couldn't be wrong, regardless of the circumstances. He couldn't let go of the best thing he'd ever wanted. He just needed to make a plan.

Chapter 12

Arie: I never know what I can and can't say to you, Charly. At times I feel as if I need to hold back on being myself with you. I feel as if I'm caught in limbo. I don't know what's real anymore. Maybe I'm losing my mind.

Charly: I feel the same way. Although, I think our profession can trigger a lot of those kinds of feelings – and most of the population is a little crazy. Nothing is real unless you want it to be.

Arie: Right. Do I make you feel uncomfortable? Do you dislike talking to me?

Charly: I think you forget I'm not overly fond of the online chatting scene.

Arie: I think you forget that I'm a woman, and
women need a little more communication.

Arie twisted her lips and sighed, the words on her
monitor fusing together as her vision glazed and
her thoughts trailed along uncertainty – a path
that was becoming all too familiar. She pulled her
hair loose from her hair tie, before clutching thick
handfuls of hair and twirling the strands between
her fingers.

What am I doing?

It was the question of the day. No – the
question of the year. This whole situation with
Charly was getting to be too much for her to
handle. It was a strange experience, and she did
feel as if she sat balanced somewhere between
here and oblivion. Charly was slowly driving her
insane, and she was beginning to suspect he
enjoyed stringing her along and toying with her
emotions.

He excelled at dishing out ambiguous
messages and double-meaning inuendo. Then,
the moment she'd feel awkward and begin to
retreat, he'd deliberately seek out her attention.
Charly was a clever man, and very creative. He
was careful at covering his ass, too, and many of
his attempts to catch her attention involved
cryptic social media posts, and subliminal
messages that he had to know only she would
understand. Yet, he did it in such a way that it

could easily be misconstrued – call him on it, and he'd eat her for dinner like a fool.

She should know – she'd been eaten a few times already. It didn't feel so good.

"What is wrong with you, Arie?" Arie asked herself, shaking her head and squeezing her eyes shut.

She was talking to herself again. Self-chiding had become a habit lately, too. She had to be crazy, right? Because she usually wasn't the type to allow herself to be treated in such a cavalier manner. But through all of the mind-bending games and constant self-questioning, Charly's soul continued to visit her – it was as if he knew how to project his energy toward her and merge with her soul. He was with her a lot of the time, and the strength of his love was unbelievable, and totally contrasted with his indifference toward her in the physical world. They knew each other intimately, and that's why Arie kept tripping up.

Meanwhile, her marriage to Brett was suffering. She was disconnecting from him and she didn't know how to stop it. Brett deserved better from her – she knew it. Funny how people could talk themselves into justifying their feelings and actions. At first, Arie had felt so guilty for having feelings for another man. So much so, she could barely stand herself. But, now, guilt had become a faded emotion, and one she seldom entertained. She knew the emotion wouldn't serve her or anyone else involved. And she knew enough to be able to say that connections this strong were more about the heart and soul, and less about the circumstances.

The soul didn't cater to physical circumstances. The soul only knew expansion.

But not at the expense of losing your self-respect, my dear.

She bit her bottom lip and swung her gaze to the window, her eyes finding the white-wash of the waves crashing against the jagged coastline. She took a breath and exhaled slowly. *Just let it go, Arie. Just let him go.* She knew it was the only way to reclaim her sense of inner peace again – the only way to salvage what was left of herself. Although the thought of losing Charly unsettled her, she knew she couldn't force him to love her the way she longed for him to love her. And she wasn't convinced he was strong enough to make it work, either. After all, it would take a great deal of trust and commitment on both of their parts to make something like this work.

When it's real, you can't walk away.

She closed her eyes and nodded, ignoring the agony burning in her heart. This was something she had to do for herself. If he couldn't be straight with her about his feelings, then this was all she could do – release him.

It's not real. It never was. He'll walk.

Arie swallowed the tears stinging behind her eyes before she squared her jaw and frowned hard. A new sense of determination circled in her belly and drowned the screaming protests churning deep within her. She didn't need to say anything, or announce her decision to Charly – she just had to execute it with her actions. Or rather, inactions. And she'd have to find a way to block him from entering her soul.

She turned her gaze back to her computer screen, ready to push Charly from her mind and get into some work. There was nothing better than the intellectual demands of writing to get her mind off him. And given the nature of their discussion and their time difference, she expected he would've logged out of their workspace by now so that she could move on with her workday. Her breath hitched and she frowned when she saw he was still online and that there was a message waiting for her.

Charly: I could never forget that you're a woman.

Despite her firm convictions, Arie couldn't help but smile.

Don't respond, Arie.

Yeah, tell that to my fingers.

Arie: I would never let you forget.

He didn't respond right away, but she could feel the delight in his reaction as his energy ruptured through the monitor and shrouded her. Then, something else – a sensual sensation caught her heart and quickened her pulse, and she closed her eyes and groaned. Wanting. His wanting. It captured her being like an exquisite rush and overpowered her senses. She closed her eyes and exhaled, consciously opening herself to his desire.

He felt velvety and unbroken, and his passion was insatiable. She moaned again as her body responded to his lustful hunger. Her nipples ached against the fabric of her bra, and she thought her panties would soak from the tingling throb of her swollen lips.

These were the moments that drove her to the brink – moments when she could fall to her knees and beg him to abuse her. Shadowy interludes when she could entangle herself in the beautiful depths of his darkness and become anything he wanted. Moments that would be her undoing.

Get a grip, Arie!

She flicked her long hair over a shoulder and tried to regain herself.

Don't fall for it, Arie... it's only words. Lovely, fickle words.

Honestly, she was absolutely puzzled with the intensity of emotions Charly aroused within her – it was as if the strength of their connection awakened an extreme love, as well as the flipside. Hate. Oh, she didn't hate Charly – but, somehow, their bond invoked her most inner sanctuaries – love. Hate. Fear. Anger. Joy. All of the above. Buried emotions brewed to the surface and confronted her like a reflection she couldn't avoid.

When his next words flashed up on the monitor, it was a shot of pure elation that caught her emotions, and her heart flew with the birds gliding past her window.

> Charly: I feel you in my mind and my soul. It won't be easy, Arie. But this can be real if you want it to be. Do you want it to be?

Arie gasped, and she smiled through her tears.

> Arie: I've never wanted anything more.

Lovely, fickle, words, and with all her heart she wanted to believe.

Chapter 13

She brought heaven to earth. Charly didn't
deserve such a thing. He'd treated her badly at
times and he knew it. Arie had remained like a
resilient light shining a path he couldn't ignore,
and now he revelled beneath her golden blaze. He
hadn't behaved that way toward her because he
didn't love her. Those actions had been born out
of fear, and the torment of wanting something he
couldn't have. But now he knew it had never only
been about attraction and desire. The connection
between himself and Arie was more about
unconditional love and spiritual growth.

It had been three weeks since Charly had typed those words onto Arie's screen, and he'd meant every syllable. Those words hadn't come easy, either. He'd never been the kind of guy who wore his heart on his sleeve – hell, it'd normally be a hard victory to find it in his socks under his feet. That's how deep he buried it. And just as deep as his emotions ran wild when his heart was awakened.

Now, his heart had awakened so much that he knew he'd never be the same. These were times where everything seemed possible. Days where he allowed himself the freedom of feeling love, and to entertain the notion of a new future. Granted, it was still the early days, and he knew carving out a life with Arie wouldn't come easy. But Charly was good at making plans, and once his mind was made up, nothing could stop him. Only, there was something that he had to conquer first – the last of his doubt.

It wasn't that he doubted his feelings for Arie. There was no question that he loved her. No, it was more about the weight of what pursuing their union represented. It would mean change. Major change. And there were many things to consider – his family, and Arie's. Their radical geographical difference. His reputation, the financial downfalls of divorce... and the worst yet – what if he went for it? What if he took all of those chances, and it still didn't work out with Arie?

Charly shuddered and pulled his collar up high before sliding his key from the car's ignition and flinging the door open. The air blew into his lungs like tiny shards of ice. *Good.* Maybe it would sharpen his brain, too. Because he knew he could create all the excuses in the world. Play it safe and just walk away from her. He was good at shutting people out when he wanted to – it was like an innate gift born into him. But deep down, he also knew that if he cut Arie from his life and never saw or spoke to her again, he would spend the rest of his days knowing she was out there without him.

There has to be a way.

He rushed along the side of the wall between the car and his house. The path was slippery and slick with sleet, but it didn't stop him from taking the porch steps two at time. As soon as Charly opened the door and crossed the threshold, though, he knew something was up.

The house was quiet, which wasn't all that unusual, but there was a stiff feeling in the air that instantly set off an alarm bell in his head. Something felt... off. Now that Jamie and Jack were older, their home had become a considerably quieter place. They were either always out at school, working their part-time gigs, or hanging out with friends. And when they were home, they did their own thing for the most part. Just like him and Mandy. Sometimes, Charly didn't know how his marriage had become the way it had. Familiarity could breed a lot of things when you allowed it – distance, indifference... contempt.

Sometimes, people just grew apart, too. But Charly and Mandy had been raised by parents who'd never separated. Both of their families held very specific views when it came to marriage, and although it had never been voiced as such, both families held high expectations for their lifelong commitment. Honestly, Charly had, too. He hadn't gotten married only to get divorced – that would mean failure. Not something he was particularity good at.

So, he hadn't ever seriously contemplated leaving Mandy. Their marriage had lasted for almost two decades now, and they'd settled into a rhythm that worked and suited him just fine. But life had a funny way of shaking your foundations when you least expected it. People and situations showed up to remind you of other possibilities – to reignite a flame or spark an otherwise dormant desire. To rock a person's world and offer a picture of what could be.

To dare to dream.

Charly slipped his bag from his shoulder and draped the strap over the stairwell balustrade before shrugging off his jacket and tossing it over his bag. His eyes hung over his jacket for a moment while unease rippled through him. He was due to leave town in a couple of days for an interview piece. The way he was feeling, the trip couldn't have landed in his lap at a better time – he was keen to put some space between himself and Mandy. But, for now, he knew he'd better go find her and make sure everything okay.

She was in the kitchen sitting on a stool and leaning over the counter with her nose in a magazine. Her shoulder-length hair was scraped back and clasped at her nape while her slender shoulders hunched forward and she cupped her chin against a palm. She didn't look up when he entered the room.

"Hi honey," Charly said, barely glancing at her as he made for the cabinets to fetch a glass.

"Hi," she said. Her voice was sharp, and traced with a hint of aggression.

Charly tensed, but he chose to ignore her brash tone as he busied himself in the kitchen with a glass tumbler and some water. Cold water.

"Nice day?" he asked, throwing her a sideways glance before he opened the fridge and deliberately took his time reaching for a bottled water.

The bottle of water chilled all the way into Charly's bones when he grasped it and carried it the benchtop. His gaze lingered over the bottle a moment too long as he set it down, before he remembered he'd forgotten to close the fridge door. The silence stretched into awkwardness, and he felt every long second as he turned back toward the fridge.

It was the way she moved that caught his attention as he pushed the fridge door closed. It was slow and deliberate, and her hazel eyes were like dark stones as she lifted her chin to catch his stare. Every one of her muscles was tight, and her nostrils flared slightly.

This isn't good. Charly's mind began to race.

"I *was* having a nice day until I received an email from Ty," she said, her voice as cool as the frigid air outside. Her gaze intensified on him and he knew that whatever was coming next, he was done for. "I took the liberty of checking myself – I know all your accounts; no secrets, right?"

Charly paced back to the bench and the water bottle, and stood facing her with the counter between them. He rubbed the whiskers on the side of his face while trying to tame the sprint of adrenaline coursing through him.

"What are you talking about? What did Ty say in the email?" he asked, his tone even.

"Isn't it obvious?"

"I'm not a mind reader, Mandy. If you tell me, then we'll be on the same page."

Her face widened – jaw dropping and twisting, thin brows lifting into her hairline. Her features froze like a static movie.

A horror movie.

"Same page? How ironic," she spat, suddenly leaping from the stool and clasping her hips. "We're not even in the same damned book!" Her chest heaved beneath her blue cotton blouse, her eyes boring into his as she lowered her chin and struck him with her next words. "I read your messages with that Australian whore – what the hell, Charly? She's talking about—"

Charly held up a palm, his head shaking as he interrupted her.

"Hold up, Mandy – Ty emailed you about Arie?" he asked. His thoughts whirled, but he fought to remain calm.

Mandy squeezed her eyes shut and took a couple of deep breaths so that her body trembled and her lashes pooled with tears. She hung her head low and swiped the backs of her hands over her eyes before she looked at him again.

"Ty is concerned about your business. He's worried this woman is leading you down the garden path – he says you're unfocused and all over the place. I've noticed you haven't been yourself lately, too," she said. She bit her bottom lip as a lone tear splashed across her cheek. When she spoke next, her voice was shaky. "I noticed you've been more distant, but I never suspected it was because of another woman."

Charly's nerves punctured his heart like deadly needles. He cranked his neck and sighed. His eyes darted over the ceiling and, for one spilt second, he thought he might find the answers in the layers of white paint. He wasn't prepared for this confrontation.

Dammit, Ty! Why couldn't you leave well enough alone?

"Charly?" Mandy asked, breaking through the torrent of thoughts scrambling in his mind.

His stomach hollowed when he looked back at her. Her pale, tear-stained face glistened beneath the kitchen lights while her fingers bunched together at her waist, and her expression was sombre. He didn't like seeing her like this. He didn't want to hurt her.

Her chest rattled with her next breath, and her voice was quiet. "Do you love her?"

It was a simple question, and yet Charly knew his answer could shatter worlds. *His* world. His *family's* world. But how could he lie to the woman who'd been by his side for most of his life?

He couldn't.

Charly's gaze captured hers, silently pleading for the understanding he knew he didn't deserve. Then, he gave a slight nod. "I do love her," he said, his heart twisting as Mandy's face contorted with pain.

Her eyes dropped to her feet and she shook her head before she clutched her temples and began heaving again.

"Mandy," Charly said, walking around the counter. He stopped beside her and rested a gentle hand on her shoulder. "I'm so sorry... I tried to resist – I did. I didn't mean for this to happen..."

She jerked away from him suddenly, stepping back and facing him. Her teeth clenched beneath the curl of her lips, her eyes shooting daggers.

"It *didn't* happen – do you hear me?" she spat. She gripped her hips and began a fast pace. All the while, her voice remained strung high as she ranted. "I'm not going to let some Australian hussy destroy our family. You can't love her – you barely know her. Ty is right, she's tricked you – she's dangled her femininity in your face and, like a brainless idiot, you've fallen for it."

"Hang on – that's not the way this went down at all," Charly said, shaking his head. "Arie didn't trick me, Mandy... she's—"

"She's what? Beautiful? Exciting? Not me?" Mandy snapped. She stopped walking and abruptly faced him, her expression darkening beneath her glare. "How dare you humiliate me this way? You will end this now – from now on,

Ty can deal the business end with her, and you're to have no more contact with her. If you don't agree, I will ruin you, Charly – so help me, god, I will make sure the world knows what a lowlife, cheating son-of-a-bitch you really are. I will drag your name through the dirt and throw you to the fucking wolves. I will clean you out and leave you begging in the street with nothing to your name. Do we understand each other?"

A cold chill sliced through Charly's heart and his stomach churned as he held the gaze of a woman who had become a stranger to him. Her lips seemed to stretch into something sinister, and her eyes were brimming with hatred. He knew she meant every word and every threat she'd just hurled at him, and his world blackened with his burning soul. He hung his head and studied the floor for a moment. Arie's image danced across his mind's eye before she disappeared completely. The dream was over, and his heart would be forever incomplete.

He lifted his chin and looked at wife, before sighing so hard that his lips quivered. "I understand, Mandy," he muttered.

"Good. *Now* we're on the same page. I want her to hate you, Charly," she said sharply. She brushed past him then, heading for the kitchen door and calling over her shoulder. "We're doing this right now – you're going to email her, and you're going to make sure there is no return. Let's go to your office, shall we?"

I guess we shall.

Charly: Hey Arie, I can no longer correspond with you. It appears you have feelings for me, but they aren't reciprocal and I am feeling uncomfortable with the nature of your messages and interactions with me. I'm not interested in pursuing a relationship with you beyond the business one we've established with Ty and Stevie to work on our project.

Moving forward, all correspondence regarding business matters pertaining to our project will be handled exclusively by Ty. Please email him directly with any questions or concerns you may have in the future.

Regards,

Charly.

"*I make love to you with song*

and word,

I wrap you in a phrase,

One I've never heard.

I feel your gentle touch upon

my mind.

You are everywhere, everything

in time."

~ From the song, "Perfect Harmony"
Twin Flames; a True Story of Soul Union.
Antera.

Chapter 14

Let the dream die, Arie.

It had been one month since she'd received Charly's email, and one month of enduring Charly's silence. At first, she'd been hurt – each word of his email had splintered her heart until it had become a fractured shell. It had hurt so bad, she'd had to escape the demands of her family and flee to the ocean shore. She'd stayed there for hours, trembling and gazing at the sea, and questioning her sanity. After that, she'd begun to get angry – angry with herself for believing he could've loved her, and furious that she'd allowed herself to fall so in love with a man who'd rejected her.

Most of all, though, she questioned the universe – how could she be shown such a divine love for another, only for it to be taken away from her?

Had she imagined the love? Had she?

Sometimes, she'd thought she had. But then she'd remember the way her spirit had been pulled into the higher realms where Charly waited for her. Where their souls united and danced to the tune of freedom and love. It wasn't his personality she knew so well; it was his soul. And, somehow, she knew she'd known him since the beginning of time.

The door to Arie's closet slid open with force, hurtling her back to the present with a gasp. She blinked toward the figure of Cara silhouetted against the stream of light behind her while reining in her thoughts as she sat on the stool in the cool, dark closet.

"Mommy, what are doing? You have to help me with my hair. You've been in here for ages and ages – and you're not even dressed yet," Cara said, stepping into the walk-in closet and staring at her with wide eyes. Her brows creased. "Are you having trouble?"

Arie forced a smile. "I am," she said.

More than you know, little one.

Cara grinned and looped her fingers through Arie's. Her skin felt warm and clammy, and she gave Arie a light squeeze.

"Then I'll help you choose something to wear," she announced, pulling her shoulders back and tilting her chin. "Sometimes, mommies need help, too."

Arie's laugh caught somewhere in her throat. She tried to say something, but the words dissolved with the sudden wave of emotion flooding through her. She looked at her daughter's face and her heart melted.

Thank god for her children!

Their presence in her life was her only salvation. She found she was filled with so much appreciation for them – more than ever before. And for Brett, too – he was the stability in her life. He was loyal, and he loved her so much. She didn't deserve him, but she knew her marriage would never be the same – how could it? She loved him still, but after experiencing the kind of love she felt for Charly, her love for Brett felt paled in comparison.

"Come here," Arie said, pulling Cara closer to her.

She wrapped her arms around her little girl, closing her eyes and pressing her small body against her chest. Her chin rested on top of Cara's crown and she inhaled her daughter's fresh, daisy scent. The people in her life gave her precious moments she would never forget, and she cherished every one of them. But she knew there would always be a barren place in her heart that only Charly could fill.

It sounded a little melodramatic, even to herself. And she knew that it was a burden she couldn't share with her closet friends – nobody would understand what she was going through. How could they, when she barely understood herself? It was an emotional pain like no other – it was excruciating and indescribable. The hurt shadowed her every waking hour, and constantly crippled her heart and soul.

How?

How could Charly deny himself to her? How long could he deny who he really was?

That was the other part she could barely fathom – her growing resentment toward him. Not only had his words peeled away her skin and stabbed her soul, but she felt as if his silence was a punishment. As if his decision to cut her from his life was also keeping her severed from a part of herself that was rightfully hers. Crazy stuff. It felt so crazy that she'd decided to talk to someone who might know more about these kinds of connections – a psychic medium. She was due to see him today.

Cara squirmed from her embrace and gazed up at her. Even in the dim closet, her dark eyes dazzled like onyx gems.

"I love you, Mommy," she said.

"I love you, too, baby girl," Arie replied, forcing her thoughts to lighter places. "Now, what am I going to wear today?"

Cara's features lit up with her grin. She switched on the closet light before she cocked her head to the side to inspect Arie's clothes hanging in rows along the rails.

"A dress!"

"I'm not surprised," Arie said, chuckling. Cara was the most girly of her girls – she was into pretty dresses and barbie dolls, and make-up and jewellery. She was much more girly than Arie had been as a child, and Arie adored that about her daughter.

Cara chose a simple linen summer dress. It was a blend of white and thick, light grey stripes. The bodice was fitted and hugged Arie's breasts before falling over her waist and spilling to her ankles. Arie seldom wore dresses, and she didn't mind wearing one today. She liked the way the fabric moved against her body. It made her feel pretty and feminine – and, god knew, it had been a while since she'd felt like that. She even added a pair of silver hooped earrings and a splash of musk body oil to her wrists. A pair of white strappy sandals were added next, and then she was ready to face another day.

It was a beautiful day – the colors of the eastern coastline were vivid and the salty air hung like a delicious haze over parts of the town. Arie adored the ocean's salt hazes. She loved the vigorous scent, and the way it misted and curled along the tree-lines – as if it whispered briny, sea secrets. She didn't notice any of it today, though, as she dropped the girls off at school, grabbed a large coffee, and headed toward the place where she was to meet the psychic medium.

The shop was located in the next town. Although it was tucked away along a little side alley, Arie had no trouble finding it. The shopfront was small and covert, yet mysteriously inviting. Arie paused and pushed away the nerves bunching in her stomach as she gazed into the store's windows. She swallowed hard and scanned the buddha figures carved from stone, rows of crystals, and ribbons of leather that wound around dreamcatchers and hung amongst hippie flags and iron windchimes. The smell of sandalwood incense drifted from beneath the doorframe and seemed to calm her – the scent was her favorite, and she took it as a good omen.

As soon as Arie entered the shop and saw him, somehow, she knew at once that he would provide the answers she so desperately needed. He was a tall, solid man, and he stood behind a small counter and looked to be about sixty years old. His thinning white hair skimmed across his scalp, and his eyes reminded her of blue, lucid crystals. His skin was slightly blotched and worn with age, and when he tilted his chin and smiled at her, his eyes reached the depths of her soul.

"You must be Arie?" he asked, his lips stretching wide as he reached for the walking stick at his side.

"Yes, I have a 9:30 appointment. Blake?" Arie asked, returning his smile.

His hands were large and appeared strong, and he gripped the walking cane as if it were an extension of himself. He moved around the counter toward Arie, stopping short of her and nodding.

"You're looking at him," he grinned. He stretched a hand toward her and clasped her palm in a gentle shake.

The moment he touched her, she felt it – a tingling shimmer that amassed at her nape and sprinkled over her cheeks before it spiralled down her spine delightfully. Her dark eyes locked onto his and she smiled. "Nice to meet you, Blake," she said.

Chapter 15

"Twin flames."

"Twin flames?"

Blake nodded, his eyes glazing someplace beyond Arie.

"Yes, thank you," he said softly, as if to himself, but Arie knew he was thanking the guides for the revelations they'd provided him. He frowned and trained his eyes back on Arie. "That's what your spirit guides are telling me. Do you know anything about soul creation?"

Arie shrugged and dropped her eyes to her twisting fingers. She immediately recalled the psychic reading she'd received months earlier, from the woman who'd predicted that her twin soul lived in America.

"Some – a little," she replied, her gaze darting back to Blake as she anxiously waited for his next words.

"Some souls are created in pairs to embark on a spiritual journey. They travel through many lifetimes before finally coming together – in union. Throughout each lifetime, they collect experiences and grow, striving to become the individual beings they are meant to be. When one or both of the twin souls have reached an awakened state of being, the universe will orchestrate their union," Blake paused, his eyes twinkling excitedly. "It is a rarity to come across a twin in union, but here you are." He leaned across the table and lowered his voice. "Charly shares the same energy as you, Arie – the bond is unbreakable and eternal. Twin souls always reunite for a higher purpose – it's never just about the twins. The love you share is not the product of this world – it runs deeper than any man-made concept of marriage. It is the lifeblood of all creation; that is why you have been experiencing such intense emotions and unusual phenomena. You're meant to face yourself and evolve from the union."

Arie was silent as she allowed the information to seep into her mind. The hairs on the back of her neck and arms raised and her entire body tingled. The reaction confirmed what her soul already knew. Blake had just articulated the information for her mind to catch up. She looked away from him, her gaze falling toward the maroon cheesecloth fabric covering the table between them. Her thoughts pieced together the unusual experiences she'd had since Charly had been in her life – unexplainable synchronicities, uncanny images and dreams, telepathic communication, and the overwhelming feeling of knowing him intimately.

She gasped, her heart thundering against her ribcage as she was overcome with a sense of gratitude – she felt honored to have met her twin soul during this lifetime. Her eyes glistened, and she smiled wistfully through unspent tears. All at once, she knew every single moment of her life before him had been always leading toward their meeting. She lifted her gaze back to Blake and frowned. His expression was curious as he watched her intently.

"If Charly is my twin flame, how could he shut me out like this?" she asked.

"He might've shut you out in the physical sense, but the soul level is a different story – there are other ways to communicate and have a relationship. You say you still feel his energy around you, and I can feel him around you, too.

He hasn't let you go, Arie. But you may need to let him go in order to heal your soul and find inner peace again."

"How do I let go of a piece of me? How do I live the rest of my life knowing he's out there and not with me?"

Blake smiled. "Look forward. Focus on your family; on your writing. You have the ability to create the life you want – we all do. Your will is strong and you have fire in your heart. I can feel you're extremely in tune with the universal laws – and your energy is so beautiful, Arie," he said. He laughed and shook his head. "And honestly, Charly can be an asshole. He should've honored your connection. He should've protected your bond – if only he realized how fortunate he is to have a twin soul in his life."

Arie swallowed hard.

"He didn't honor me, or our connection. He made me feel like a deranged idiot – as if I concocted the entire experience in my head," she said. Her heart lurched as all the painful emotions simmered to the surface. "And now he won't give me the time of day. He hates me."

Blake reached across the table and took her hand. His fingers were long and thick, and his touch instantly tamed Arie's erratic feelings. Despite his smile, her expression was somber when she peered up at him.

"You're not an idiot, Arie, and he doesn't hate you. You're in love – thank him for showing you the highest form of true love. Look at what's he done for you."

"What? Shown me how bad pain can really be? Because I've had broken hearts before, but nothing compares to the way this man has hurt me." Arie shook her head and gave a rueful laugh. "If that's true love, then I'm not sure I want it."

Blake laughed and gently pulled his hand away from hers. He straightened his back, and tilted his head to the side, gazing at her fondly.

"He's shown you the kind of love that can only be likened to our very source energy – pure, unconditional, higher love. Doesn't that exhilarate you? Doesn't it charge you with a sense of excitement?" He paused, his broad chest inflating with his next breath. Then, his lips stretched into a smile. "Learn from it – take your lessons and grow. But don't waste your days waiting for him; it may never happen in this lifetime. What you do with your experience is your choice."

Life is full of choices.

Arie sighed and nodded. He was right.

"I know what I have to do," she said quietly. "I know I have to be true to myself, and to my family."

"Being true to ourselves can often be our hardest undertaking.,"

Life is what we accept it to be.

"I don't know if I can stay married anymore..." Arie's voice trailed off. It was the first time she'd said those words out loud, and every syllable she'd uttered shook her heart. She grazed her teeth against her trembling lips and lowered her eyes. How could she remain married to Brett when she felt this way about another man? It wouldn't be fair to either of them.

"There are many changes coming up for you, Arie. Trust in the universe and follow your path with faith – you don't have to make any decisions right now, so go easy on yourself," Blake said. "You know, the universe has a funny way of steering us in the right direction. Send Charly love and move on... but most importantly, don't let others take away from you. Believe in yourself – what you experienced with Charly was real. Don't ever doubt that."

For some reason, the last of his words took Arie's breath away. Her eyes flew up to meet his, and a wonderful sense of gratitude instilled itself within her. It was remarkable how one meeting could dramatically change your perspective. Blake had given her permission to forgive herself. He had handed her a slice of hope when her heart was too bruised to see beyond the pain, and he had validated her experiences and feelings for Charly. She wasn't going crazy after all.

She reached across the table and wound her hands overtop his, before her gaze intensified on him. The corners of her lips stretched, and she gave a half-laugh. "You are wonderful – thank you so much, Blake," she said.

"Anytime, Arie. Call on me anytime you need me," he replied.

Arie left the small shop feeling lighter than she had in months. It was as if Blake had somehow set her free of the guilt, the constant confusion trickling through her mind, and most of all, he had given her a glimpse of what could be. With faith and trust in the universe, she knew anything was possible.

She didn't go home right away. Instead, she drove along the roads edging the rugged cliffs that overlooked the sea before she stopped at her favorite lookout. Once there, she trekked along the rough trail, pushing against the sea breeze whipping at her dress and catching her hair. She found a secluded spot right on the edge of the cliff, between long blades of grass and low shrubs, and folded her legs beneath her as she sat down and gazed at the Tasman Sea.

The ocean stretched before her like a deep blue abyss, meeting with the lazy white clouds that hung on the horizon whispering secrets to her.

The sounds of the waves crashing against the rocks below filled her senses and seemed to affirm every mystic sigh of the universe. She smiled, and she knew then that no matter what was to come, everything would be okay.

Chapter 16

One Year Later

"Mia – no social media after 9 p.m. on school nights, and please help your father out with your sisters," Arie said, pushing her luggage into the back of the cab.

Mia rolled her eyes and grinned.

"Ma, I've got it, you've only told me a thousand times already," she said. Her smile turned wicked as she leaned closer to her mother. "You realize the rules at Dad's house are different than yours, right?"

Arie closed the boot and saddled her hips with her hands. Her eyes narrowed with her glare. "Mia, don't," she said, shaking her head. "You've all got him wrapped around your fingers as it is... just let him believe he calls the shots. Males like that," she added with a grin.

Mia laughed before her eyes glistened and her expression grew serious.

"I'm gonna miss you, Mom," she said, stepping closer and folding her arms around Arie in a hug. "Good luck in the States – I know you're gonna knock them dead with your Aussie attitude."

Arie's chest tightened as she squeezed Mia, her lips brushing against her forehead as she spoke.

"I'll miss you, too... and your sisters. Give them another kiss for me when they wake up, okay?"

"I will," Mia replied, snuggling her nose against Arie's neck and sighing hard. "I'll look after them with Dad. Promise."

Arie nodded before peeling Mia away from her and holding her at arm's length.

"I'll be back before you know it. Now, go back to bed and get some more sleep. I love you," she said, almost choking.

Why are goodbyes so hard?

It wasn't like she'd be gone forever. It was only three weeks, for crying out loud. She was being ridiculous.

"Love you, too," Mia said. "Call as soon as you arrive at the hotel."

Arie swallowed the lump in her throat and pulled open the car door. She forced a smile and nodded.

"I will," she said before climbing into the backseat of the cab and closing the door.

As soon as the car pulled away from the curb, Arie's heart fluttered. Goodbyes might be difficult, but as the cab drove through the quiet morning streets toward the airport, it was the acute spike of excitement throttling through her veins that she had trouble containing.

She pulled on her sunglasses and gazed out the window, smiling secretly as she spotted a flock of white cockatoos scattering over a rolling green landscape. She loved birds and the freedom they represented – she was a bird, too. Or, she'd liked to be. She stifled a laugh at the absurdity of her thoughts and glanced toward the driver. He gripped the steering wheel and peered stolidly toward the road beneath a pair of dark sunglasses. Thankfully, he was the silent type. Which suited her just fine – she could be alone with her thoughts as she contemplated the past and the future.

A lot could happen in a year. Her life had changed dramatically, and it hadn't always been easy – but sometimes, one had to sift through the dark and confront the deepest of fears in order to emerge into the light.

For the first time in months, Arie felt as if she could finally breathe. It hadn't been long after seeing Blake that she'd found her own house and separated from Brett. The transition had been difficult for the entire family, and Brett had been devastated. Her honesty had hurt Brett, and she'd felt awful about it. But she didn't regret her decision to leave him – life was fleeting, and he deserved more from her than what she could give. Above all else, she wished her husband the kind of love she'd experienced with Charly.

Arie hadn't heard from Charly since that last email – offering the words that'd shattered her heart and rattled her world. Oh, she'd been aware of his online presence on social media platforms, and she'd even noticed a few of his posts that she thought might have been for her benefit. But she couldn't afford to put her faith in cryptic messages and false promises anymore – she had to protect her heart. So, she'd scolded herself before taking the measures of removing her connection to him on those platforms, and tried very hard not to have a peek every now and then. Still, his continued silence was deafening.

After settling with her daughters into their new home, Arie had thrown herself into her work and writing. She'd continued to write articles as a freelance journalist while drafting a romance series between the gaps. It hadn't been long before she'd discovered her love for writing fiction. A passion that'd opened new doors and publishing contracts, finally leading to this trip to America.

An independent American publishing house called Dark Dream Publishing had come across Arie's work and decided she was the best person to get involved in a collaborative-fiction writing project. The man putting the project together was named Adrian. He'd contacted Arie the month before, and had been so excited about her writing that he'd offered to fly her to the States in order to connect in person and start creating a dark fantasy thriller series. The publishers were so invested in this project, they'd expressed hopes in selling the film rights and gaining international recognition.

Who was she to turn down such an amazing opportunity?

Nothing ventured, nothing gained, right?

A ripple of delight shimmied down her spine as Arie spotted the airport looming up ahead. She pushed aside the niggling bouts of anxiety and deliberately focused on the end game – she couldn't afford to doubt her abilities to pull off this project. She just couldn't.

Believe in yourself.

Those words had become her daily mantra since she'd taken the steps to change her life, and for the most part, they'd helped her overcome a lot of her inner fears and blockages. Now, she faced a new beginning – a new chapter in her life. She had no idea where her path would take her, but she trusted it, and she was excited.

Chapter 17

The flight from Sydney to Los Angeles was long and brutal, and after enduring the connecting flight to New York, Arie was a complete wreck. As soon as she checked into her hotel room, she called home before she showered and collapsed in the bed and slept like a log until the following morning.

For the first meeting with the publishing team, Arie chose to wear a sheer black blouse and smooth grey pants that hugged her legs and tucked into black leather, knee-high boots. She applied light make-up to her face, using charcoal eyeshadow and black mascara to emphasize her dark eyes, before she glossed her lips and added silver hoops to her ears. Her breath stalled when she peered at her reflection. Her dark hair tumbled over her shoulders and framed her face while her eyes stared back at her like a stranger. Sometimes, she barely knew who she was anymore – without him. Even though a year had passed, Charly's absence from her life still hollowed a corner of her heart. Now that she was back in the States, he was on her mind more than ever.

She gulped a large breath and buried her feelings. No amount of pining would bring him back to her. He had made his choice – he had chosen to turn his back on her, and she couldn't change that. Still, in the quiet hours when she was alone, his soul continued to whisper to her and she felt him caress her heart. She figured it would always be that way – feeling him from within. But a recipe would not bake a cake, and it was the cake that she wanted.

By the time Arie hit the New York streets and grabbed a coffee, she felt somewhat humanized. She waved down a cab to head downtown toward her meeting with Adrian and the publishing team. Her nerves bunched in her stomach like a tight ball of twine, and she tried to drown them down with large sips of coffee.

Who am I kidding?

All the coffee in the world wouldn't take away the torrent of apprehension jittering through her system; that's how nervous she was about meeting Adrian and the publishing team. She inwardly scolded herself, using a few four-letter words to add fire to the insults as she reeled in her thoughts and the taxi came to a halt at their destination. By the time she paid the driver and stood up outside, staring up at the tall building where her presence was due at any given moment, she was feeling slightly more at ease, and a little more courageous. Four-letter words *did* have their uses.

Arie walked along the office corridors with much more confidence than she felt. The air in the building was warm, and raced against her skin like hot needles. Well, that's how it felt, but she wasn't sure if was really the warm air causing her to perspire like a dripping tap.

Damned nerves.

Stupid deodorant.

She should've applied an extra thick layer of roll-on before dressing that morning. *Hold up – where am I going anyway?* She had followed the sign pointing in the direction of the publishing company when she'd alighted from the elevator, but now she felt as if she wandered around corridors aimlessly. Arie stopped walking, gathering her thoughts and peering along the spacious office hallway. She frowned and noticed the spread of light coming from the windows at the end of the corridor. Above the threshold archway was a sign that read 'Dark Dream Publishing'. That's where she needed to be. A light sigh of relief escaped her lips and she started for the end of corridor.

As Arie rounded the archway that spilled into a vast room, she paused abruptly to look around. The first thing she noticed was the startling glare of the windows, and the New York cityscape that spread like a concrete jungle as far as the eye could see. Then, she heard her name called and turned towards the smile of a man she recognized as Adrian as he strode in her direction.

His face was clean shaven, the thick skin of his cheeks riddled with fading pock-marks. He was average in height, with a generous helping of ginger hair and silver streaks that caught the overhead lights and glimmered. A light grey blazer and matching pants swished with his movements as he walked with a slight bend to his gait.

"Arie, welcome. How was your flight?" he asked, stopping short of her and clasping her hand.

Arie shook his hand and smiled, feeling her nerves dissipate with the warmth of his greeting.

"Hey," she said, shaking his hand before she shrugged. "Ah, you know, it was a long flight and I'm glad it's over, but I'm super excited to be here – thank you."

His green eyes widened with his grin. "We're super excited to have you here – come and meet the team, and your co-writer," he said, slinging an arm around her shoulders and steering her further into the room toward a group of people sitting around a large circular table.

They chatted amongst themselves – three men of various ages and two women who appeared very serious and business-like. They all paused to look her way as Arie approached the table with Adrian. He began to make the introductions, and Arie smiled and nodded, and made all the right noises, and then she saw him and her heart stopped and her legs suddenly felt like pudding. Charly Alba.

He stood beyond the table, by the big windows... watching her. His face was neither happy nor serious – it was steadfast and intent, and his eyes seemed to drink in her image while his chest heaved slightly beneath his black sweater. His long hair was tied at the nape of his neck, and his hands were stuffed deep in his pockets. He didn't move an inch when Adrian gestured toward him.

"Arie, meet Charly Alba. He'll be working closely with you on this series; he'll be your co-writer," Adrian said.

What the hell?

She couldn't stop the scream in her mind, nor her bottom lip from slackening. Her heart had decided to move again, and now it pounded against her ribcage as if it had gotten a shot of amphetamines – which Arie might've considered not to be a bad alternative in that moment, because the man she loved and had lost stood in front of her like it was the most natural thing in the world, and she was totally out of her comfort zone.

"Hello, Arie," Charly said, finally moving away from the window and walking towards her.

Arie eyed him as coolly as she could, lifting her chin and fighting the urge to bite her bottom lip before responding.

"Charly," she muttered, swinging her gaze from him back to Adrian. She noted the frazzled expression on Adrian's face and forced a smile. "We've met before. We've worked together before."

Adrian grinned. He raised his arms, the sleeves of his blazer falling to his elbows as he waved his hands through the air in an animated display.

"Wonderful!" he exclaimed. "This gets even better – Charly, you didn't tell me you knew Arie."

The whiskers around Charly's lips curved with his smile. When he spoke, he looked at Arie and held her gaze. "I wanted it to be a surprize," he said.

Arie scowled. Suddenly, it was rage filling her gut and escalating through her heart, and she couldn't stop it from spilling over her tongue.

"Achieved," she said sharply, shaking her head and taking a step backwards. "I'm not into surprizes – especially when it involves someone I don't trust. This isn't fair, Charly. I—"

"Wouldn't have come if you knew," Charly said, cutting over her words and stepping closer to her. His tone lowered and eyes darkened. "I didn't mean to upset you, Arie. I had to see you again."

For a few long moments, Arie said nothing. The room was utterly quiet, and she became aware of every pair of eyes watching the scene play out before them. Then, she squared her jaw and narrowed her eyes, turning to Adrian and giving him a dazzling smile.

"I'm so sorry, Adrian. Shall we begin with our meeting?" she asked, brushing past Charly and making for the table with as much dignity as she could muster.

Screw Charly Alba and his tricks.

She was here for business, and she wasn't about to make the same mistake twice. Still, she couldn't subdue the elation quickening in her blood stream. It was good to see him again.

Too good.

He's going to kill me all over again.

Chapter 18

The morning passed in a series of interesting discussions, as well as amazing interactions. Arie loved exchanging ideas and crafting the imprint of an outline with other like-minded people. The publishing team members turned out to be smart, intelligent individuals with a lot of side funk that made for compelling conversation. By the time the lunch hour had arrived, they'd formed a solid plan, and Arie couldn't wait to get into the guts of drafting the story.

The only drawback?

Drafting involved time alone with Charly.

She'd spent the majority of the morning trying hard to ignore him. She'd taken a seat as far away from him as possible, and focused purely on the tasks at hand. Well, that had been the idea anyhow. And, outwardly, she knew she'd pulled it off – a cool face plus determination was a winner every time. Her inner world was a totally different story, though. Evading his intense stare and strong presence was near impossible. She could only hope he didn't realize how much he actually affected her.

When Adrian called a break, Arie wasted no time in gathering her gear and making for the elevators as fast as possible. She needed to widen the space between herself and Charly – to think and breathe, and get herself together before their afternoon writing session. The elevator doors remained stubbornly closed as she stood in front of them, repeatedly jamming her finger against the button while muttering beneath her breath.

"Please hurry. Please," she pleaded, wanting to stamp her feet in frustration. A quick glance over her shoulder and the discreet bell signalling an arriving elevator chimed above her. She lifted her eyes heavenward and sighed with relief. "Oh, thank goodness!" Neither Charly or any of the other team members had made it to the elevator lobby in time to catch the first lift down to the ground level.

As soon as the doors slid open, Arie rushed inside the small space and immediately began hitting the button to close the doors. Just a few more seconds, and she'd be in the clear. She knew she'd be able to avoid him once she was on the busy city streets – vanishing into the New York crowd was easy. The race of her nerves began to ease with the sliding doors as they started to close. She grinned and relaxed her shoulders, leaning back against the mirrored wall and exhaling.

Then, the doors halted suddenly and began to slide apart. Arie gasped, her heart dropping while her stomach flipped as she tensed all over, and Charly stood there smiling at her. His grin was brilliant and white, and it captured her mind and held her thoughts ransom as she struggled to keep her resolve.

"Hey," he said, casually walking into the elevator and leaning against the wall beside her.

"Hey," she mumbled. She swung her gaze toward the floor-level numbers above the doors as the car shifted into motion and began its descent. Every one of her senses went into overdrive at his close proximity, and they completely went off the grid when he turned to gaze down at her. The scent of his citrus-woody cologne began to make her feel heady.

"It's good to see you, Arie. I've waited so long to see you again," he said.

His voice was hollow and raw, and every chord reached into her soul and squeezed. She titled her chin and looked up at him, half expecting to see mockery in his eyes. Maybe that's what she hoped to find. An obvious clue to support the heartlessness of his actions – he'd hurt her, severing from her world as if she meant nothing, and she was utterly terrified he'd do it again.

She shook her head and forced herself to look away from him. "Doesn't make sense. You cut me from your life – walked away without a backward glance. Why would you even care to see me again?" she asked.

"Because you are all that's real to me, and I can't deny the truth any longer," he said.

Arie fought to contain her trembling hands; she wrung them together and darted her gaze back to him, her dark eyes glinting. "And what exactly is the truth, Charly? That you'll screw with my head some more until the truth cuts too close and you run for the hills again?" she snapped.

He shook his head and sighed.

"No, I'm done running. I'm done with fear, and I'm sure as hell done hiding in the hills," he said. He stepped closer to her, reaching to brush away a lock of hair falling across her brow. "I'm done with being apart from you."

Arie swallowed and dropped her eyes to her feet. Her heart began to swell with the tide of emotions flowing through her. *This isn't fair – he can't do this me again.* Her thoughts twisted, and she felt as if a vine of thorns tore through her chest and ripped out her heart. Those were the words she'd dreamed about. Words she'd longed to hear pass from his mouth and into her ears... and, now, she wanted to believe him.

Please. Please be real.

When she lifted her gaze back to face him, the clarity in his eyes stole her breath and rocked her core, and she knew he was speaking from the heart. She took a breath and titled her head.

"But... but it's impossible. We live in different countries, you're married, we both have families... and—"

Charly shook his head and cut her short, "And it can be real if you want it to be. I know it won't be easy, but we can make work – together, we can figure it out," he said. He paused and smiled. "And I'm not married anymore, Arie... and I've noticed you longer wear your ring."

Arie smiled. "I'm not married anymore, either," she said quietly.

Charly grinned so widely that she thought his face might spilt in two. He broke out in laughter before he grew silent and his eyes held hers, and he cupped his palms over her chin and leaned toward her. His forehead pressed gently against hers and he closed his eyes as their breaths mingled.

Hot. Sweet. Delicious.

Their lips were inches apart, and their souls danced along with their drumming hearts, and they breathed together for the first time in union. Then, a tingle caught around Arie's neck and shimmied along her spine as his lips met hers and she parted her own to receive him. He was smooth, yet rough, and he tasted like heaven, and his tongue pushed against hers lightly before his kiss deepened and his hunger exploded to the surface as he groaned.

He sounded throaty and ungraded, and his appetite spiralled into her body like a rocket of desire. She moulded herself into him and entwined her hands around his neck while she drank him in with her tongue and her heart went crazy. She could barely breathe, and she no longer wanted to. He filled her up with all of his emotions, and her heart brimmed and exploded, and all she could see was him – and flames. Red-hot, burning flames that scorched her skin and set her soul on fire, and her wanting was almost unbearable.

Then, the elevator doors flew open and they were suddenly confronted with several sets of wide eyes and gaping jaws. Arie pulled slowly away from Charly, and they exchanged a long look before laughing. He grabbed her hand and gently tugged her forward before they brushed past the people waiting for the elevator, ignoring their odd expressions and indiscreet smirks as they burst into the lobby.

"What do you say we skip the afternoon session and head back to my hotel room?" Charly asked, glancing down at Arie as they emerged onto the street.

Arie grinned, her dark eyes twinkling as they locked onto his.

"I say, I couldn't think of anything better."

Her heart pounded and her pulse raced, and Arie knew their obstacles were only just beginning – that there would be long stretches of separation and an avalanche of details to work out in order for them to be together. But, also, she knew it would be worth the endurance, and that the rewards would be their happiness. Charly was the love of her life. Her twin flame, the piece of herself that made her whole... she could face anything as long as they faced it together.

Anything is possible in love – anything.

The End.

About The Author

Kim Petersen is USA Bestselling Author of Dark Soul, an Ascended Angels Chronicle. Her debut novel, Millie's Angel received a gold award in the 2017 Dan Poynter's Global eBook Awards.

Based in Australia, Kim forces herself out of bed in the wee hours to walk the oceans roads of the NSW sleepy south coast town where she lives with her family. She is always grateful she did because she thinks there is much to be said about those small hours. She loves to explore the meta-physical aspects of life, and the universal bonds of love and friendship – then find expression through creating works of urban fantasy, paranormal romance and dystopian fiction.

Contact.

Visit Kim's website and receive a free gift when you subscribe to her newsletters.
Website: http://www.kimpetersen.com.au
Facebook:
https://www.facebook.com/kimpetersen11
Twitter: https://twitter.com/kimpetersen_

Storm Struck By Catherine Evans

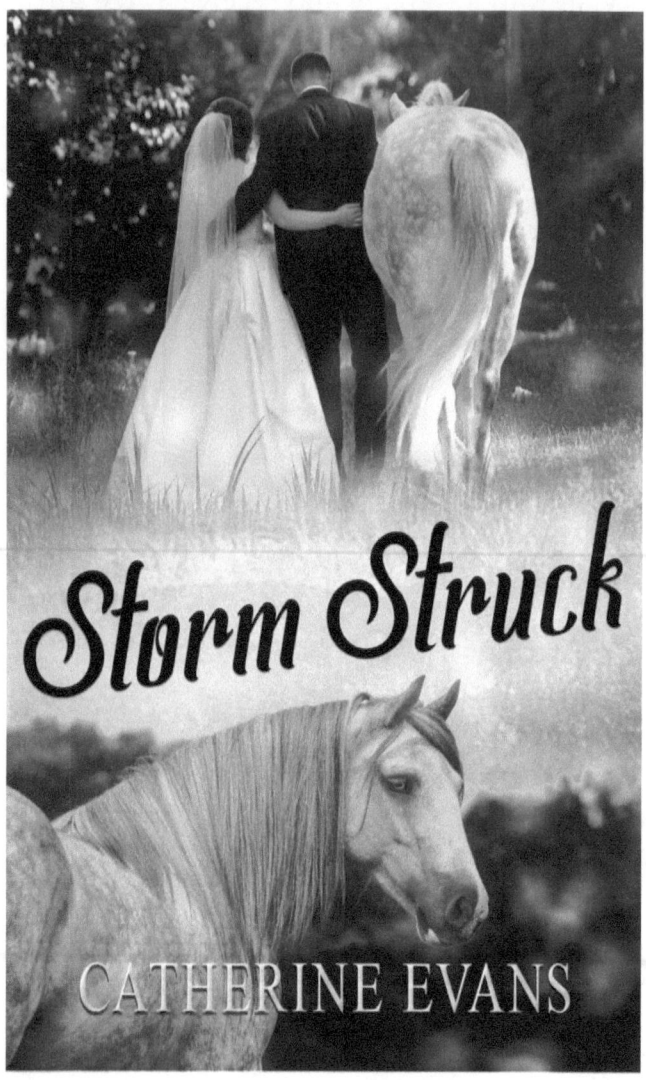

Acknowledgements

This story came about through fate. I was at a workshop on day 1 of the Wollongong Writers Festival and met Kim Petersen. On day 2, I met Kim again. Since we lived near each other, we caught up for a cuppa. She asked if I wanted to write a story for an anthology with her friend, Beth Prentice. Life is about taking chances. This was one of the best. Thank you to: Kim and Beth, but also South Coast Writers Centre, Wollongong Writers Festival, Diane Cassar, Australian Romance Readers Association, Romance Writers of Australia, and Kim's mum!

Kim and Beth are amazing women and great anthology partners. I've learned so much and have thoroughly enjoyed working on these stories. I can't thank them enough for including me in their project, and being patient as I was swamped with tasks, files and self-publishing know-how. I hope you enjoy their stories as much as I have.

Ainslie Paton and Jennie Jones read in a hurry and made useful comments on my story. Thank you, my awesome writing friends, for taking time away from your work to help.

Editor extraordinaire, Belinda Holmes, took on the editing job when she should have been making New Year's resolutions, relaxing and sipping coffee. Thank you for polishing my words, making me smile during edits, and for your encouragement and support.

Patti Roberts from Paradox Book Cover Designs did an amazing job with the anthology cover and with my cover. Thank you for being a dream to work with and finding a gray horse!

I've drawn inspiration from Pippa, Kori and Laurie, three horses I've owned and loved.

With much thanks to my family and friends, great supporters of my writing bug. Special thanks to Pete. I wouldn't be able to do this without your backing.

To all Readers, thank you for picking up our anthology and for reading our stories. I'd like to give a particular mention to Bev who always prompts me to write when she sees me on

Facebook, and to Sue, Deb, Janine, Linda, Juliette, Debbie, Helen, Lyn, Barbara, Karen, Len, Nat, Sarah, Lu, and the many others who are vocal and supportive of Aussie writers—thank you!

I couldn't share my stories without everyone's support. My heart-felt thanks.

Dedication

For Kim and Beth
and
Pippa, Kori and Laurie

Chapter 1

All her life, Tamara had run in the mornings. Lately, an extra afternoon run was essential for her sanity. No matter what time she got home from work, she stretched as she got changed and then loped around the suburb. When she was warmed up she often headed to the beach for a run along the sand, and if it was hot enough, maybe a swim. Today she needed the swim not just to cool down her body but cool down her mind. The day had been a trial. A new job and a new town was tough, add in a highly demanding boss and some days it was almost unbearable.

The track that cut through the dunes was a bit rough, so she slowed her pace and kept an eye out for tree roots that poked through the sand. A couple of weeks before, unfamiliar with the place, she'd almost rolled an ankle and wasn't keen on doing that again, especially not when work was chaotic. As she rounded a bend there was movement in the trees to her left. Expecting a bird or maybe a kangaroo she was startled to see a horse. A big dappled gray horse. A gelding. His head lifted, then he snorted. Not the panicked snort of a horse about to run, just a friendly snort asking who she was. She murmured softly, his head turned, and his gaze locked with hers. Her breath caught.

"Aren't you beautiful." Tamara maintained eye contact with the horse and took slow steps forwards. Whenever he snorted, she stopped. "Easy there, I'm not trying to hurt you." His ears flicked but otherwise he remained still. She consciously slowed her breathing and eased the tension from her body. Horses picked up every little feeling. She had to tune into what she was projecting and make sure she wasn't threatening or concerned. This fellow looked a little shaken, a bit unnerved. She needed to project a calm, quiet care. Years of Grandpa's instructions flooded back.

It was slow progress, but eventually she had her hand under his nostrils. He greeted her with a sniff, before blowing his warm breath against her cooling flesh.

"Hey gorgeous boy." She said the words as softly as she could, and he seemed to respond. The soft velvet of his nose brushed across her hand. She closed her eyes. It had been years since she'd felt that kind of touch. Slowly, she moved her other hand and gathered the dangling reins in her fingers. Exerting no pressure on the bit, she allowed the horse to sniff along her arm, up her neck, and across her face. That fresh grass smell, warm breath, tickling whiskers, and velvet softness brought so many memories. Her eyes prickled but she squeezed back recollections and tears. This wasn't the time, she had a horse and a missing rider, to deal with.

"How about we walk carefully out of here and see if we can find who you left behind." She lifted her hand and ran it along the horse's cheek. When she glanced at the reins, they were not joined, but were still attached to the bridle, and the bit didn't seem to have damaged the horse's mouth. His legs looked fine too, and he stepped without problem. With no saddle, she figured someone had been riding bareback and had come off on the beach. Either they were trudging up the sand to find their lost steed, or injured somewhere on the beach. She hoped for the first option.

Tamara led the horse carefully along the track and out onto the open beach. The horse had manners and led well, which was a relief because if he took off down the open beach she had no chance of catching him.

She looked to the left, scanning the beach for a body or someone walking. No one. She turned to the right and saw a couple of people walking with dogs but no one who looked like they were missing a horse.

"So big boy, where did you dump your rider?" The horse didn't have an answer. He seemed to be looking up and down the beach the same as she was.

Although she smiled at the horse, an uneasiness settled in her gut. "Please tell me you didn't kick them off in the water." That was the last thing she wanted to find. She'd spent all day with a demanding, often furious, boss and dreaded her time being sabotaged by the same type of person. Someone dumped in the surf was not going to be happy. She took a deep, steadying breath. "Let's go check the shallows."

She walked to the water and turned left, hoping if the rider was to the right, the people with the dogs would have seen them by now. She walked along the beach talking nonsense to the horse while she scanned the water and the sand, hoping for the best outcome. Up ahead was a large clump of seaweed in the shallows bobbing and moving with each wave. She frowned, squinted and peered. "Crap, you ditched them in the water." She walked a little quicker, and although she tried to remain calm, the horse picked up the jitters. Not that he spooked or did anything stupid, he just picked up the pace, snorted a few times, and gave off a vibe somewhere between bravado and apology.

The lump was definitely a person. A very much alive person. The vibe he projected was not happy, but something like fury or pain. He'd taken off his shirt and was rigging it into a sling, the kind of sling for a collarbone break. There was absolutely no hardship in looking at his chest. It was packed with muscles, nicely tanned, and beautifully etched with dark shadows and hair trails. That he was still sitting in the shallows wasn't good. He must have a leg injury to go with the broken collarbone.

Tamara closed the gap between them desperately trying to think of something useful to say, but what do you say to a man in pain? While she tried to quell the butterflies dancing in her stomach, she realized the horse wasn't reacting. If the horse expected a beating, he'd be reluctant to come near the rider. She looked between man and beast. The horse showed no reluctance at all. No matter what her body was telling her, she trusted the animal. The man was in pain, not furious or angry, and not likely to react badly.

"Hi, I'm Tamara." She cringed. Of all the stupid things to say.

He actually laughed. The corners of his eyes crinkled, his lips curved, and his white teeth flashed. "I love a girl who can handle a crisis." His grin and words relaxed her immediately. "Thank you for catching Storm. I'm Rob."

"Hey Rob. Broken collarbone and broken ankle, or is it sprained?" She decided it was best to ignore the crisis comment and focus on injury management. As for the horse's name, she'd think of that later. Catching a storm while running was something her grandmother had told her when she was a kid. She could almost hear her grandmother's voice, but a deep male interrupted.

"I don't know if either are broken but neither of them feel good."

Storm moved close to his rider, who soothed him with quiet words. Rob's fingers tickled across the horse's nose and the long curve of face. The gentleness in the caress made Tamara's chest tighten. Then Rob ran his hands down each of the horse's front legs. Any man with suspected broken bones, sitting in the shallows of the ocean, who took the time to check his horse for injury or inflammation was a good person. A man Tamara could trust. Someone she had to help.

She looked at the ankle, the water, Rob's pale, clammy face, and took in his lack of clothing. She had a T-shirt with a bra/crop top underneath, and one of those was excess. The T-shirt gave more fabric to wrap around his ankle. The crop top wasn't going to offer much in the way of a bandage, it would be more useful for pressure, but since he wasn't bleeding she could leave that on. She had to get him out of the water before she could strap his ankle. She let the reins fall to the sand, and gave Storm a look, hoping he'd interpret it as a stay.

"He'll walk up with us," Rob said as he took hold of the ends of the reins.

"I'm sorry, but this is going to hurt," she said softly to Rob. Squatting behind him, she wrapped her arms around his ribs being as gentle as possible with his injured side. "Take a deep breath, and when I pull, scream if you have to. And drop those reins the moment that horse pulls." Before Rob could respond, she yanked him up the wet sand. It hurt her, so she had no clue how much it must have hurt him. She repeated the maneuver, twice more, but didn't have the strength to do it a fourth time.

They were both sucking in deep breaths, but he seemed to recover faster than she did. "You don't look like you have anywhere near that much strength."

She hadn't known she had that much strength either, but it had to be done. She looked up at Storm. His big soulful eyes were staring back at her. Her grannie's voice came through clear as a bell, *"You'll fall head over heels in love after catching a storm while running."* Goosebumps skittered down her spine. It had been years since she'd allowed herself memories of childhood, and they were flooding back.

Now wasn't the time for a walk down memory lane. She had an injured man to help, a horse to get home, and a home of her own to go to before a deep sleep ready for another trying day at the office.

"Let's wrap your ankle and give it some support." She expected an argument, but there was none. She tied her T-shirt around his ankle, over the boot, giving it as much support as possible. "I don't suppose you have a cell phone, do you?" Since all Rob wore was a pair of boots and shorts, both of which were wet, she knew the chances of a phone working, if he did have one, were slim.

"Not here. Do you?"

She shook her head. She never brought a phone when she ran. Running was a time to disconnect, and that meant from all forms of technology. Her boss was not going to interrupt her hour of solitude and sanity.

"I'm going to have to run somewhere to call an ambulance for you."

Rob clucked with his tongue and the horse's ears pricked. "No ambulances. Storm will get me home."

"How on earth will you do that?"

"I'm pretty confident he'll stand right there, and if you can help me to get upright, I can use him to anchor me and take some of my weight off you. Then we can limp over to the dunes and I hope you might help me on. I won't be able to get on unless there's a decent height difference. Storm's too big for me to clamber onto from the ground and I can't leap with the injuries. Will that work for you?"

"You've only got one arm and one leg."

He gave a bit of a grin. "Technically, I have two of each, it's just that one arm and one leg may be rather incapacitated."

She closed her eyes, took a deep breath, and bit back the smart alec response she wanted to give.

There wasn't a lot of choice. Working with what they had was the best plan. If Rob could lean on the horse and her, they probably could get him upright, and maybe even moving. She looked at the dunes. If the horse stood in the right position, maybe she could leg Rob on, maybe they could get home, but he still had to get to a hospital. She didn't like the idea that he might have broken bones unattended to.

"Let's try. What's the worst that can happen? You break more bones and end up in hospital via the ambulance anyway." She tried to make it a little humorous with the touch of a laugh at the end, but it came off sounding sad.

"Please believe me when I say it's not your fault. I can do this. It's not my first broken bone, not my first fall, not the first time I've had to get myself out of a situation like this."

She gave him a stare. He sounded so resigned to doing everything alone that it struck a chord deep inside her. She needed to help. She was here to help. This was meant to be.

Lifting Rob wasn't easy but she pushed, levered, and exerted herself, while he did the same. Storm stood rock solid. Allowing Rob to push against him.

It was an act of bravery on Rob's part. His courage made her realize that it had been a long time since she had trusted anything, or anyone, as much as he trusted Storm.

When Rob was standing, she saw the absolute futility of what they had just achieved. His injured ankle and injured collarbone were on the same side. When he slung his arm over Storm's back to support himself, there was no way he was going to be able to move. She had no hope of supporting his other side.

As she stood wondering how this would work, Rob gingerly tested his foot on the soft sand. His breath sucked inward, and he bit his lips hard, but he kept pressing down until his foot was flat. A few breaths were sucked in through his teeth, before he took a deep breath and exhaled slowly. Sweat beaded across his forehead and dripped off his chin. It was really hurting him, and there wasn't anything she could do to make it easier.

Tamara moved towards Storm, gathered up the reins, and stroked the horse's neck. Focusing on the horse was much easier. Watching Rob battle through the pain was too personal. She keenly felt his need for privacy even if he hadn't said a word.

After what seemed like forever, he said, "Okay, that was as bad as it probably looked." Rob sucked in another breath. "I don't know if I'm going to be able to take a step. Can you hold Storm still while I try?"

She gathered the reins, put a hand across Storm's chest and whispered softly to the horse. Rob grunted, his breath hissed, there was a gasp and she winced. All the time, Storm stood still.

"I can walk. It's just slow. Let's do this." The words seemed as if they were gritted out between clenched teeth. Tamara wanted to argue but it wasn't her body that was injured. He was an adult and capable of making decisions, even if this wasn't one she would have made.

Storm, still perfectly behaved, and Tamara moved at a snail's pace across the sand. It was excruciating listening to Rob. His ability to move given the pain, was quite phenomenal. Every suck of breath, every tightening of his throat when she was sure he was swallowing down a moan, every tiny hiss caused her to flinch. If she could have borne some of his pain, she would have. Seeing anyone, or anything, suffer was difficult, yet Rob handled it admirably. Okay, maybe not admirably, maybe it was stupidly, but she had to give him credit for backing up his claim.

When they made it to the small rise in the sand, she called a halt. They were a long way from the edge of the dunes, but this small undulation might give them enough height difference to get him mounted. And if she excavated a little sand...

"You lean on Storm and have a breather. I'll just dig a little deeper here." When Rob opened his mouth, a deep frown on his forehead, she knew he was about to argue. "No. Not this time. I'm not putting my back out lifting you when I can scrape along here a bit and get an inch or two extra height difference." An extra inch would make the hill about a foot higher than the flat. The sand, away from the edge, was quite stable, not like a sandcastle that would flatten with Rob's weight. The extra inch might allow Rob to get his stomach over Storm's back without putting any extra pressure on the ankle or catching the bandaged arm during mounting. She could only hope it might help.

Rob gave a pained grin and bobbed his head. The way he was breathing, she didn't think there was much fight in him. His face was a green-white color, and perspiration beaded on top of the sheen. She had to get him mounted, and get him to hospital, regardless of what he thought of his invincibility. If his horse wasn't so damn obedient, she'd have called a stop to this whole ludicrous business.

As she scratched away at the sand, making something like a flattened trench, she tried to rationalize what she was doing. If anything happened to the guy, how would she explain why she'd let him call the shots? The beach was deserted now. The people with dogs had moved way beyond where she could see them, if they were still on the sand. Neither she or Rob had a cell phone, so to get help she would have had to leave them. It was an option. But somehow, the three of them were in this together, and she felt some crazy need to see this through. It had nothing, nothing at all, to do with the words her grandmother had said. Nothing to do with her attraction to the man with the naked chest and stubborn nature. Nothing to do with the pang of desperate longing she had when she connected with his horse. Nothing at all to do with the flood of beautiful childhood memories she'd so long suppressed.

"Thanks. That looks better." Rob's voice dragged her mind from regret and into the present. He sounded better. His breath wasn't gaspy. It was almost like he had his pain under control.

Well that'll last only moments.

"Can you lead Storm down there, and I'll clamber on him from here?"

She stared at him. "Don't you think I could give you a leg up or something? How are you going to climb with the use of only one arm and one functioning leg?"

"Please, trust me. I'd rather you stood with Storm than legged me up."

No matter how long she stared at him, unblinking, he didn't change his mind. He was serious. After one shake of her head, she went with trusting him. Of all the idiotic, stupid things for her to do, she was trusting an injured man, whose mental capacity was affected by pain, and who she'd known for all of what, twenty minutes?

Storm stood perfectly still on the lower section of the beach. She explained what was happening, more for herself than any hope that the horse might understand, blocking out the soft groans and grunts coming from the man moving against the horse's side.

Storm let out a deep exhalation as Rob sprawled across the horse's back. When she went to help him, a gritted, "No," stopped any thought of movement. She kept talking to Storm, trying not to notice the excruciating way Rob slowly maneuvered into position.

She didn't think anyone would have the ability to do what he had just done. His skin had gone from a pale green-white to something quite deep, making her wonder how much more pain he could endure. His Adam's apple bobbed, and she imagined he was swallowing bile. No one could be that color green without feeling ill.

They waited. She wasn't moving until he was settled, and she was half expecting him to lose his lunch, or whatever else he may have eaten in recent hours. He only breathed. Long, slow, deep breaths. After quite a few, they seemed to be less pained. She glanced at him. His color was back to the pale green-white.

"Let's see how a few steps go." She said it slowly, still hoping that he may ask her to run and get help, but he only nodded. She looped the reins over Storm's neck, passing them to Rob. He gathered them in his good hand, and she took hold of the cheek strap on the bridle. "Right?" she asked and waited for Rob's nod before she asked Storm to walk on. After a few steps Rob nodded again, so she kept moving slowly up the beach, through the dune scrub where she'd first met Storm, and out onto the dirt track that skirted the town.

"At the end of this track, there's horse paddocks. Any chance you can walk us there?"

Biting back an acerbic comment, she responded with humor. "Well, I was just going to leave you here since you're both so capable, but I suppose, since you asked nicely, I could help out."

A slight chuckle from Rob made her glad to have chosen comedy.

She brushed her hand along Storm's neck and walked them towards home. Their home.

About halfway there, she turned. "If you're going to pass out, please let me know before you hit the ground." When Rob grunted, she knew she wasn't too far from the mark. The pain was swamping him. He'd gone that darker shade of bile. She could only hope he held on until they got home, or someone drove down this dirt track, which hardly seemed likely since the tracks were old and filled with grass.

The sun was beginning to set, pretty soon they'd be in that twilight shadow phase. Hopefully Storm would remain sensible and not spook at shadows. Rob had his eyes closed, his body was hunched, and with only one good leg, he'd hardly be in a position to stay on a prancing beast. If he came off, there was no way in the world she was getting him back on. She'd have to leave them and get to a phone. What would happen to Storm then was anyone's guess. She muttered all this to Storm as they walked. If he didn't understand a word she said, she didn't mind. It got her fears out in front of her, so she could face them, and not have them inside making her jittery. She couldn't afford to project any fear; Rob and Storm needed her strong.

At the paddock on the left at the end of the track was a gate. Storm went to it and waited patiently while she wrestled it open. He took his burden through with a calm gentleness that made Tamara think that he took his responsibilities seriously.

I'm going mad, talking to a horse, and now anthropomorphizing his behavior.

As mad as it seemed, she let Storm lead the way. This was home, and horses were always keen to get back to their feed, water, buddies and shelter. He led her towards lights, so she knew she'd find people, or at least phone access, even if it wasn't the right place.

Lights were on in a building that looked like stables. She could even hear the murmur of voices. *People. Thank goodness.*

Two people walked out of the shed towards a car.

"Excuse me," Tamara called.

Both stopped and stared. "Is Rob okay?" A woman about her age asked quickly, concern lacing her words. Tamara explained the situation as briefly as she could. The woman had a phone out and was calling the ambulance as Tamara explained.

The other person, a young girl, went out to meet the ambulance, reassuring Tamara as she left, telling her to stay with Rob and Storm and that she'd bring them right in as soon as possible.

While the woman remained on the phone, Tamara slid her hand along Rob's thigh, gently squeezing the tense muscles to get his attention. "Rob, the ambulance is almost here. Just hang on until they get you off Storm. They'll have pain relief. I'll look after your horse and make sure everything is locked up before I come to the hospital. Don't worry about anything." A flutter of his eyelids was the only acknowledgement. She couldn't believe he'd made it this far.

It took long moments but eventually she heard the siren in the distance. The woman pocketed her phone and came towards Tamara. "I'm Patti. My daughter, Mila, you've already met."

"I'm so glad you were here. I didn't have a phone, neither did Rob."

Patti glared at the injured man and then stared at Tamara. "I thought he was the only idiot who went out without a phone."

Tamara bit her lip and refrained from replying. Patti was entitled to be angry and frightened and worried. Anyone would be, if a stranger brought your half-unconscious husband home slumped on the back of a horse.

When the ambulance arrived, Patti asked Tamara to control the animal while they looked after Rob. That was fine, truly it was. She had no claim over him. She and Storm were no more than vehicles to carry the injured home. When Rob was on the gurney, she led Storm into the stables.

Mila was there in an instant. "You should hose him down first. The wash bay's here." She led Tamara outside and pointed to the cement area just to the edge of the light. "When you walk out there, a sensor light will come on. Then Storm's feed is on the chart on the wall in the feed room. The tack goes in the tack room after you wash it. Sorry I can't help, but we need to go." She smiled apologetically, after she'd dictated the demands like a drill sergeant.

"That's okay. Go with your mom. I'll fix Storm, lock up here, and then I'll check in at the hospital. Thank you." Tamara's thanks was called out to the departing back of the girl. She'd run off no doubt to join her mother and head to the hospital to be with her father.

After Tamara had settled Storm into the wash bay, she turned on the hose and it seemed like water sprang from not just the tap. Her chest overfilled and tears spilled up her throat and out of her eyes. Her heart had swollen with memories, and the pain and ache of those lost years tore at her. She thought she'd dealt with it years ago, but it seemed she'd only papered over the hurt and this afternoon had ripped that to shreds. At least there was only Storm to see, and with the hose gushing more than she was, she wet herself and him.

Storm kept close, nudging her with his soft nose and snuffling along her neck, making her chuckle. After washing him, removing the excess water, giving him a brush down with a rippled glove she found in the wash bay, she fed him and settled him for the night.

"I'll go check up on your master, and report back in the morning," she promised as she turned out the lights and closed the stables up for the evening. To others, it may be madness talking to a horse, but it was the most natural thing in the world. Tamara's grandfather had always treated his horses as friends, she knew nothing different.

After a quick shower at home, followed by a bite to eat, she was off to the hospital. A phone call may have been quicker but she wasn't sure they'd give her any information. At least in person she had a better chance of explaining the situation or running into Patti or Mila.

At the front desk, she explained to one woman who then called another. "I found him on the beach after he fallen off his horse." She sounded as exhausted as she felt, and hoped the women didn't take it as her being patronizing or annoyed. She knew they were doing their job, all she really needed to know was that Rob was okay. "If you can't let me know how he is, could I leave a message for him, or Patti or Mila to say that I've locked up, fed his horse, and I'll check on them again in the morning?"

The nurse seemed more interested after the name-dropping. "What's his horse's name?"

Tamara's eyes widened. "Storm. A big gray gelding."

"Insanely attached to Rob, doesn't want to go near anybody else. A crazy beast."

Tamara couldn't tell if she was being baited, so she went with the Storm she knew. "He was quite respectful and I had no problems with him, but you're right, he adores Rob."

The nurse's hand flew to her chest, and then across her open mouth, before she nodded as if Tamara had passed some test. "Come with me. I'm Maxine. You can see him, but he's asleep and dosed up on pain medication."

Tamara had no intention of waking him up, she just wanted to see that he was okay. She followed the nurse into the room and sat beside him in the chair the nurse indicated. She sat and waited while the nurse took Rob's observations.

The adrenaline dropped out of her body and she sank into the chair. It seemed to clasp her in a warm hug, drawing her into a deeper relaxation.

She stared at the man in the bed. She may only know his name was Rob, but she also knew he was tough, courageous, had a good sense of humor, a strength beyond belief, was kind to animals, and was stubborn. So very, very stubborn.

He'd be okay. The nurse whispered that to her and she tried to reply, or maybe she did; the chair was claiming her.

Chapter 2

A slow incessant beeping that wasn't his alarm roused Rob to consciousness. He slowly brought his eyes into focus, peering through the slits of his eyelids, and knew he wasn't in his bedroom. His body ached. One hand seemed attached to his chest, the other was wrapped in something warm and silky. Someone's hair? His face hurt a little and might be a bit swollen, but he couldn't seem to move either hand to touch it. As he catalogued his body, it seemed his chest and ribs, stomach and hips weren't overly affected. He could wriggle his thigh muscles and his left toes moved okay, but the right ones caused pain. Sharp-edged pain that made his eyes close and his breath catch.

He cast his mind back. He'd come off Storm. Someone had helped him. Not someone. A woman—part guardian angel, part dream girl. Competent, relaxed, calm in a crisis. Anyone who could keep calm in that situation, and keep Storm calm, was someone Rob wanted to know.

Tamara.

Tamara without a T-shirt.

Tamara with the fine, lithe, athletic body. Eyes the color of alfalfa, hair the color of molasses.

The drugs were making him delirious. No girl should be compared to horse feed.

He must have napped because the next time his eyes opened, one hand was free of silky confines, the pain wasn't quite as intense, and he felt almost human.

"Welcome to the world, Rob."

The voice sounded familiar. Rob rolled his head to the side and a grin broke across his face. "Maxine, are you a sight for sore eyes." Maxine had horses on agistment at his place.

She chuckled. "How are the drugs going?"

"Better than they were last time I woke."

Maxine bustled around the room doing his observations, and he took the time to breathe and wake more fully. His head felt full of cotton wool, so the pain medication was doing its job. When

Maxine dropped the folder back at the foot of his bed, she looked up and gave him a grin. "Did you come off Storm just to meet the girl?"

"I don't know what you mean." He had half an inkling of what she was implying, but he couldn't see how she'd know about Tamara.

Maxine adjusted his pillows. "Sorry. I shouldn't jest while you're drugged. I was talking about the girl who came in to check on you last night. She's lovely. Left not long ago after she fell asleep in the chair. She left you a note, but she's looked after Storm and she was heading back there to feed him this morning. Said she'd be back this evening after work. She wanted to catch up with Patti and Mila."

He let all the words swim around his head before they slowly settled and made some sense. "Who is she?"

"That new girl in town. The one who bought the old Mason place." She gave Rob a folded page, and promised to look in before she left. A gleam in her eye told Rob that the news of Tamara saving him would be around town in no time at all. Tamara staying beside him all night would probably be around town too.

Oh boy. I have to let her know what she's in for.

Rob opened the note. She'd left a phone number so if she didn't show up tonight, at least he could let her know that everyone in town would be gossiping about them.

The next time Rob wrote woke, the doctor was telling him the damage he'd done, and the plans for the future.

"The collarbone's broken but there's not much we can do for that. You have to wear the collar and cuff sling for about six weeks." A frown danced across the doctor's forehead. "The ankle's more problematic. I don't think it's broken, but there's a lot of swelling. We've got you in an ice boot to reduce the swelling, then we'll X-ray and see what the damage is."

Rob nodded even though the information was taking time to soak into his brain.

"We'll keep you here a couple of days to reduce the swelling. I know that won't happen if we let you home. Hopefully we'll get you in a moon boot to protect the ankle and give you some movement. Then it'll be physio."

"Okay Doc." Rob slurred the words as he drifted off again.

Rob dozed the day away. Sometimes he woke when people were in the room, but when he did, he wasn't sure he made sense of what they said or what he said to them. He couldn't get things straight in his head. He'd worry about it tomorrow when the pain meds wore off, the cotton wool disappeared from his brain, and he was more like himself.

The dinner tray had just been left when there was a hesitant knock on the door. He glanced up, wondering why the catering staff had knocked.

"Oh, you look so much better." She didn't move her feet, but her face broke into a beautiful smile.

The quiet calm of the voice seeped into his brain. Reassuring and strong. "Tamara?" She nodded. "Come in, please."

As she walked, he tried to read her body language. Although she didn't seem overly confident, she wasn't lacking in it either. She didn't look anything like the tousled-haired runner he'd met. She was neat, prim, business attired. He wasn't sure he knew this woman, even though he was comfortable with her here.

He tried to follow her progress around the bed to the chair but movement was awkward while lying flat and immobile.

"Can I prop the bed up a little for you?" she asked.

He nodded. She seemed competent so he let her pick up a gizmo resting on the bed. He began to sit upright, without any pain or exertion. She was a magician. A no doubt loopy grin appeared, but he couldn't stop it. She'd done something that seemed miraculous. "These drugs are messing with my brain. Thank you for helping me, now and with the fall."

She smiled as she sat down. This one was a softer smile, almost shy. "It's no trouble." She waved her hand as if brushing off the thanks. "And I'll take that as a warning. Anything you say, I won't believe until you're non-drug addled."

The grin was absolutely gorgeous and he couldn't help grinning back. "Perfect. So I can say all sorts of things and get away with them." He watched green eyes sparkle and knew exactly what he wanted to get away with. "You saved my life. Storm was perfectly behaved with you. Will you marry me?" He laughed, but even as he joked, he felt a strong sense of the words being right. There wasn't a hint of panic inside him.

Pretty cool drugs if they make that so easy.

She froze. Her face contorted and her arms crossed over her body. She swallowed, before wriggling uncomfortably on the seat. Then she leaned away from him. After a few seconds where he wasn't sure what to do, she made a poor attempt at laughter.

"I don't think I saved your life, and I absolutely adore Storm, he's a beauty. Thank you for the offer, but I'm not looking for marriage." The prim businesswoman was here. Even if she was smiling and pretending to rebuff his joke, she'd put up walls. Thick, impenetrable walls.

Part of him was mightily offended. He had been joking about the proposal, but her rebuff hurt.

"How are you feeling?" Tamara's voice was soft, almost apologetic, but there was strength there too.

Which reminded him. "What you did yesterday was incredible."

"Incredibly stupid, I think. Please tell me that you didn't do any worse damage when I listened to you and helped you ride home." The way she bit her lips as she finished the sentence made him think that she really was scared he'd done further damage.

"I did all the damage in the fall. Broken collarbone, ankle injury unknown at this stage. There's too much swelling."

"That's probably because you walked on it."

He grinned. He couldn't help himself. "You sound just like my sister."

"You've done this before?"

"I've probably broken every bone at least once. Mostly when I was a kid. Seems to go hand-in-hand with horses, rodeos, breaking in, and general living."

She was relaxed and grinning by the time he finished, which was exactly what he'd hoped. He wanted those green eyes flashing and twinkling, the dimples digging into her cheeks, and the rosy tint that brushed across her cheekbones.

"Is that your dinner?" He nodded. "Why are you waiting?" He shrugged. He could hardly say he was too exhausted to open the covers, could he?

She wheeled the trolley closer, then lifted the lids, examining what lay beneath. "Doesn't look that bad." She didn't wait for him to respond. "It's hard to cut up food if you've only got one hand. Why don't people think of that? I'll cut it up, then it'll be easier for you."

Once she started cutting, the aroma got to him, and his stomach grumbled. She glanced at him, lifted a forkful of food, and he opened his mouth. He should be mortified, but it was easy. She made it easy. A sip of water. A little more food. No chatter. He was being fed, his horse was being looked after, and all was okay in the world.

Chapter 3

When Tamara got to Rob's the next morning, a crowd was gathered. Before she could turn around, Patti waved and headed towards her. *Patti. Great.* She needed to explain her visits to the hospital. Not that she had any legitimate explanation. Surely falling asleep would account for the first night. Last night, with the intimacy of feeding, had no worthy explanation that she could think of.

"Tamara, hi, I'm glad you're here."

"I'm sorry. I shouldn't be. It's just I haven't been able to catch up with you."

Patti frowned briefly and then waved a hand. "I've been running around like a crazy person. Rob and Maxine said you'd been in, that you'd feed Storm, and that's great. One less job for me." Patti smiled, and Tamara had the distinct feeling that she was missing something. Patti pressed on. "We're here to work out a roster system. Rob's going to need help, and we hoped you'd be involved too?"

Without waiting for an answer, Patti headed into the milling crowd, whistled, and addressed everyone. "This is Tamara. She found Rob, brought him and Storm home, and will keep looking after Storm." Everyone turned, and Tamara wasn't sure where to look, so she gave a bit of smile, bobbed her head, and then looked quickly at the ground.

Patti was the ringleader and organized people into groups of those who'd provide food and those who could handle the horse and business management. Patti seemed to have no interest in horses. It must be an interest Rob shared with his daughter.

Strangely, Tamara found herself as Patti's second-in-charge. "I'm quite happy just looking after Storm," Tamara said softly so only Patti would hear.

"I know but I need someone to help with Rob, and I think you're perfect for the job. Unless someone will object, like a husband or boyfriend."

"The only person who'll object is my boss, and right now I'm not sure I care." Tamara blurted without thought. It was too late to take it back, but Patti didn't seem at all worried by the outburst.

"Perfect." Patti gave her a key to the stables, which also had the key for the house. "Now, you go and feed Storm, and I'll see you this evening when you pop in to visit Rob."

Tamara nodded and went to feed the horse.

Later that night, when she got to the hospital, Tamara was relieved to see Rob sitting up in bed, gamely wielding a fork, and feeding himself. He smiled when she knocked on the doorjamb and waved her in.

On the tray were a couple of slices of dry toast with unopened containers of butter. With a sigh and a head shake, she opened the butter and buttered the toast. A large warm hand closed over hers and gave a squeeze, she dropped the knife and squeaked.

"You're not cutting soldiers."

Tamara gave half a laugh. Her heart was galloping and she wasn't sure if it was caused by the fright of a hand closing on hers or from the unexpected growl. She glanced up at Rob's widely opened eyes. He looked shocked, a little amused, and still in some pain. Her galloping heart didn't slow. There was another possibility for the gait change but she wasn't thinking that. He was a married man, and no matter how odd his marriage to Patti seemed, she had to respect the bond.

Rob growled again. "I'm not three or one hundred. I can eat a slice of toast without it cut to soldiers."

She nodded to show her comprehension, but she wasn't understanding anything about this moment. She should be stepping away, withdrawing her hand from his, yet she remained, frozen. The squeak from a footstep behind her was all that stopped her moving closer to Rob.

"Have you had nursing experience, Tamara?" Patti's voice from behind her turned her blood to ice. She stepped back quickly, lowering the knife to the plate with the toast.

Tamara bit her lips together as she nodded and turned to face Patti. "As a carer, not a nurse."

Patti made a sound in her throat that Tamara felt was something self-congratulatory, even if that made no sense. It must have been a different noise about staking territory.

Patti walked to the opposite side of Rob. Tamara glanced at him and his glare was harsh as it flicked between Patti and her. "Why are you asking, Patti?"

"You're going to need help."

His whole body stiffened, and the muscle at the back of his jaw bulged and ticced ensnaring Tamara's attention. When muscles went like that, either control won or it was blown to smithereens. She took another step backwards just in case.

"Broken bones take about six weeks to heal. Surely you know that, Rob. You won't be able to do anything for weeks." Patti sounded as if she was speaking to a child and Tamara kept an eye on that beating jaw muscle. This wasn't the way she'd speak to Rob. It seemed to enflame his emotion, which wasn't going to aid his healing.

She spoke before she could stop herself. "The first few days will be the worst, when you're trying to get used to only have one working arm, and a hobbly leg."

"What?" He glared at her. "Days?"

Tamara remained silent as she met his gaze. She'd deliberately said "days" to make him a little more accepting of his incapacity.

"It'll be weeks," Patti said, rather unhelpfully. Rob swung his glare to her, and Tamara changed her mind about the helpfulness of Patti's comment. If it took his ire from her, surely that was a good thing.

"What?" Rob's word was a growl of complete denial, anger and frustration. The rawness of the word seeped into Tamara in a way she hadn't expected. She hardly knew him, yet his emotions seemed to so easily readable.

"What's your opinion, Tamara?" He didn't take his glare from Patti, but Tamara felt as if he was looking right inside her.

"Um, I'm no expert. I think some people adapt to incapacity fairly quickly. After seeing you deal with the injury, I thought you'd be capable of many things within a few days...but I don't know you as well as your wife."

The room went utterly still. Tamara saw Patti's eyes widen, her mouth open, and then her attention fell on Rob as he spun his upper body towards her. "What wife?" This time his growl almost took her knees out.

Patti's laughter drew Tamara's attention. "You think I'm his wife?" she spluttered between guffaws.

Tamara knew her face was flaming without the burning stare from Rob. Maybe she'd made an incorrect assumption. She wasn't sure what to say next, how to apologize, or get herself out of the mess she'd spectacularly landed herself in.

"Patti is my sister. My annoying, pain in the ass, older sister." Rob broke the horror of the moment with his amusing comment, and Patti smacked him in retaliation. "And, I prefer her prognosis to yours," he told Patti with a forced grin.

"Good." Patti didn't bat an eyelid. "You won't mind if she helps out with your care."

"No." Tamara and Rob said the word in unison. She jumped back, as if the word had scalded her.

"Excellent that you don't mind, Rob." Patti gave him a shark-like smile. "I've given her a key already, and she and Storm are firm friends, so you won't need to worry."

Rob's jaw muscle ticked like a bomb. Fast and furious. Tamara's heartbeat seemed to speed up to keep pace. She had to stop this.

"I can't, Patti," she said in a breathless rush. "I have to work."

"I know. It's okay. I'll help out in the day, but I can't do overnights without uprooting everyone. Most people are in the same boat. I was hoping you might do the overnighters."

Tamara searched for an excuse. She had no kids. No connections in the town. Everyone knew that. She was the newcomer, arriving alone. Yes, she needed to sleep at night, but Rob would be doing the same. Unless she was willing to admit to night terrors, she had nothing. She looked to Rob for help, but she only had his profile as he still glared at Patti.

"At least she won't drive me nuts like you and your cronies." Rob's growl caused skitters to again dance down Tamara's spine, yet Patti seemed oblivious to his discomfort.

"That's settled then," Patti spoke with the conviction of someone who'd had a monumental win.

Tamara would work things out with Rob. For all his growling menace, he was no threat. The whole town would know she was staying with him each night, and that reduced any threat to nothing at all. Except, he no longer had a wife.

Chapter 4

Hospital was the worst place to be trapped. Rob hated the smells, the isolation, the cleanliness, the institutionalization. Why would anyone design a building where every corridor looked the same, where every room was identical? Wouldn't you want to create a space where healing and individualization were important?

Each nurse treated Rob with personal care and concern, but he was part of a system, where he was a patient, or rather an injury, with an expected duration and a discharge date. For Rob, that couldn't come quickly enough.

Although, as Patti drove him home and he realized that he'd now be swapping institutionalization for feminine care and smothering, he wondered if it was worth heading back to the hospital.

"...so all the meals are in the freezer for you." Patti drew a breath after explaining how every person he knew had done something for his welfare.

"Thanks, Patti, but you really didn't have to organize all of this."

"How were you going to care for yourself?"

"I'd manage."

Patti gave a snort and continued to drive, lecturing him on every aspect of his life and listing almost every failing. He knew it all came with a big dose of love and caring, but that didn't make it any easier to swallow. As a captive in the car, and hindered by his lack of movement, Patti was making best use of the time. He was doing his best to shut her out.

"...Tamara will be here after five." Except when she mentioned Tamara, then his ears tuned in. He glanced at his watch, five and a half more hours.

"Don't you have school pick-up and running around with the kids?"

Patti gave a huge sigh. "I just told you that. You'll have to fend for yourself for a couple of hours because I'll go at three, and Tamara won't be here until after five. Were you listening at all?"

"Sometimes the drugs vague me out." It was the best he could come up with, but it did the trick. Patti became apologetic and when they got to his place, after she'd helped him to bed, she left him alone to sleep. He could have done with a trip to the stables, but he was exhausted, so maybe a few hours rest wouldn't hurt.

He woke sometime later to find a thermos mug on his bedside table, and a note propped in front of it. He slowly reached for the note with his useful arm. Patti had gone, and Tamara would be here soon. He looked at the clock, only ten minutes before she got here. He'd had a ridiculously long sleep. In the middle of the day. He wasn't even in hospital. He had hoped it was the environment that was sending him into daylong naps, but he may need to reconsider that.

It took an inordinate amount of concentration and energy to get out of bed. His ankle might not be broken but the moon boot, that made walking possible, was difficult to manage. His foot didn't move properly, actually, his whole leg wasn't moving right. His balance was off kilter. He wobbled and put both arms out to help himself and searing pain shot down his body. His chest was on fire. He let rip with every swear word he knew.

Hands closed around his waist, tight. They steadied him, held him until he found his center of gravity again.

"Do you have to try to make things worse on your very first night?" The thread of amusement softened the blow of her admonishment and almost made Rob smile. He had other things on his mind.

He kept walking, or more precisely, hobbling. "I've no time for chitchat. I have to get to the bathroom." He paused at the bathroom door. No matter how he thought about things, he couldn't think of a way he could undo his jeans in the time he needed to have them undone. He had to ask her, yet how do you ask an almost stranger, who in other circumstances you may ask for a date, to undo your trousers?

"Let me get your jeans, then I'll wait out here and you yell when you need a hand doing them up." Tamara made it sound so matter-of-fact. As if he was a body in need and she was here to help. He should feel relieved, and yet he didn't.

He turned a little and let her expertly unzip him. His eyelids came down to shut out the vision before him, and the other visuals his mind supplied.

"Will you be right?"

"Yes." He was abrupt and even though she deserved a thank you, he didn't have anything polite in him. He wobbled to the toilet and took care of his needs. Or at least he did what he could. He couldn't manage the zipping up part. He could barely manage the hand washing. The turning wasn't all that easy either. A string of words raced through his mind but he couldn't let them loose. He hadn't managed to close the door. He hadn't even thought of it. He'd not left himself time enough to make his way to the bathroom. That was a lesson learned.

The mercy was that Tamara wasn't standing at the doorway, nor anywhere close to the open door frame. The kettle was going so he made his way down the hall. She met him as he turned into the kitchen. "Here, let me." Her hands were raised, but she waited until he'd moved his hands to the side before she did his zip up. "If you have track pants, you could wear them for a few days. You'll get used to one-handed things in a couple of days and can get back into jeans then."

She turned to the sink, washed her hands, and then gestured around the kitchen. "Would you like a tea or coffee? If so, where is everything?"

He pointed to the cupboard above the kettle. "Coffee for me, please. Everything is in the cupboard."

She took down the coffee beans, the grinder and the single cup plunger. "Do you mind if I have tea?" Her hand hovered over the mugs.

"There's bags in there. Is that okay?" He was surprised that she'd taken down all the coffee gear when a jar of instant had been positioned right next to the tea bags. Maybe she understood a coffee drinker's need.

She nodded and went about grinding his beans before making the drinks. She was efficient, economical in her movement, and easy to watch. He'd thought that about her at the beach too, but he'd been worried it had been his pain-filled mind romanticizing his savior. She was calm and careful. The perfect temperament to work with horses. He needed new staff. Tonight wasn't the time to offer her a job. He needed to get to know her better, even if what he'd seen was very pleasant.

"Milk or sugar?" she asked, bringing his focus back to her hands as she held the mug of coffee just off the bench.

"Neither, thanks."

"That makes it easy to make and easy to remember." She smiled as she placed the mug in front of him.

"I don't suppose you'd allow me to go out to check on Storm."

She looked up and gave him a shake of her head. Although he'd known that would be the answer, it brought a heaviness to his chest.

"Not until they all leave," she said it simply so that it almost whooshed past him. Then the words sank in.

He looked at the clock. Five-thirty. It was one of the most popular times for owners to tend to their horses or ride. Agistment really meant that his place was the second home to everyone who boarded their horse with him. Kids came to ride their ponies or horses. Cars came and went as kids got picked up and owners arrived to feed their horses, then left. She was right. It was a crazy time to head outside. He'd be swamped by people.

"You're right."

"I'll help you outside later, when they've all gone, but only if you promise never to tell Patti."

He mimed zipping his lips. Then frowned. "Why would she care?"

"I may have, kind of, almost, sort of, promised not to let you out there." She looked apologetic, sheepish, and more than a little naughty.

"You what?"

She sipped her tea. "Pretty much lied to your sister. I tried to skirt around it but she seemed to know I was hedging my bets. She made me promise not to let you out for at least a few days."

"And how did you get around that?"

"I promised not to let you out." She shrugged. "I figured if I took you out, then that was totally different to letting you out."

Laughter burst from him. "You're something else, Tamara...oh, I don't know your last name. Do I?"

"Probably not." She smiled. "We've had an upside-down way of meeting, haven't we? Tamara Hancock."

"Rob Richmond." He stuck out his uninjured hand, but it was the wrong hand to shake with and they both fumbled a handshake, finger squeeze. "Did I do that any better on the beach?"

She grinned. "I have no idea. I was shocked you were alive, surprised at how calm you were, and then astounded that you wanted to ride home. Pleasantries weren't high on my agenda."

"I was a bit of an ass. Sorry."

"I wouldn't have said 'ass' but if that's how you see yourself, fine by me." She gave the sauciest wink that had his heart skipping a beat. Then she looked down at her tea, her head shook just the once in a tiny motion he almost missed. "Patti said your ankle needs icing every few hours. Should we be doing that?"

He should be. The constant ache had become a little sharper since he'd been upright. "Thanks, yes." He let her get the ice pack and made his way to the couch. He unsnapped the boot but waited for Tamara to take it off. He hated being dependent but there were so many things he just couldn't do.

"It'll be easier in a few days," she said as she wrapped the ice to his ankle after settling it up on a pile of pillows.

"So you keep saying." He was growling but he couldn't stop it. Incapacitated. Useless. Cranky. In pain. They were all legitimate excuses, but really, he was just being an ass. Again.

"Can I get you anything?" His mind stalled. Thankfully she filled in the gaps. "Do you eat dinner early, or would you rather it later? Patti said your freezer was full and I only needed to heat something up, but if you want something different just let me know."

Okay. He was following now. He was the patient, lying on the couch like a sick person, and she was his carer. The witty banter had ended. "I don't even know what there is."

She passed a notepad to him "It's all catalogued here."

He groaned. Patti and her freaking lists. He'd bet she'd added to the one up in the stables, probably with colored stars. "Anything will do. I don't really care what I eat."

"Never?"

He shrugged. "Should I?"

"You don't ever get a craving for, say a bacon, avocado and tomato sandwich?"

His body had a moment on pause. Craving? That was one of those code words, wasn't it? But Patti had told him she was single. He checked her stomach—still flat. "I think only women get cravings." Even the way he said it sounded like he was treading carefully through a minefield. He hoped she didn't hear his caution.

Her eyes rolled. "Not pregnancy cravings." She gave a sort of annoyed sigh. "Why does the word craving always do that to men?" Thankfully she wasn't after an answer because she kept right on speaking. "A hankering, a mouth-watering need for a certain food. Don't you ever get that? Waking up and needing bacon and eggs? The desire for chocolate cake? Your mouth watering for strawberries?"

He'd never felt like that—not for food anyway. "Maybe bacon and eggs if I'm hungover, mostly I only think of something if I smell it cooking."

She shook her head as if he was missing out on some major necessity in life. "It's a wonder you survive," she said in a tone that showed him exactly how amazing she felt his living was. She could be on to something, because with the crazy things he'd done in his thirty-two years, it was truly incredible that he was alive.

"If I pull some random meal out every morning to defrost, you'll be happy to eat it heated up of an evening?"

"I eat everything that's on the list." He grinned. "You know Patti wouldn't let people just rock up with anything. Everyone in town has a meal they always bring to any catastrophe. You aren't allowed to turn up with anything else."

"What's your specialty?"

Rob rocked back. "Men aren't involved in that."

Her head tipped to the side and little lines etched themselves across her forehead and between her fine brows. "Why not? You cook for yourself, don't you? When you're not injured, that is."

Yes, he cooked for himself. Anyone could cook meat and vegetables, couldn't they? That's what he cooked mostly. In winter he threw a casserole or two together. He cooked pretty well for himself when he stopped to think about it. He glanced again at the list on the bench. He probably could cook all of it. "I don't know why men aren't involved. I can cook stuff like that." He waved his hand at the page. "It's just that it's...umm..." He faltered. Her stare was drilling holes into him and he knew if he said the words, "women's work" or something similar, it would probably set off a time bomb. Better to just let the sentence trail away. Then he had a flash. "So, right. Next time someone needs something, I'll make something. I'll repay everyone's generosity."

She held her hands up and took a step back. "I didn't say a word."

He may have sounded more defensive and grouchy than he'd intended. "Sorry. I figured you were going to have a shot at me."

"For what?"

"Um…" What had he been expecting? She'd done nothing to indicate that she'd jump on her high horse and give him a serve. Where had his expectation come from? Patti. His sister was the one who jumped on him at any hint that he may be excluding her because she was female, and yet she was one of the main people encouraging the divide with only women caring for others in the community. What was with that? "Sorry. Nothing to do with you. My own force of habit." When her eyebrow lifted in clear encouragement to continue, he kept his mouth shut. In some ways, this town maintained old traditions because no one thought to change them. He didn't want to get into that sort of a discussion tonight. He wanted to know more about Tamara.

"What made you move here? It's a quiet little backwater."

She shrugged. "Maybe that's what I needed."

"I thought everyone always wanted the bright lights and fast pace."

"Not everyone." Her smile came across as if she was tired, or maybe burned out.

"Where were you before you moved here?"

"Are we playing twenty questions?"

He grinned. "May as well play something while we wait, and heaven knows there's not much I can play with a gammy arm and a crook leg."

She gave a puff, as if she'd almost laughed again. "Then we go one at a time, question for question. I don't like being grilled."

"Fair enough." He waited for her answer.

She took her time, perching on the edge of a chair and balancing her tea on her knee before she answered. "I was in the city before I moved here." She seemed incredibly reluctant to give him that much information and she'd given him nothing at all. "Have you always lived here?"

"In town and in this place. I grew up here, inherited the property when Dad died and Mom moved into town." He ran a fingertip around the rim of his coffee mug. There were so many questions he could ask, but he wanted something that was easy for her to answer. Something where she might give him more than a one-word answer. Or a question to catch her off balance. "What's your favorite color?"

He'd definitely caught her off balance if her flared eyes and succession of quick blinks was any indication. "Red. What about you?"

"Blue."

She scrunched her nose. "Typical."

"Are you paying out on my color choice?"

"Yes. Do you work elsewhere, or is this place your full-time job?"

"Hey, isn't it my question?"

"No," she said with an impish grin. "You asked if I was paying you out and I answered."

He gave a mock groan. Even though he hadn't realized that she'd counted that as a question, he was glad she was relaxing and getting into the spirit of the conversation, or game, or whatever it was. "This is full-time. I breed, break in, agist, train, give lessons, and event. It keeps me busy. Sometimes too busy. But I don't think I'd do anything else. I love horses. I've been around them all my life. I need to fund the eventing, and this manages the bills. And eventing showcases some of the young horses I've bred or broken and need to sell. So it all dovetails nicely." The easiest question would have been to ask what she did, but there was something about the way her face softened and her eyes became half-closed that made him change his question. "Do you love horses?"

"Always," she answered quickly. "I grew up with them and adored every moment." Then she seemed to draw herself together. Her gaze snapped back to his and she gave a tiny shake of her head. "You're lucky to do something you love."

"Yeah, I know. I count my blessings every day."

"Even when you're down a leg and an arm?" She gave a bit of a sad smile.

"Especially then. Because I was saved by a guardian angel, dragged from the ocean by an Amazonian warrior, and taken home by a good Samaritan." He hoped his big grin would make her laugh and it did. She softened when she laughed. It seemed to shed the hard covering she held tightly in place. There was so much more to her than he was allowed to see. Sure, she was a stranger and entitled to her privacy, but he was inquisitive about her, and she brought out something inside him that made him want to know every detail about her.

"So, how about you, what do you do for work?"

"I'm an executive assistant."

He waited for more but there was nothing more coming. Not even a question. It was as if she'd turned inside herself, hard cover firmly back in place. "I guess that's not your dream job." She said nothing, but her lips tightened. "If ever you need to come and work with horses, you give me a yell." It was a lighthearted comment, but as he said the words, he felt a rightness about them. He noted the small jerk of her head, as if she was momentarily keen but then changed her mind.

He stopped to think more seriously about his offer. She would make a nice fit in the business. Maybe. He hardly knew her, yet he held a lot of stock in first impressions and she'd made one heck of a one. But he couldn't afford to make a hasty offer of a job, and she didn't look as if she was ready to open up to him, so he needed to bide his time.

"I might be late tomorrow." Tamara gave him a look from beneath her eyelashes, as if she was worried admitting it. Then she twisted her hands together. "I'm sorry. I tried to tell Patti that sometimes I get busy but..." she paused as if unsure what to say.

Rob knew what to say. "Patti's often out of control. I reckon it's best to let her plough ahead and sneak around behind her, and you seem to have worked that out quickly."

Tamara grinned. "It's not like I had a chance to work stuff out. It was all I could do."

"And that's exactly how I feel about her." Rob smiled and hoped she felt a similar camaraderie to what he had blooming in his chest.

Tamara grabbed the cups and spent quite some time putting them into the sink and cleaning up.

She'd gone funny again. If she was a horse, he'd be backing off before now, and yet because she was human, he hadn't been paying the same attention to the signals. "I'm going to read a book. In about an hour everyone will have left. Would you be able to help me outside then?"

Tamara nodded. "I'll get that ice from you and put the boot back on." When she'd done that, she stood in the doorway almost twitching. Energy thrummed from her and it hit him. She needed to run. She needed to burn off the day. That's what she'd been doing when she found him. He understood the need to burn energy.

"This place is pretty big and the roads that run around most of the paddocks are fairly flat, good for running. Feel free to run wherever you want to. You can't get lost. The house is on top of the hill, and you can see it from anywhere. I'll give you my phone number in case you get stuck, but you'll be fine."

She stared as if she wasn't sure he knew what he was saying. "I'm here to care for you, not go for a run."

"I'm going to lay on the couch and read. Pretty sure I can manage that without a carer." He gave her a wink. "And a promise not to tell Patti." He was relieved to see her lips twitch.

"Are you sure you'll be okay?"

He rolled his eyes in an exaggerated motion, stretched out his hand for her phone, and when she gave it to him tapped in his number. "Now go."

"I'll be back in half an hour."

"Make it an hour, and then everyone'll be gone." The smile she gave him told him that he had guessed right.

Chapter 5

The place Rob had was impressive. The pastures looked healthy, the fences were well maintained, and the horses in good condition. She could only ever imagine working somewhere like this. She had no skills for outdoor work. She'd left the farm as a twelve-year-old, and fourteen years later she'd become an indoors person, adept at photocopying, filing, computer work, and living in rarefied air, without sunshine.

She may have escaped the bars of the city, but she hadn't escaped prison. There was no way she was lucky enough to have run across an escaped horse, an injured man, and found herself in heaven. As much as her heart had flown when Rob made the quip about giving her a job, reality was never going to be that good. However, if she made a friend and could spend a little bit of time here, that may rejuvenate her soul.

Running in the fresh air, without traffic or people, was bliss. This town wasn't big, so she never battled hordes when running, but there were people around. Not out here. Here there were horses. Some snorted at her, but most kept their heads down and grazed. It was beautiful.

As she headed back to the house, she detoured via the stables to ensure everyone had left. The lights were out, and the place looked spick-and-span. She turned the lights on and open the doors wide. A nicker came from the far stall, the deep rumbling welcome sound causing happy goosebumps to dance along her arms and upper spine. A big gray head stretched over the half door.

"Hello Storm." Tamara walked up to the big horse with her hand outstretched. "I have a surprise for you tonight. I'll be back in a moment with it." She rubbed her hand along Storm's cheek, pressed her lips to the middle of his face, and inhaled the scent of hay and horse.

She hurried towards the house and met Rob at the back door. "You are not walking down those steps by yourself."

When he glanced up, she saw the surprise in his widened eyes, the guilt in the twist of his lips, and the effort it had taken to get that far in the sheen across his brow. She ran up the stairs and stood right in front of him. He didn't move a muscle, and neither did she. Surely he'd know the damage it could cause if he fell down the stairs. She bit back all the words she could lecture him with and put a hand under his elbow instead.

"Let's take this slowly. One step at a time. I'll go down and you follow." She read disgust in his facial expression and felt the tension in his arms. "I promise this isn't forever. It's just for a few nights. Then you'll have your balance, and you'll be able to do this by yourself."

It seemed to pacify him. And if it didn't, walking down the steps took every bit of his concentration, and hers. Thankfully, there were only five steps. His body brushed against her each time they came down a riser. It set her afire. It shouldn't. She was his carer. She met him only a few days ago. There was nothing between them, except in her imagination. Yet it didn't feel like that. Whenever she was near him, she felt like that Amazonian warrior he spoke of earlier. All woman. All-powerful. Yet she also wanted to curl in his lap and purr like a kitten.

At the bottom of the step mountain, she tucked herself under his good arm and held on while he caught his breath. That was a mistake. Her arms slid around his middle as if they were meant to be there. Her chin almost rested on his shoulder; their height was perfect, it was just that there was no way she was resting it there. As it was, her body seemed glued to his side.

She had to distract herself from this feeling of rightness. "Storm is going to be so happy to see you."

"I hope you've managed to look after him okay."

"He's been perfect, even if everyone seems to think he's some wild beast." She shrugged.

Rob's eyebrows lifted and he tipped his head to the side. He slowly nodded. There was something guarded in his gaze that made her want to probe, but she wasn't here for that. Rob seemed steadier, and had gotten his breath back, so she stepped away. Distance was a much better plan. Together they walked into the stables.

Storm whickered and then snorted. Tamara chuckled. "I only get a friendly hello, it's you he's desperate to see. Head down there, and I'll mix up his feed."

Rob didn't spare her a glance. He hobbled down to the stall where an impatient gray horse was throwing his head and snorting as if telling Rob to hurry up. She waited, watching and listening to the deep timbre of Rob's crooning and the rumbling of Storm's responses. She was definitely not watching the way Rob walked, the way his backside fit snugly into his jeans, or the way his shoulders stretched out his T-shirt. She was purely watching in a carer's role, in case he fell.

Mentally, she snorted louder than Storm. The last thing she was thinking about was being a carer.

She mixed Storm's feed in his bucket, added a biscuit of hay, and wandered down to join her two favorite males. They were watching her. One had his gaze firmly on the bucket in her arms, the other watched her face, her body, her face, her body. She had to fight back the grin that threatened to explode. Was he as interested in her as she was with him?

No. He couldn't be.

Storm whinnied, making Tamara chuckle. "Hold your horses. What have I told you every night?"

"Stand back and wait until I get the bucket on the ground?" Rob's voice held a touch of laughter.

She stopped still and stared. "Have you heard me?" But he couldn't have. Rob hadn't been here.

Rob laughed. "No. It's what I tell him every night."

Tingles ran down her neck. Surely he didn't mean he used those exact words. She brushed off asking the question, set the bucket on the ground and placed the hay in the hay net. Then she allowed Storm to eat and went to join Rob.

"He likes you," Rob said as if it was a surprise to him.

"Believe me, the feeling is entirely mutual." She smiled as Storm chomped ferociously on his feed before snatching a bite of hay. "It's like he thinks his food will disappear."

"He was pretty emaciated when I bought him."

She wanted to wrap her arms around the horse who'd suffered, but her grandfather had never let her interfere with horses when they ate. He always said it was their personal time. It was even more applicable to Storm. If she interrupted him, he may think she was there to take his feed away. "Poor boy. He probably is worried his feed will vanish. How long ago was that?"

"Six years."

"He was young?"

Rob nodded. "A bad-tempered, starving colt. Someone wanted to break him through deprivation. I heard about him, got him cheap, and it took a while to build a relationship with him."

Although she didn't want to end the conversation, Rob's skin was becoming pale and a couple of lines were digging in beside his lips.

"Let's leave him to eat in peace. You need to ice your ankle again."

They made it inside without mishap and Tamara went through the icing ritual again. When she'd cared for her grandparents, her body had filled with warmth, love, caring, compassion and concern. She'd known them all her life and she repaid them by giving them all she could, yet there was none of the tingling awareness, the overwhelming energy, the burning need not to cause pain, that she felt for this man. A man she'd known for a handful of days.

"Tell me about Storm?" she asked, mostly to keep her mind on something other than the twitch of calf muscle as she carefully lifted and adjusted Rob's leg. The abrasive brush of his dark leg hair against her soft, city hands. Thank goodness he kept his eyes closed through most of this process. It meant he wouldn't see the blush that heated her cheeks. Or the stray movements of her eyes when she forgot she was a carer.

Rob told her about Storm and the work he'd done to bond with him. The passion, determination and stubbornness she'd already seen in Rob was in every word. He'd taken an angry, injured beast, and earned respect. Although most people didn't believe animals could love, she thought they could. She could see that between Storm and Rob.

One thing bugged her. "So why does everyone still see Storm as some wild beast and not the animal you've tamed?"

Rob bit his lips together; not in pain, because his eyes were twinkling. It was as if he was fighting a grin. "Yeah. That." He shifted on the couch. "I need to explain that...it's kind of awkward."

Awkward? "More awkward than everything else we've been through?"

He chuckled. "Well, you have a point."

When he didn't immediately speak, she got up. "It's almost time for the ice to be off. So let me put dinner in the microwave, get the boot back on, and you can tell me while we eat."

As she headed to the kitchen, she could have sworn that he muttered, "And that'll make it so much easier," but when she turned and asked him, he denied saying anything.

She got dinner, cut Rob's food into small portions, exchanged ice for the moon boot, and when they were eating, she asked the awkward question. Instead of sitting in the chair, turned towards Rob, she sat on the floor closer to him in case he had trouble with his meal. He was still on the couch, sprawled with his leg up, like an emperor or king.

He had no regal presence after she asked the question. This question about Storm was making him horribly uncomfortable and she couldn't think why. She waited for him to explain and ate the meal someone had provided.

"Storm is still a wild beast. He bites and kicks. He trusts no one else, or he didn't. No one gets close to him. No one ever goes into his stall. He's been a one-person horse. Mine alone." The words came out slowly, and she desperately wanted to argue or query, but something told her she should be quiet and hear him out. She held all her questions inside and listened.

"Mila is probably the only person Storm tolerates. She'll feed him if I'm away, but she just hooks the hay net around and fills it. She never gets in his stall, and never gets too close for long."

Tamara scraped the last of her dinner and set her plate aside. She folded her legs and wrapped her arms around them as she listened.

"Patti made a comment about Storm needing to approve of any woman in my life, and everyone in town knows what she said. You might have noticed how quickly gossip spreads in this place. My sister is one of the worst culprits, but she has a gaggle of friends who are equally as bad." He shifted again, placed his fork down before lifting the plate. Then he seemed to realize that he couldn't reach the coffee table, or anywhere else to put the plate. Tamara grabbed it from him and sat it on top of hers. She wasn't missing the end of this conversation or interrupting his story. She had a feeling this was leading into the most awkward part and she hadn't been able to work out what it was, although she had an inkling now.

Rob pinched the bridge of his nose, and rubbed his thumb and forefinger down the length a few times. He then slid his hand, flat, across the couch. It reminded her of him stroking Storm's neck. She regretted that they weren't having the conversation in the stables. Rob seemed more comfortable out there.

"Hell, Tamara. I'm really sorry about this." He turned away, rubbed his nose again, before glancing back at her. "Patti says that whenever Storm finds some woman he likes, I'll find my wife."

She should laugh. That would be the response she should give, yet there was nothing to laugh at. The air around her stilled. Her breath stalled. Every muscle seemed to vibrate with some sharp, sweet sensation. Sweat made her palms sticky.

"It's crazy, I know." Rob sounded as if he was miles away.

Her heart began to pound furiously. Saliva pooled in her throat and she forced a deep swallow. "My grandmother told me I'd fall in love when I caught a storm while running."

The world stood still. Rob's gaze locked with hers. She couldn't breathe, and then they both gasped together.

"What? When?" he asked with something like horror in his tone.

"She died when I was twelve. I forget when she said it first, but it's something she often said. It made no sense." She shook her head. "Most people get told not to stand in a storm and catch a cold. I got told something insane."

"Except you caught Storm when you were running." This time he sounded like he was in a trance. His words came slowly, like he had to carefully think of each word before they formed.

"I can't do this." She snatched up the plates and bolted for the kitchen. Although she knew she shouldn't, she shut the kitchen door. If there'd been a lock on it, she would have turned that too.

The burning in her chest threatened to overwhelm her.

Chapter 6

Rob fell back against the arm of the couch. "That went well," he muttered as the back of his head clunked onto the cushioned armrest.

He should have said he wasn't after a relationship. The trouble was that Tamara fascinated him and he wanted to know her better.

So he should have said he wasn't after a wife. At the time, all he'd seen was the sheer panic in her eyes and he'd frozen. The panic itself wasn't what had stalled his mind. It was that a heap of other little flares of panic he'd seen from Tamara had made sense. It was like another piece of the puzzle-of-Tamara slotted into its rightful place.

For the last few days, she'd been haunted by her grandmother's prophecy, which was a much more telling thing than Patti's flippant words. And when he thought he was warning Tamara about the women in town matchmaking, what he really did was terrify her into believing a prophecy more than a decade old.

That hurt a bit.

He was already feeling miserable and sorry for himself with his injuries, but it didn't explain the dagger to the heart he was experiencing now. *Would it be so bad to fall in love with me?*

He was pretty realistic about himself, he thought so anyway. He was fairly well setup with his business and property. He wasn't bad looking. He was fit and healthy, barring present injuries. The biggest block to his love-life was his insistence that his horses came first, or if not first, then a very close second.

Tamara loved horses, and she was capable. She'd make a perfect fit in his life. She'd probably put horses right up there on the list too.

So why was she panicking?

He pondered that while she spent a ridiculously long time locked in the kitchen. When he needed to go to the bathroom, he didn't wait or call. He unzipped his jeans while he was lying on the couch and made his way slowly down the hall. He took an inordinate amount of pleasure in successfully completing his mission. Maybe she was right and in a few days he would get the hang of being one-armed and hobbling.

He was heading past his bedroom doorway when a wave of exhaustion hit. Knowing not to ignore it, he hobbled to bed rather than back to the couch. Sitting on the edge of the bed, he realized that he'd celebrated too soon. His jeans weren't going to come off over the moon boot, and he couldn't get the moon boot off without help.

He could undo them and shove them down as far as the boot. That would at least be more comfortable for sleeping. He did that. Extricating one leg and leaving his jeans caught at the top of the moon boot. He contemplated sleeping in his jocks but he was sick of that after the hospital. He slept comfortably naked, and if he covered himself with a sheet, no one would know. Besides, Tamara was unlikely to be out of the kitchen this side of midnight, and he'd probably be awake again by then. Comfortable, he closed his eyes.

He became half-conscious as his leg was lifted, then the straps were undone. The moon boot sliding off brought a moment of discomfort and that passed. Ice tingled. He shuddered, but that too passed. He slept.

Later the ice was removed, his clothes brushed as they slid from his leg. He woke properly as the moon boot was fitted over his foot. Not a terribly pleasant experience. He blinked in the half-light.

He'd opened his mouth to ask if she was okay when he noticed her properly. She'd tipped her face away from him. A tiny sniff told him that she wasn't okay, but everything about her posture warned him from asking, from commenting. So he feigned sleep and let her go.

He had to give her points for courage. He'd expected that she would have rung Patti and begged off duty. Although, maybe he was the lesser of the evils... and that wasn't any pleasant consolation.

Patti.

His mind stumbled.

As a teen, she'd fallen deeply and deliriously in love. Often. Always ending with heartbroken sobbing and drama. It was like love was an addiction; she kept going back for more. Her marriage wasn't much different. In recent years, after the drama of the break-up, she'd avoided love. Avoided men, really, and devoted herself to the kids.

Was Tamara like that? Hurt and afraid of love?

There were few similarities between her and his sister, but he hardly knew Tamara so it wasn't fair to comment. But she did sometimes show those same skittish tendencies that Patti had shown.

He went to roll over, only to be reminded of his incapacity by the heavy tether on his leg. He could deal with the one arm far better than he could with the stupid leg. He had to get up again.

Would Tamara be asleep? She'd been gone twenty-five minutes and he hadn't heard a peep, so surely he could get up without disturbing her. She was taking the caring role quite seriously, if she bothered to ice his ankle at the required time after such a tense misunderstanding.

He hobbled to the bathroom again. This time faster than before and he was feeling pretty good about that. And then he heard her. Not a footstep, just the sharp intake of breath.

Oops.

Nudity. He should have thought of that part when he'd wondered if she was awake. When he finished, he grabbed a towel and tied it around his hips before making his way to the kitchen.

"I'm sorry I woke you." Tamara spoke softly from the shadows of the darkened lounge room.

"I'm not. Thank you for putting your care of me ahead of anything else."

A sniff, almost too faint to hear, and then a swallow. "I overreacted. I'm sorry."

It wasn't what he expected. Although he couldn't say what his expectation was. Having lived with Patti, a quiet dignity certainly wasn't it. "I'm not looking for a wife, Tamara. I wanted to explain why everyone would be matchmaking. I didn't explain it properly."

"I shouldn't have told you what my grandmother said."

The pain in her voice hit him hardest. He wanted to wrap his arms around her. "Why not?" He headed towards her, slowly, hoping he wouldn't trip over anything.

"It was silly." She whispered the words, but there was something in her tone that made him think she didn't believe that at all.

He reached her and brushed his hand lightly across the top of her head. It wasn't the hug he wanted to give but with only one functional arm, it was all he could do. Hauling her up and pinning her to his side, one armed, had crossed his mind but it seemed a little too caveman. "It's not silly. It's something your grandmother gave you. A precious memory."

She nodded.

He ran his hand across her head again. "Tell me about her." He said it softly so she could ignore him if she wanted, but he felt her nod and swallow deeply.

"Okay." She sounded so brave, and so sad.

He slid his hand down the side of her face, gently brushing his thumb across her damp cheekbone, before cupping his palm gently beneath her jaw. When her hand reached for his, he held on.

"I was raised by my grandparents. They had a farm. My grandfather loved horses, my grandma did too but nothing like Grandpa did. Grandpa lived and breathed for his animals, and Grandma lived and breathed for him." Her voice caught on the last words and he ached to bundle her against his chest and take her pain away.

"You loved them very much." It was all he could offer, short of the caveman act.

She gasped, grabbed his hand and stood up. "Rob, get off your leg. Lie on the couch or go back to bed. I'm fine. Truly."

"I want to know what happened." He said it gently, while he held her hand in his and slid his thumb across the back of her knuckles.

"It's not a bedtime story." She bristled, but he didn't react. Just stroked her hand. "Couch or bed?" It was said like she was snapping but he knew she'd settled. He'd won a tiny piece of her trust, her respect.

"The bed's more comfortable for me, but I'll pick the couch if you'll keep talking to me," he said softly.

It took an age for her to decide. When she did, she let out a sigh. He had another piece of her trust. She shook off his hand but followed him to his room. When he sat on the side of the bed, preparing to swing his booted leg up, she called from the hall. "Chuck your towel out when you're in bed and I'll hang it up in the bathroom."

He could have done a victory dance. A huge chunk of trust. "Thank you." He even made that sound normal. Once he was covered, he bundled the towel and hurled it to the doorway. "Incoming."

A puff of what may have been a laugh was the only response.

He'd hoped she might lie beside him while she talked, and he could put his arm around her, maybe have her head rest on his chest, but he'd won so much from her he wasn't about to push. If she held his hand, he'd consider that a major victory.

In the end, she sat beside him and talked of the horses of her childhood. Of learning to ride. Of her grandfather's passion, and her grandmother's love. Her hands waved as she spoke. Sometimes she'd catch his arm or brush his fingers. He left his hand on the bed between them, open but not expecting contact. Every contact felt like another tiny piece of trust handed over.

When he began to drift towards sleep, she noticed. "Thank you for letting me talk so much." She leaned across and pressed her lips gently to his brow. "You're a lot like my grandfather."

Before he could gather his softly drifting thoughts, she was gone.

Over the next four nights, Rob discovered more about Tamara. Her life, her care, her kindness, her fears and her grit and determination. He learned to acutely dislike the boss who seemed to take advantage of her good nature. He wanted her all to himself. He itched to hold her close. Ached to feel her lips on his. For heaven's sake, he was jealous of Storm and the attention she paid his horse.

Patti even remarked on his tolerance. "I don't know what drugs they put you on, Rob, but you're handling this recovery much better than any other one." He fobbed her off by saying it wasn't the eventing season so he wasn't worried about missing out, but given her sharp-eyed glare, she suspected it was more than that.

On the fifth night, they were talking over dinner when Tamara said, "You're doing everything on your own now, Rob. And the swelling is out of the ankle. I don't know that you need me here any longer."

The bottom fell out of his world. His first instinct was to tug her close, tell her he didn't want her to go, but he'd never do that with a horse. This was a break for freedom. The last gigantic burst before they gave you all their trust. The worst thing to do was to hang on and drag them close. The hardest thing to do was to let them throw themselves away. If you had every piece of trust bar the last one, they wouldn't leave you. They'd come back on their own, stand and wait for your attention.

He'd done this with dozens of horses, even with Storm, but it had never been this difficult.

"I've enjoyed your company, Tamara. I can't say that about too many people." He gave a grin that he hoped looked sincere and not too cheesy.

"I feel the same way. Do you think we could remain friends?"

He bit back all the words he wanted to say. "Sure. That'd be great. Storm and I would love to see you whenever you stop by. Maybe we could go for a ride when I've got the all clear."

Watching her closely, he saw her eyes crease at the edges and her lips tighten. *Good, she felt that as sharply as me.* Going riding together in some distant future was a perfectly lovely invitation, unless you wanted more from a friendship—a relationship.

The routine was the same, the conversation similar to every other night, but something stretched between them. He'd call it a need for a closer bond, but he wasn't sure if she felt the same way. The next move had to be hers, except he was impatient.

In all the conversations they'd had, with all the confidences she'd shared, she hadn't told him what had happened to her grandparents. He hadn't asked because he wanted her to give him that piece freely. She hadn't. Tonight was his last chance. She wasn't a horse. His gut told him he had to ask before it was too late to do so. But another part of him worried about pushing. Was scared of losing her. Didn't want to back her into a corner.

As she did up the moon boot after his last ice session, he faced his fear. "You haven't told me what happened to your grandparents." He held his breath.

She gave him a brief glance. "I know." Although the words were "I know", he heard it as "I can't". She walked away with the ice pack, and he let her go. Lying in bed, flat on his back with his booted foot up on pillows, he posed the least threat to her. It was a good time to prod. She was free to walk away or to tell him the story.

She'd walked.

He closed his eyes. There was emptiness.

He didn't know how much later it was when his bed dipped. Cool fingers brushed over his. He closed his hand, capturing them before they darted away. He tried to breathe slowly, evenly, to control his building emotion.

"I was twelve. We'd argued and I lost. I went to boarding school. They wanted me to go so I'd have a better education, more friends of my own age, modern influences, and exposure to the city. I understood why they chose to send me away, but all I wanted was to be with them and farm with them." She gripped his fingers so tightly. "They died. There was a bushfire. Everything gone."

He had no way of holding in his shock. Not when she'd choked those few words out as if they cost her everything. "Angel. God. No." He tugged and she lay her forehead against his chest. Moisture pooled on his skin from her tears. He needed to wrap her tight but she clung to his hand. He growled, ducked his head and tried to slide the sling from his injured arm. He growled louder as the pain hit.

"No," she cried. "You leave that on." She put the sling back in place and settled his arm where it should be.

Since she'd let go of his fingers, he curled his arm around her, which was where it needed to be. He stroked her spine. Up and down, slowly. She curled beside him and settled her head against his chest. He stroked her hair, held the back of her neck and massaged gently. "I'm so sorry that happened to them. To you. It must have been horrific."

She made a move against his chest and a hiccup of a sound. They lay together and he held her and gave her what comfort he could manage. His offerings were insignificant. How did anyone go on after such loss? Her bravery and her calmness in a crisis hit him harder. She was an incredible person. He didn't want to lose her.

"The school was good. The town too. I had no one. I didn't know what I wanted. I've never known what I wanted. I lived one day to the next." Her heartbreak tore at him. He held her close, trying to convey his emotion with just the soothing strokes of his hand. It was nothing.

She lifted her head from his chest, stared at him in the half-light. "You've given me hope. Being here with you, talking to you, looking after Storm, running in the paddocks, it's been a miracle. At first it was too much, but now I know what I want."

He held his breath. He gulped.

She smiled through her tears. A glorious smile. "I want to do something with animals, or horses—"

"Then come and work with me."

She rested her chin against his chest for a second and then pressed a chaste kiss to his chin. "Thank you. You're incredibly generous but you don't need an employee."

"Actually, I do." He winced. "Let me explain properly. In the eventing season, I always employ a groom and usually they stay through the off-season and help out here. But the groom I've had for years has gone traipsing around Europe and I was waiting for the season before advertising for a groom."

"Then maybe I'll apply when you advertise."

He was making a hash of this. "I could do with someone while I'm laid up. Please consider it?"

There was a long pause. She searched his face. Expectation filled the air, and he hoped it was something she was feeling, not just him.

"Are you serious?" she asked a little breathlessly.

He nodded. "This is a no pressure offer. It doesn't come with any strings."

"You mean we can't be friends?"

He took a punt that it was sauciness in her tone. "I'd like to be friends. We just don't need to listen to any of the matchmakers."

"What if I want to?" Her breath caught, as if she said it by mistake.

"You want more?" Okay, so he sounded slightly desperate, but he didn't want her to run off. He had to see if she cared for him. No. Not cared. More than cared, she'd been caring for a week now. He needed to know... He was being a romantic fool.

"Do you have a policy against romance in the workplace? If so, I might have to decline the job offer." How could she sound so matter-of-fact?

He shifted so he was closer to her, so he could curl his hand easily around her nape. "Is this romance with Storm?"

She shook her head as she chuckled. The sound surrounded him like a wave sliding on to the shore. She seemed to have lightened since her tears. He hoped that sharing her heartache had lessened it.

"Are you sure?" he asked as his lips brushed lightly against hers.

A whimper came first. "I'm sure." She moved then so their lips caught better. So their mouths could fit perfectly in a kiss that threatened to melt him. She gave her trust, fully and completely. Her lips opened to his questing tongue. Her hands cupped his jaw, brushed his face, slipped into his hair. He held her. He never wanted to stop.

Chapter 7

Rob's recovery took six weeks. During that time, Tamara's certainty about her grandmother's prediction only strengthened. She quit her job and accepted the position with Rob. There were moments when things weren't all roses, but they sorted those out quickly. She and Rob had so many similarities, and so much of him reminded her of her grandfather. He had the same patience, the same gentle kindness, the same singular focus especially when working with a young horse. Tamara thought if the world ended when Rob was training one of his yearlings, he wouldn't notice at all.

She loved her new life. Every aspect of it. Working closely with a romantic partner was something she wasn't sure she could manage, but she enjoyed it. They weren't always together. She'd go off and do things away from Rob, and that made seeing him again so much sweeter. If someone had told her of such a relationship, she would have found it sickeningly saccharine. Living it was a joy.

The day he was given the all clear to ride, she hung around the stables, making sure he really was okay to ride. Rob rode Storm and watching them working together was every bit as stunning as she'd imagined. They had a seamless connection. Afterwards, she couldn't tell which of them enjoyed the ride more.

Rob worked around the stables for the rest of the day but didn't ride any of the other horses.

"Did the ride hurt?" she asked him as she packed up for the day.

"Not too much. Would you like to come for a ride with Storm and I?"

"When?"

"Now. If you don't want to run."

She grinned. "I can be talked into riding instead." Although Rob had been helping her regain her confidence with riding he'd been on the ground giving her instructions not riding beside her. Riding with him made her heart trip over itself.

"Storm's waiting for us." Rob waved to the stall where Storm waited, already bridled.

"Who will I take?" None of the other horses appeared to be geared up and waiting for her.

"Will you ride with me?" The hesitation is his words made her stop. He led Storm out in just a bridle. No saddle.

"Bareback? Together?"

He nodded. "Is it asking too much?" He shrugged. "I just thought maybe you'd like to—"

"I'd love to." Rob must need to show her he could ride. Not that she needed convincing, she'd seen them earlier. She had no qualms about riding Storm either. She'd ridden Storm under Rob's guidance many times in the last few weeks.

She gave Storm a pat down his face. "Are you right to take us both?" He rubbed his head against her, and she took that to be his acceptance. She grasped Rob's hand and swung up behind him, glad she'd been swinging up on fences, as well as riding, for the last few weeks.

She slid her arms around Rob and lay her head against his shoulder. His scent always made her smile. There was so much horse to it, then beneath was the spicy tang of the man. A little something from his soap, lemony freshness from washing powder, and earthiness from hard work.

Her eyes closed and she breathed him in. She'd never tire of the deliciousness of him.

Through the arm wrapped around his waist, she felt his stomach muscles tighten and relax with each sway of Storm's gait. With no fear of hurting him now his injuries had healed, she slid her hand over his stomach and settled it against his left pectoral muscle; over his heart.

She loved him. It was ridiculous to be in love so quickly, but she had no doubt about it. As if he knew her thoughts, he gently lifted her hand and kissed each knuckle before placing her hand right back where it had been. Gestures like this made her certain that Rob felt the same way.

"It's a beautiful evening," he said, and she knew he was grinning as he looked around; she heard the happiness in his tone. "As much as I've appreciated all your care, especially all the times you've helped my outside, there is nothing like being able to do things with your body intact."

She squeezed his waist. "There's nothing quite like seeing you happy."

Rob laughed. "As opposed to the grumpy, cranky, impatient ass you've had to put up with for weeks. I don't know how you managed."

Sliding her hand over his chest, she internally debated how to answer. It was too soon for raw, romantic honesty. She'd like to be looking at him when she bared her heart and soul so she could see how he felt. "It wasn't so bad." Almost complete honesty. "You weren't always a grumpy, cranky and impatient ass...sometimes you slept." With a touch of humour. Rob laughed, just as she intended. He always managed better when there was a sense of fun, or a dry comment. It was another thing she loved about him.

They were on the beach now, and she held Rob tighter for a moment.

"Scared?" he asked.

"No. Not one bit." She inhaled deeply. "It's a little lovely, being back here with you and Storm. It's like we've come full circle." She'd have loved to be facing him now so she could guess what he was thinking. All she had was a tiny hitch in his breath and the squeeze of his hand around hers to give her any indication of how he received her comment. She hoped those meant that he'd put some thought into the destination and it wasn't Storm's random meandering that had brought them here.

"Are you game to come into the shallows with us, or would you like to hop down and run on the beach?"

"I'm game." She was sticking with him, not out of fear but because sitting here wrapped around him was the best place to be.

Storm splashed in the shallows, lifting his legs high and causing water to spray over them.

"How did you fall off that day?"

Rob shrugged, his shoulder blades moved against her breasts making her even more aware of him, and she hadn't thought that was possible. "I don't know. I've replayed it in my mind so many times because it was unusual. Mostly I know the moment a fall's happening but can't stop it. That day, I knew I was falling only after I'd hit the ground."

They were silent as Storm waded through the small waves licking at the beach. Their boots weren't too wet, so he wasn't in deep. She wondered if Rob ever came down and swam with the horses. Maybe that's how he'd come off. "Were you swimming with him?"

"No. Walking like this." Rob took her hand from his waist and threaded his fingers through hers. "It's crazy, but all I can think is that it was fate. I had to fall so I could meet you."

Her heart tripped. She pressed her hand tighter against his chest. *What a beautiful thing to say.* "Oh, Rob."

Storm stopped at the edge of the water. Rob twisted around to face her. "Falling off Storm was the best thing that's ever happened to me."

She chuckled. "I doubt that."

"It meant being saved by you." She thought he'd kiss her but instead, he held himself away from her mouth and kept speaking. "I know it's only been six weeks, and this is all so quick, but your grandmother was right, I have fallen in love and I'd like nothing more than to spend the rest of my life with you."

She gasped. Her hand flew across her mouth as tears prickled her eyes.

"Tamara Hancock, will you marry me?"

She couldn't say a word. They were all tangled up in a huge knot in her throat.

"If you can't say yes because it's too soon, then I'll ask you again, I promise."

"No," she said. Then realized what she'd said. She grabbed his shoulder. "Yes, I mean. Yes, I'll marry you. The no was because you don't need to ask me again."

"I don't?"

"No. Grandma was right. She was always right. Catching Storm while running was perfect. Maybe I didn't fall in love with you right away," she grinned, "even if you do have an impressive chest, but I love you, Rob. I haven't been anywhere close to this happy since I was a kid. I'd love nothing more than to have you in my life. Permanently." Storm gave a whinny and a toss of his head. "And Storm too, of course."

Rob's kiss had her clinging to him. It was breathtaking. He was magnificent.

Storm began the walk home, and she and Rob hardly broke their kiss.

Life was going to be pretty close to perfect.

The End.

Thank you for reading *Storm Struck*

I really appreciate the time you've given to read Tamara and Rob's story. I hope you enjoyed it.

About The Author

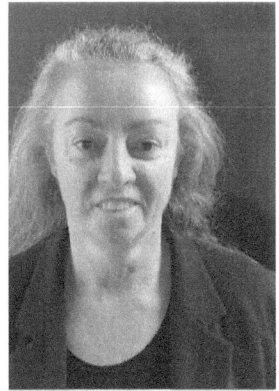

Catherine Evans writes stories set in Australia's outback and country towns. Although she grew up in Sydney, she moved to the country as soon as she could and loves it. After working in agriculture for many years, she now works with her creative side and writes about the places she loves. She lives with her husband in a small town on the coast of New South Wales, Australia.

Contact.

You can find more about me on my website:
http://www.catherineevansauthor.com/

I'm not the greatest at being social, but I love readers. So
please say hello, even if I'm being quiet.

Email: catherine@catherineEvansAuthor.com
Facebook: https://www.facebook.com/CatherineEvansAuthor/
Twitter: https://twitter.com/cathevansauthor

AMAZON: https://www.amazon.com/Catherine-
Evans/e/B01D39PVNA

Other Books by Catherine Evans

The Healing Season
https://www.amazon.com/gp/product/B01AUJUW4E/

Long Game https://www.amazon.com/Long-Game-
Catherine-Evans-ebook/dp/B076C6PN2B/